STRIKER
No Prisoners MC Book 1

by Lilly Atlas

Copyright © 2016 Lilly Atlas

All rights reserved.

Lilly Atlas Books

ISBN-10: 1-946068-00-4
ISBN-13: 978-1-946068-00-2

For Sam.
Without you, all I'd have is a messy word document and
an email address. Plus, I'd never have known to do a
CT to rule out an orbital fracture.
Love you.

Dr. Lila Emerson is finally free of the shadow of her politically connected family, with her new job in a small town Emergency Room. But her new peace is shattered when she encounters the dangerous, but compelling Striker. He's everything she should stay away from, but all she craves. And since he keeps turning up in her ER, he's hard to avoid.

As Vice President of No Prisoners outlaw motorcycle club, Striker is no stranger to violence. But when it touches the pretty doctor he wants in his bed, he'll do anything to keep her safe. When Striker and Lila are thrust together, sparks fly and passions ignite. Before long they find themselves entangled in a relationship neither saw coming.

The MC can and will eliminate any threat against Lila, but what if they—and the man she's falling for—are the reason she's in danger?

STRIKER
No Prisoners MC Book 1

Chapter One

The doors to Desert Community Hospital slid open with a whoosh. It was a sound Dr. Lila Emerson heard countless times each shift, so she didn't bother to look up, focusing instead on completing a written proposal for the concussion and sports safety program she hoped to institute at the local high school. Another forty-five minutes and she would have it completed, and be on her way home to the bottle of Cabernet and warm bath that promised to soothe her tired body after a hectic week. She couldn't wait.

"Stitch." Jester's booming voice bellowed through the lobby. "We need you, girl! Gumby's face is all busted up."

Lila groaned. Again? Perhaps the man needed a new nickname. Gumby didn't seem fitting, considering the number of times his body cracked.

Members of the No Prisoners motorcycle club had burst into the lobby of the emergency room. She could always tell the moment they came through the doors, even without the inevitable *we're here* announcement made by Jester. There was a change in the energy of the room: a charge of fear and distrust from some, a nervous respect from others, and a buzz of sexual energy from all the testosterone they seemed to

1

emit. There was a strong possibility she was the only one who noticed that last point.

Jester led the pack of two leather-clad, boot-wearing men as they tromped through the waiting room, and up to the admissions desk. Silence descended as the patients awaiting treatment gaped at the intimidating duo. Jester was a mountain of a man, topping out at no less than six foot five inches, and probably weighed close to three hundred pounds of solid muscle. He had the body type of a serious weight lifter, and could have been one, for all she knew about him. Both arms boasted full sleeves of tattoos, and additional ink peeked out from the collar of his T-shirt. Jester's dark brown hair was long, past his shoulders, and thick, though usually contained in a ponytail at the base of his neck. He was a formidable figure, and not someone she'd want to meet in a back alley at night, despite his apparent jovial demeanor.

He reached the admissions desk, and braced his meaty hands on the counter. The action placed him directly above poor Anna, the middle aged receptionist who worked the night shift. She had to tilt her head way back to meet Jester's fierce gaze.

"Um, if you wouldn't mind filling out these papers." Anna's voice shook as she fumbled with the clipboard that contained the intake paperwork. "Then please have a seat, and we will call you back soon. There are only a few patients ahead of you, so the wait shouldn't be more than an hour."

"That's not gonna work for us. We'll just head back to an empty room, and Stitch can meet us in there."

Jester was the first to call her Stitch, after a number of club members had required stitches following a particularly brutal bar brawl one night a few months ago. The moniker stuck, and spread throughout the town.

The No Prisoners. Their name came from the phrase *take*

no prisoners, an expression the club was rumored to live by. Lila's patients loved to pass along town gossip, and she was regaled with numerous grandiose stories about the club's penchant for making their enemies disappear. Typically, she took what patients told and believed about half of it, but these rumors she didn't doubt. Each club member she'd met was able to laugh and joke with her, but there was always a deadly undercurrent that couldn't be ignored. They all carried weapons, and she'd often wondered how they got them past the security guard, but she wasn't about to ask. No point in getting on their bad side.

Lila rolled her eyes, and stood, intending to intervene on Anna's behalf, when her gaze landed on the man rounding out the group. Striker shook hands with the night security guard as he came through the double doors. In its typical fashion, her heart rate kicked up a notch at the sight of the No Prisoners' vice president.

Her eyes widened as she watched Striker pass what looked like money to the portly guard who glanced around before sliding his hand into his back pocket. Well that explained how they got their arsenal in the building, and why they were never asked to leave, no matter how many patients complained of being uncomfortable by their presence.

If Webster's had a definition for sexy bad boy there would be a picture of Striker. He stood around six-foot-two, with muscles galore and dark, almost black hair that was short and a bit unruly. Combined with a strong jaw, piercing blue eyes, and leather, he made for one mouthwatering package.

"Ah, there's no guarantee that, um, Dr. Emerson will be the one to see you." Anna's face was flushed, her voice wavered, and her eyes shone with a glimmer of unshed tears. Jester still hovered over her, a scowl on his face.

Lila sighed. Her schedule had been crazy this week and

she'd had to squeeze in work on the proposal anywhere she could. It was just about finished, and she had planned on it being done by the time this shift was over. So much for that.

She moved toward the reception area to rescue Anna before the unassuming woman broke down under Jester's glower. "Anna, it's okay." Lila put a hand on the older woman's shoulder. "There's no one else in line to check in. Why don't you run and grab a cup of coffee from the break room, and I'll get these gentlemen's information and get them settled."

The look of relief on Anna's face was almost comical, and she scurried away the second the offer was out of Lila's mouth. The club members were imposing for sure, but in all the times they'd been into the ER, Lila could be honest in saying they never actually caused any trouble. They just always looked like they were on the verge of it. Still, the patients in the waiting room stared at the floor and out the windows, anywhere but at the hulking men in leather and chains. Most of the staff reacted the same way, and Lila realized, aside from the worthless security guard, she was alone in the shared admissions and charting area.

She shifted her attention to the three men standing by the desk. Jester wore an ear-to-ear grin on his face, like flustering the receptionist had been the highlight of his evening. Gumby, the injured party, stood next to him and held a blood soaked rag under a rapidly swelling eye. Striker leaned against the wall off to the side, arms crossed, face unreadable, and Lila forced her attention away from him.

"Just head on back to room four," she instructed. It was best to get them taken care of quickly. Tension would leave the ER once they were back outside on their motorcycles. Plus, she'd be able to go home as soon as she treated Gumby. "You know the way. I have to talk to the nurse for a minute and we'll be right in. Try not to scare away too much of our business on your way back there."

"Aww, Stitch, Gumby's face doesn't look that bad," Jester said.

"I was talking to you," she shot back with a smile.

Jester laughed, threw an arm around Gumby's shoulders, and steered him in the direction Lila had indicated. Striker lingered at the admissions desk. When she met his gaze, one corner of his mouth lifted in the arrogant grin she had come to expect from him. Her breath caught in her throat and she forgot what she was supposed to be doing. She barely remembered her own name when he looked at her like that, and lately the heated gazes seemed to be coming more frequently.

Part of Lila, the part that had moved across the country in hope of having the freedom to live her life her way, told her she loved the attention. She was free to make her own decisions for the first time in her life. Taking this job in a small town hospital where she could really affect the lives of individuals in her community was the first step in exerting her autonomy. The next step would be finding a man to spend that life with.

She really didn't know Striker, but the idea of the tough-looking biker wanting a picket fence and two point five kids was almost laughable. Lila could admire the attractive packaging from afar, but she shouldn't be thinking about the desire that shone in his eyes, as she did far too often. There was nothing but trouble down that road. Especially since he probably spent much of his time on the wrong side of the law.

"So, Doc, I hear you have a big presentation coming up," he said.

Pride swelled with the knowledge that there was talk

5

around town about her program. It was her baby. She'd seen too many high school athletes come through the ER with serious head injuries due to the school's ignorance about concussions and equipment safety.

"I do! I'm presenting my idea in front of the school board Monday night. If all goes well, I'll form a committee and begin putting a program together. It's so important. Did you know that the majority of the sports equipment at the high school is over ten years old? There is no way it is in any condition to keep the kids protected."

Her face heated. She was passionate about this project, and could talk about it for hours, to anyone apparently, even sexy bikers who normally had her tongue-tied. "Sorry. I can ramble on about this until your ears fall off. I'm sure you're not interested, so I should probably go tend to the bleeding man."

She turned to flee toward the treatment rooms, but stopped when Striker's voice sounded behind her. "Actually, Doc, some of my guys have kids in the high school. A few of them play football. I think it's great what you're doing."

And damn if her heart didn't do a happy dance at the look of admiration on his face. With a nod in his direction, she turned and headed down the hall.

Cammie, her friend and one of the best ER nurses she'd ever worked with, came up the hall as Lila went down it. "Cammie, can you grab a suture kit and meet me in room four? I'll also need lidocaine and saline to irrigate the wound. Looks like Gumby took quite a shot to the face."

At the mention of Gumby's name, Cammie paled a bit, but she nodded and walked straight toward the supply room. Lila wasn't sure what that was about, and didn't want to waste time speculating.

She pushed the door to exam room four open and walked

in. The miniscule room was even smaller than usual with two very large males filling the space. Gumby sat on the treatment table directly opposite the door, the blood soaked cloth still pressed to his face. Jester was off to the side, sitting in a plastic chair that was built for a man half his size. Striker hadn't followed her into the room, and she breathed a small sigh of relief at the lack of distraction.

"Hi, Doc. Miss me?" Gumby asked. He tried to smile but winced when the action caused the skin around his still expanding eye to crinkle.

"Hey there, Gumby, I see you're here for our standing Friday night date. I gotta tell you, it wouldn't hurt to bring a girl flowers every once in a while," she said with a wink.

Jester laughed. "You may want to take it easy on Gumb tonight, Stitch. Not only is his pretty face all busted, he got his ass handed to him in the ring. He's been a tad cranky ever since."

"Fuck off, Jest," grumbled Gumby. "Fucker got in a few lucky shots."

"Sure he did, Gumb." Jester patted him on the back like he might a petulant child, and shot a quick wink Lila's way.

"Lie down on your back for me please, you are way too tall for me to reach your face all the way up there." She adjusted the angle on the treatment table as she spoke, so he wouldn't be flat, but would lay at about a thirty-degree incline.

Gumby did as she asked while Lila donned a pair of nitrile gloves. Before she moved to assess him, she opened a drawer beneath the table, and pulled out a few four-by-fours of gauze and ripped the packages open. When Gumby was in position, Lila placed her gloved hand over his to remove the saturated cloth.

His eye was badly contused and swollen shut. The color

palette was spectacular. Various shades of purple and blue mottled the skin surrounding his entire orbit. A two-inch laceration stretched across Gumby's cheekbone as well. The gash cut deep, but not jagged, so it would be easy to approximate the edges and he'd have minimal scarring. She pressed the clean gauze over his eye while she waited for Cammie to bring the suture kit.

"Did you get knocked out, Gumby? If so I'll need to do a CT scan of your head."

"I'm good, Stitch. Just need my face sewn up so it will stop fucking bleeding."

"Well, I'd really like to—"

"Doc." A gruff voice came from over her shoulder. "He's fine, just do your thing, and put his face back together so we can get out of your way."

She'd heard him approach and had tried to ignore the star of too many of her late night fantasies, but apparently Striker wasn't going to let that happen. A dueling sizzle of awareness and annoyance struck her as he stepped in between her and her patient.

"Thank you, Striker. As usual I'd be lost in my job without your sound medical input."

"Man, I love coming here." Jester laughed. "Too bad one of us needs to get all jacked up or I'd be here every day to be on the receiving end of your charms, Stitch."

Lila turned her attention back to Striker, and narrowed her eyes to let him know she was serious when she expressed her dislike of his interference. Once again she was met with a one-sided smirk she would like to smack off his face. Okay, there was a chance she'd like to kiss the smirk off his face, but she wasn't ready to admit that out loud.

Cammie knocked on the door before she entered, and wheeled in a cart with the supplies Lila had requested. Lila often teased her about her curly red hair and how it bounced as she walked, mimicking her bubbly personality, but tonight she was stiff and rigid as though she was being walked to her doom. "I have your suture kit, Dr. Emerson. What can I do to help you?" she asked.

"Thanks, Cammie, I can take it from here."

Cammie shot Lila a grateful smile, and was out of the room in a flash, apparently not wanting to miss out on the reprieve she was given. Lila made a mental note to ask Cammie why she seemed so uncomfortable when Jester mumbled. "Yeah, Gumby, probably shouldn't have climbed on that ride, knowing how often you end up here."

Well, that explained why Cammie lit out of there like the floor was caving in. Given how the members of the MC flirted with any female staff between ages nineteen and fifty, she was surprised there weren't more awkward encounters.

Lila gifted Gumby with an innocent grin. "Oh crap! I'm so sorry, Gumby, I forgot I have a meeting to get to. I'm just going to call Cammie back and have her stitch you up. I'm sure she won't forget to numb you, and she'll be very gentle." Her snarky statement would have been better believed if she hadn't burst out laughing halfway through at the look of horror on Gumby's face.

Behind her, Striker laughed. "Ouch, Doc, way to hit the man when he's down."

Lila chuckled. She always had fun when these guys were here. "Okay let's get down to business so you can get out of here, and ignore my instructions by mixing your pain killers with booze." She grabbed the bottle of sterile saline off the cart, and irrigated the wound. Gumby hissed out a curse. "Sorry, Gumby. I can't see exactly how deep it is unless I clean out the blood. There's a chance you have an orbital fracture. I recommend a CT."

He shook his head. "Just close it up."

Surprise, surprise. "Sometimes you guys are very annoying."

They all laughed, and she used the lidocaine to deaden the area around the wound. When he was numb, she ripped open the suture kit and got to work. Lila could feel Striker's eyes on her back and she had to concentrate to keep her hands from quivering like a third year medical student. Thankfully they remained quiet, allowing her to focus, and in ten minutes Gumby's wound was closed, the stitch job quite impressive, if she did say so herself.

"Okay, Gumby, you are the proud new recipient of fifteen stitches. I'll have a nurse bring you something for the pain. It will hurt like a bitch when the lidocaine wears off. The nurse will also have your discharge instructions. You can leave when she's done."

Lila knew how they operated, and didn't expect a single instruction to be followed, but protocol was protocol and she'd obey it. As she turned to leave the room, her gaze collided with Striker's. His heated stare affected her more than she was prepared to admit so she shifted her gaze and broke the connection. Neither said anything as she left the room, but she felt the lingering effects of having him so near in her racing heart and wobbly legs.

Her shift was officially over, and she could go home as soon as Gumby's paperwork was complete. Now she just needed to get Striker off her mind long enough to finish her proposal and still get some sleep tonight.

Chapter Two

Striker prowled the half-full waiting room while he waited for Gumby to emerge. He spotted Lila behind a desk to the right of the admissions counter, typing away on a computer that looked like it should have been replaced ten years ago.

He should leave. Jester could stay with Gumby, and he could go meet up with the rest of his brothers at the party he was missing. The only reason he stuck around was because Lila drew him like a junkie to the needle.

It was pointless. Lila was the marrying type, not the type to fuck a biker once or twice. And that's all it would be. Striker didn't do anything more than that. As vice president of the MC there was no shortage of women eager to bang him, and that's exactly how he liked it. Someday he'd be president, and maybe he'd consider getting an ol' lady then, but there was no point in it now. He had all the easy pussy he wanted, but he had to admit the challenge of getting into Lila's pants was appealing.

The emergency room at Desert Community Hospital was often surprisingly busy for such a small town, but tonight was a pretty slow night. Taking a rare moment to study the doctor without her knowledge, he wondered, not for the first time, what the hell she was doing in his Podunk town.

Lila seemed so much…bigger than Crystal Rock, Arizona, a tiny, off the grid desert town known for its one percenter motorcycle gang. True, a portion of the town rested along a gorgeous lake, an oasis in the hot desert that was a tourist attraction. But for whatever reason, possibly the MC, their town wasn't included in the area where tourists flocked. Hell, Crystal Rock didn't even boast a motel for travelers to stay.

The first word that popped into his head whenever he looked at Lila was, classy. Her clothes gave the impression they cost her a good few bucks, and even in her scrubs she gave off an air of sophistication. When she was working, she kept her long dark hair neatly pulled into a tight bun at the top of her head. The look was supposed to be professional, but it exposed the smooth skin of her neck, and Striker wished he could lean in and nibble her elegant jaw. Striker's fantasies about the sexy doctor often began with him yanking that bun out and tangling his fingers in her thick dark hair so he could pull her head back and feast on her mouth.

Jester strode into the waiting area, and Striker lifted a hand to catch his attention. Conversation among the five or so patients waiting to be seen came to a dead halt, similar to when he and his brothers first arrived. Jester often had that effect on a room.

"Should be about fifteen minutes. Nurse Cammie got stuck bringing Gumby his pills and showing him how to take care of his boo-boo. I figured I'd step out and give them a few minutes alone." He grinned and rubbed his hands together as though Gumby's further discomfort pleased him.

"Not sure who will hate you more for that one, Gumby or the redhead."

Jester snorted. "Gonna go out and have a smoke. You coming?"

"Nah, I'll hang here."

After shooting him a curious look, Jester shrugged and made his way outside. Striker saw him through the window, near the bikes.

Striker turned his attention back to Lila. Damn she was just plain hot as fuck. There hadn't been a legitimate reason to stay in the room while she stitched up Gumby, yet as soon as she bent over the table to work on his face, Striker got a close up view of her tight ass and decided to stay for the show.

Even the baggy lab coat and scrubs couldn't disguise what a luscious ass it was. Lila was tiny, couldn't have been more than a few inches above five feet. They teased her often about her miniscule stature when she was fixing up one of his guys. Most of them were fairly big men, and she looked like a child when she was surrounded by them.

Maybe child wasn't the right word, seeing as how he never failed to notice she was all woman. Despite the fact that she was short, she had a banging body, with a tight, curvy figure he wanted to run his hands, and mouth, over. The few times he'd seen her out of scrubs, he'd had to clench his teeth to keep his tongue from lolling out and panting after her like the dog he was.

What was new for him was the fact that he admired her, as a person, not just her body. She was intelligent, quick witted, and, in the few months she'd lived in Crystal Rock, her combination of compassion and skill as a physician had earned her the respect of the entire town. Striker didn't meet many women of her caliber; the ones he met were in the market for a good party and a good fuck.

From where he sat, Striker could see Lila's face, drawn in concentration. She shook her head at the computer before a smile lit her features, and she increased the speed of her hands on the keyboard. She was probably putting the finishing touches on her upcoming proposal for the school board.

As he watched her type, he couldn't help but check out her breasts in the snug black shirt she had on. It was warm in the ER, and she had shed her white coat and rested it on the seat back behind her. For some reason tonight she had scrub pants on, but not a scrub top. Her breasts were just the size he preferred, slightly more than a generous handful, and he had to bite back a groan as he imagined what she had on under her professional attire.

Fuck, another second of those thoughts and he'd be stuck standing in the waiting area with a telltale tent in his jeans. Striker decided he'd stroll over to the desk, and see what trouble he could get into with the doc.

~ ~ ~ ~

"So, Doc, you think my boy's gonna live?"

Lila jumped when the deep voice rumbled above her. She was two sentences away from completing the in-depth proposal documents, and had been so focused on her task, the rest of the room blurred into background noise. Concentration broken, she peered up at Striker, and there was no way to miss where his gaze was directed. He slowly lifted his eyes to meet hers. Not an ounce of repentance showed on his face for the fact that she'd caught him blatantly checking her out.

Unfortunately, instead of feeling insulted, her body reacted to him as it always did, growing warm and flushed. Her breath caught as she looked at his handsome face, and his question fled her brain.

Lila saved her document and closed out the program, using the task to buy her a moment to remember what it was he asked her.

"Doc?" Striker lifted one eyebrow and smirked. "You okay?"

She coughed in an attempt hide the chuckle that escaped at her teenage behavior. Thankfully Anna was focused on assisting a patient with their paperwork, and didn't seem to be aware of the awkward conversation taking place just ten feet away. Lila could feel her face heating, and knew it had to be red. The way she flushed was the bane of her existence, always betraying her emotions. "Oh, um, yes," she sputtered. Smooth, very smooth. He'd find her inarticulate ramblings attractive for sure, not that she was trying to attract him. "Gumby will be fine. Back to normal in no time, and ready to have his face smashed in all over again."

Striker barked out a laugh. "Bit of a smartass there, aren't you, Doc?"

"Well, I call it as I—"

An eager voice Lila knew well interrupted them. "Oh, Doctor Emerson, I'm so glad you're working tonight."

She sighed, and couldn't hold back a tiny groan of annoyance. Would she ever get out of here tonight? Embarrassed by the unprofessional reaction, she glanced at Striker to see if he'd noticed her blunder. If the grin on his face was any indication, he had. There probably wasn't much that slipped by him.

Lila slid her professional mask on, and looked at the man who had stepped up to the desk holding a bag of ice and a towel over his left hand. Mr. White was about forty, average height for a man, which was much taller than Lila's five-foot-two, and he was a bit overweight. Despite his larger size, his clothing always looked too big for him. Greasy, mud-brown hair sat atop his head, and thick glasses rimmed his eyes.

White was a frequent flyer, a patient who visited the ER nearly once a week for myriad complaints, many of which proved to be benign. Each time he came in he refused to be treated by any doctor other than Lila. In fact, he basically refused to speak to anyone in the ER aside from her, including the receptionist. Everyone who worked there was familiar with him, and gave his eccentricities a pass. He may have a little crush on her, and Lila tried to be sweet to the man who was often so alone.

The problem was, his visits often proved to be a waste of her time and he tended to drag out each encounter, adding extra concerns to his initial complaint once she was ready to discharge him. It was almost always a Friday or a Saturday night that he came in, and she had the impression the poor man used the hospital as a way to have the attention and social interaction he probably lacked otherwise.

"Yes, Mr. White, I'm working tonight. Looks like you hurt yourself there." Lila tried to be patient and keep the frustration out of her voice. The evening had been pleasant so far, and she just wasn't in the mood to deal with what had the potential to be hours of Mr. White. As usual, he'd avoided the receptionist and ignored the other staff in the hospital.

"Oh yes, Dr. Emerson, I did indeed. I was making dinner for my mother—you know how I do that every Friday because her hands aren't what they used to be—and the knife slipped." His green eyes welled and his lower lip quivered. "I think it needs stitches, and I'm so worried they'll hurt, but now that I see you're here I can relax. You're the best, and I know you'll take good care of me. I've never been to a doctor as gentle and skilled as you are."

Lila resisted the urge to roll her eyes. Mr. White was the polar opposite of her previous patient. Gumby hadn't flinched when she'd injected the anesthetic right into his open wound, and Mr. White was as fearful as a young child.

He might even expect a lollipop before he was discharged.

The overblown compliments only served to embarrass her, especially since Striker failed to give them any kind of privacy. She risked a glance in Striker's direction, and found a wide grin on his handsome face.

"I agree." His eyes glittered with mirth and he did a poor job of steeling his features. "While I can't comment on all the doctor's skills...I can say she's an excellent physician."

Okay, time to end this encounter before her face caught fire. Striker's teasing did not help the situation. Right now she was sure her face could have passed for a tomato, it was so warm. Lila narrowed her eyes at Striker, and shifted her attention over to Mr. White. His pupils were dilated wide, and his body was rigid as he stared at the taller man adjacent to him. Striker hovered, muscular, handsome, and very alpha male. Humble Mr. White probably felt inadequate in his presence.

"Mr. White, why don't you wait in the first treatment room over there." She gestured in the direction of the room as she spoke. "I'll be right in to examine your hand."

With a last, timid look at Striker, Mr. White thanked her profusely, and made his way down the hall, cradling his injured hand.

Lila turned her attention back to a snickering Striker. "You need to behave yourself," she admonished, but couldn't keep her own smile off her face.

"What can I say, Doc? You're fun to tease. You better go. You wouldn't want to keep the president of your fan club waiting. I'm gonna go check on my boy. See you around, Doc." He threw a wink her way as he ambled off.

This was the first time she had really spoken to Striker one on one, and she got the distinct impression he was flirting with her. That could pose a big problem. Despite what her rational side told her about not getting involved with a bad boy with whom there was no future, he'd be nearly impossible to resist if he ever decided to act on those smoldering glances.

Chapter Three

Lila stood, and slipped her lab coat back on. Might as well get on with it, the sooner she tended to Mr. White, the quicker he'd be gone, and she could finally conclude this never-ending night. Her shift had been officially over twenty minutes ago. Such was the life of an ER physician.

When she reached the treatment room, Lila raised a fist and placed a soft knock on the door. "Mr. White? It's Dr. Emerson. May I come in?"

"Oh, of course, Dr. Emerson."

She entered the room, and found him seated on the plinth, tapping his foot against the leg. The towel, loosely wrapped around his hand, remained stark white, without a trace of blood. As she approached him, Lila indicated the towel. "May I?"

He nodded his consent and gave her a beaming smile. After she pulled on gloves, Lila peeled the towel back from his hand. A clean slice split about a half-inch length of skin across the hairy knuckle of his middle finger. Lila probed around the wound, and asked Mr. White to flex and extend his finger. The joint moved fluidly, all tendons intact. The wound itself was shallow, and there was minimal edema of the knuckle. It was as she expected, the laceration was no longer bleeding, and hadn't warranted a physician's attention.

"I heard about your idea to implement a concussion and safety program for the high school sports teams, Dr. Emerson. I think it's such a wonderful idea. With all that you already do for our community by working here and being the best doctor in town, I can't believe you have the time for extra selfless projects. When the school board gives you the green light, and I know they will, I'd like to be on the team that works with you to implement the program."

The idea of Mr. White on her task force was not an appealing one, but she didn't have a clue how to discourage the notion without insulting the poor man. Thankfully he didn't seem to notice her predicament and continued speaking. "It's a bad cut isn't it? I knew I did the right thing by coming straight here. How many stitches do you think it needs?"

Her head spun at his rapidly fired questions, and Lila did her best to humor him. "It's a doozy, Mr. White, however I don't think it will require any stitches. I'll get it cleaned up and bandaged, and you can be on your way."

"Oh, okay, Lila, if you're sure that's all it needs." He frowned as though disappointed with the news. "Hey, is everything all right with you tonight?"

Taken aback by the change of subject, and the use of her first name, Lila stopped working and looked at him. "Me? I'm great. Why do you ask?"

His face flushed, and he twisted the towel in his uninjured hand. "Well, I saw who you were talking to. Do you realize who that was?"

"Do you mean Striker?"

"Yes, he's the vice president of that motorcycle club. He's

not a good man. That gang is a bunch of dangerous criminals. I don't want you to get hurt."

"It's nice of you to want to look out for me, but don't worry. I'm perfectly fine."

He took a deep breath in, as though gathering courage, and looked directly into her eyes. "Would you like to go to dinner sometime?"

Lila swallowed the groan that threatened to crawl from her throat. The man was all over the place tonight. This was not what she wanted to deal with, but she had been expecting it for a while. He never spoke of any people in his life besides his mother, and she knew she had to tread carefully to avoid hurting his fragile feelings. "Mr. White, it is so sweet of you to ask, but you are my patient, and it would be unethical." There, that was succinct, clear and professional.

A look of sadness crossed his features, but the conversation couldn't be continued because shouts from the lobby diverted their attention. Agitated male voices filtered through the door causing Lila to grow concerned. What the hell was going on? Was it a patient hopped up on drugs? She hoped not, those situations were always precarious, and tended to unnerve staff as well as other patients. "Mr. White I need to check on all that noise. Please sit tight for a few minutes, and I'll be back to get you fixed up so you can return home."

Lila swung the door open, and marched toward the waiting area, only to come to a dead stop at the scene before her.

~ ~ ~ ~

"Oh shit," said Jester. "What the fuck are they doing here?"

Striker had the same exact thought as he watched three men dressed similarly to him and his brothers step into the lobby. Christ, he did not want to deal with this tonight. Five

21

more seconds and they'd have been riding back to the clubhouse.

Striker didn't know the men by name, but he recognized the image of a wolf's head with a hooded cape centered on the back of their leather cuts. It indicated they were members of the Grimm Brothers, a rival motorcycle club from the next town over. His club had taken a lot of shit from the Grimms in the past few months. They were running drugs through No Prisoners' territory. It was starting to get ugly, and Striker worried it would lead to an all-out war.

One of the men, the only one who looked like he showered regularly, stood near the doors, blocking the exit. He had short brown hair, no visible tattoos or piercings, and lacked the cold dead eyes most of the Grimms had. The other two spilled into the lobby and waiting area, glaring at their surroundings. The security guard was nowhere to be seen. How much had it cost them to get him to split? Striker made a mental note to deal with him at a later time.

Thankfully, there were only a handful of citizens in the waiting room, and about four staff members standing wide-eyed and unmoving behind the desk. Striker had no idea how this was going to play out. He stood beside Jester and Gumby, and stared down the man closest to him while they waited to see what move the Grimms would make.

A man about Striker's height with a long black mohawk, and a wicked-looking piercing through the bottom of his nose spoke first. The smile on his face was arrogant and smug, and he addressed the room in general. "Good evening, folks," he said, his voice loud, tone mocking. "We were just in the neighborhood and wanted to stop by to familiarize ourselves with the place. We're planning to be in town more, and you never know when one might need some medical attention."

The third Grimm Brother clapped his hands together once and rubbed them back and forth, like he knew an evil secret the rest of the room wasn't privy to. He was scruffy, with shaggy blond hair and an equally scraggly beard. Holes in his jeans and a stain on the shirt under his cut topped off the slob presentation.

It was bullshit plain and simple. There was no way three Grimm Brothers just happened to waltz into the hospital on the same night some No Prisoners were there. This trio had followed them. Their presence was a show of force, a smack at the No Prisoners, telling them the Grimms were moving in on their territory. The taunting would have to be dealt with soon, but for now he wanted this altercation over without any escalation. Starting a brawl to see whose dicks were bigger would only scare the patients and staff at the hospital, and it wouldn't get the clubs any closer to solving their problems. Plus, he did not want Lila anywhere near a situation that could get her injured.

"Fuck off," countered Jester, his voice hard. He stepped toward Mohawk, and placed his hands on his hips, an impenetrable wall of muscle. "This little show supposed to intimidate us?"

The last thing they needed was for someone to call the cops. Striker was about to step in and diffuse the potentially volatile situation when he heard a soft gasp behind him. Without moving his body, he turned his head a fraction, shifted his eyes, and caught sight of Lila in his periphery. Shit, he'd hoped she wouldn't hear anything, but Jester's voice carried like a foghorn and he should have anticipated her coming to check on the noise.

"Well, well," chanted Mohawk. He fixed his attention on Lila, and licked his lips while adjusting his cock. "Looks like this hospital hired themselves one gorgeous doctor. Come closer and introduce yourself, lady doctor."

"Did you seriously just do that? Get out of here before someone calls the police. Where the hell is security?" Lila's voice reflected how pissed off she was, but Striker picked up on a small tremor of fear beneath her outrage. What the hell was she doing antagonizing these guys?

Striker took a step backward and to the side, taking Lila out of Mohawk's line of sight. He placed one hand on her soft hip, and felt her fingers curl into the waistband of his jeans in what was probably an effort to keep him from moving away.

Mohawk snickered. "There a reason you don't want me to meet the doctor, Striker? Got some kind of claim on her?"

Striker ignored the question. His impulsive move to protect Lila no doubt looked personal. Mohawk would take that information back to his club and use it to their advantage. The thought of this Mohawk character getting anywhere close to Lila infuriated him for reasons he didn't have time to delve into. "You guys want to sit down and discuss our business, fine. Name the time and place. This is not it."

Mohawk smiled. "You're probably right. Let's go boys." He motioned for the two men to leave, then looked right at Striker. "You'll be seeing us." He turned, and strode out after the other two. "Sorry to interrupt your work, pretty doctor," he called out over his shoulder as he left.

Striker clenched his jaw against the anger brewing inside him. Lila released a shaky breath that blew against his neck, and her hand was still latched onto his pants. "Go outside. I'll be there in two minutes." He nodded toward Jester and Gumby.

"Got it, VP," replied Jester. "Fucking Grimms," he muttered under his breath as he stomped after Gumby.

Striker turned abruptly, gripped Lila by the arm, and half-dragged her into the hallway where the treatment rooms were. "What the fuck did you think you were doing, Lila?"

~ ~ ~ ~

Lila was so stunned by what had just transpired, she didn't think to protest Striker towing her down the hall. She blinked at him without answering his question and her insides quaked from the lecherous and calculating look the man with the mohawk had had in his eyes.

"I asked you what the fuck you were doing?" Striker kept his volume low, but his tone was hard and demanding. It matched the frown on his face.

"Excuse me?" she asked as anger began to chase away the fear. Who did he think he was, questioning her like she was a naughty child? "I heard arguing and came to make sure everything was okay in my place of business."

"Well, little lamb, you walked right into the lion's den, didn't you?" Striker was in her face now, and he was practically snarling while his hand was still wrapped around her arm in a vice grip that, while he wasn't hurting her, didn't allow her to step away, either.

Lila twisted her arm in an attempt to break free. "Can you please let me go?"

A startled look crossed his face, as if he didn't realize he was still holding her. "Sorry." He released her immediately. "Did I hurt you?"

She dropped her arm to her side she blew out a breath. "No."

Striker ran a frustrated hand through his hair as he paced in front of her, and it hit her. He'd been worried for her safety. His face was drawn in a mask of agitation, and, if she was being honest, Striker in alpha mode was sexy as hell. Who knew this badass biker would get protective over her? A warmth bloomed in her belly at the thought.

She wanted to reach out and stop him before he wore a hole in the ground. She also had an urge to hold him, and remind him that everything turned out fine. What would he do if she wrapped her arms around him? What would he do if she kissed him?

God, what was she thinking? She should not be entertaining thoughts of kissing Striker. Hadn't she just given someone a speech about unethical relationships between providers and patients? The difference was, in the first instance she had no desire to engage in any type of relationship with the man, and in this case, she practically salivated after him.

"What just happened, Striker? Were those men friends of yours?"

Lila waited as he took a few deep breaths, in and out, until he had himself back under control.

"Fuck no. They're from a rival club. They were flexing their muscles and sending us a message. Don't mess with them, Lila. Those are some dangerous fucking men. They come near you I want to know, got me?"

"I've been told the same about you, that you're dangerous." Why did she say that? It sounded way too much like she was flirting with him.

Striker stopped his pacing directly in front of her. Lila held her breath as she waited for his reaction to her statement. Standing in the corner of the deserted white hallway, they stared at each other. Lila could have sworn a magnetic force drew him in when he bent forward, and leaned so close to her ear, a gentle puff of air caressed her as his lips moved. "You're a fucking temptation, Lila. One I should stay away from, because whoever told you that was right. I am dangerous."

26

Her breath hitched at his declaration and the fiery look on his face as he pulled back until their gazes met again. Hot lust burned bright and undisguised in his eyes. She was captivated by his stare. Her lips involuntarily parted to release the breath she had been holding. Striker groaned, and all rational thoughts fled her head. In the same instant, he slid a hand to the back of her head and fused their mouths together.

Desire exploded through her system as his insistent mouth met hers. Lila snaked her arms around his neck and pulled his body flush against her. His skillful tongue swept into her mouth and tangled with her own, making her dizzy with desire. Just as her body registered the delicious sensation of his hard male torso pressed against her breasts, and his strong arms surrounding her, a voice boomed from the lobby.

"Striker! Where the fuck are you, brother?"

Lila jerked her head back, and would have stumbled if not for his arms around her. Holy shit, had she just been kissing the vice president of the No Prisoners? And at her work? Anyone could have walked by; she was surprise no one had.

Striker tensed around her before he allowed his arms to fall away. Lila took a step back on shaking legs, and noticed that she wasn't the only one who seemed to be affected by their burst of passion. Striker was breathing just as hard as she was, and there was an unmistakable bulge in his pants. Her face heated for a different reason as she ripped her gaze from that impressive package back up to his face, but of course he'd noticed her staring at his very obvious erection.

"Good luck on Monday, Doc." With a wink and a grin, he turned and strode back to the lobby. Seconds later the roar of motorcycles tore out of the parking lot.

Lila brought hands to her heated face as she tried to regulate her breathing. She chalked the kiss up to a moment of insanity brought on by an adrenaline rush from the tense conflict in the lobby.

Monday? What was on—oh my God! Had she really forgotten the school board presentation? She needed to stay far away from that man if one kiss could wipe months of hard work from her mind.

"Dr. Emerson?" A voice laden with concern and disappointment called her name from behind her.

Shit! Mr. White. She'd completely lost sight of what she was supposed to be doing. Had he seen Striker kiss her? She hoped not. The poor man would be crushed. With her fingers crossed, she started toward the treatment room only to observe Mr. White standing in the doorway, his gaze on her. There was a tearful sheen in his eyes and both corners of his mouth turned down in a dejected frown.

Lila sighed, so much for getting out of here before the sun came up.

Chapter Four

"So, what do you think?" Lila cradled her smartphone between her ear and her shoulder as she reached for the bottle of her favorite Chilean Cabernet and filled her wine glass.

"I think it's fantastic, Lila. You have this in the bag. There's no possible way they can pass. It directly impacts student safety," Cammie said.

Lila had been running ideas by her friend for the past few months, and her input on the school sports safety project had been invaluable. Cammie grew up in this town, and knew a lot of the bigwigs on the school board. She had some great insight into what buzzwords they'd want to hear. Lila had wanted to run the final proposal by her last night, but with the way her shift went, time ran away from her.

"Thanks, Cammie. Let me run through it one more time. I'm not thrilled with the way I worded the part about coaches allowing students to return to play with a possible concussion."

Cammie's laughter floated through the phone. "No, Lila. I'm cutting you off. We ran through it three times. You have it nailed. You need to put it away, and go drink some wine before you psych yourself out. Practice it one more time tomorrow before you present, and you'll do great. I'll be there to cheer you on. Maybe I can even dig out my old Crystal Rock High cheerleading outfit. Seems fitting."

"You were a cheerleader? Why am I not surprised?" Lila appreciated her friend's attempts to talk her off the ledge. Panic had set in about midday as she finished writing up the pitch. Lila had put her heart and soul into this project, and the idea of it not succeeding was unacceptable.

"Hey! Don't be a hater just because you were in the polo club or whatever it was you rich kids did after school."

"Excuse me, spirit girl, I was not in the polo club. But you're right. I'm putting it away for the rest of the night. Thanks for the ear, Cam."

"My pleasure, Doc. See you tomorrow."

"Goodnight." Lila took a sip from her glass, and leaned her head back against the couch. The wine was delicious, and she let her mind wander as the light, oaky flavor with a hint of cherry tickled her senses.

It was vital to her that the school board accept this project. For the first time since she'd moved to Arizona from Washington, DC, actually for the first time in her life, she had something that was all her own. Something she'd put thought, and hours of hard work into without the backing of her father's money or the influence of his name.

She'd had plenty of reasons for leaving home, and no plans to return. Being out from under the influential power of her parents was freeing. In addition, Lila found fulfillment being on the staff of a small town hospital. The position challenged her more than she had anticipated, coming from a busy metropolitan medical center. And now she had the opportunity to take something she was passionate about and turn it into a reality. Getting too nervous about the presentation would be the kiss of death, so she needed to remain calm.

"Do not think about kissing, Lila," she scolded herself out loud. Throughout the day her thoughts had drifted back to the previous night's events, the kiss from Striker in particular.

She couldn't pinpoint the exact reason she was so drawn to the man. Well there was the fact that he was gorgeous, with a body that belonged in the biker calendar she'd found herself sneaking a peek at in the bookstore last week. But what concerned her was the knowledge that she was attracted to more than his looks. She loved the way he made her feel when he looked at her and spoke to her—sexy, desired and just a little bit naughty.

Was that the reason she was drawn to him like a fish to the sea? Because he was so different from any man who'd shown an interest in her in the past? Was this a bit of rebellion bucking against her conservative and formal upbringing? She sighed. This wasn't a problem she'd solve tonight, so she'd try to let it go for now.

A loud pounding on the door yanked Lila out of her musings. Her heart lodged in her throat, and her hand flew up to reach for her phone, prepared to dial 9-1-1.

"Stitch! Open up! It's an emergency!"

Lila felt faint as relief coursed through her when she recognized Jester's voice. He continued to bang on the door without pause, while calling for her. Used to handling emergencies, and the rush of adrenaline that accompanied them, Lila collected herself, and ran to the door.

"What the hell is going on?" she asked as she threw the door open. Her eyes landed on Striker and she saw heat flare in his face.

"Damn, girl." Jester whistled, as he raked his dark, nearly black eyes up and down her body.

Lila followed his gaze and glanced down. Shit! In the excitement of having unexpected late night visitors, she'd forgotten she wore nothing more than a skimpy tank top and boy short panties.

"Shut the fuck up, asshole." Striker's expression was lethal. "Lila, we need your help, right now. It's an emergency. We need you to come with us."

His words were all business, but there was no mistaking the appreciative way his gaze traveled over her body.

"Tell me what happened." Lila chose to ignore their admiring stares as best she could. They needed her in a professional capacity, so she'd try to be professional despite her state of undress.

"We got a prospect who needs medical attention."

"Guys, that's what the hospital is for. I really can't...I mean...why aren't you at the hospital?"

Striker pierced her with his intense gaze, and it was akin to being burned with a laser. "Sometimes we need to handle our shit quietly."

"Right...okay," she muttered as she ran a trembling hand over her hair, which was loose and flowing down her back. "I'm not sure about this. Do you have any idea the kind of trouble I could get in?"

"Yes, Lila, and we wouldn't be here if we didn't really need your help. I promise you'll be shielded from any blowback. All parties involved want this kept quiet, so there's really no risk to you."

Lila wanted to decline, but she couldn't, not while there was an injured man who might not get treatment otherwise. These guys would probably slap a Band-Aid on him and hope for the best if she didn't help. She prayed she wouldn't come to regret this later. "Give me thirty seconds to not look like this. There is a very extensive first aid kit over there in the hall closet. Grab it while I throw some clothes on."

"No need, darling, you can come as you are."

"Jester, I told you to shut the fuck up."

She ignored them and dashed into her room, and threw a gray sweater and black skinny jeans over what she had on. Not bothering to check a mirror, she ran back to the hall and stuffed her feet into boots. As she strode toward the door, Lila wrapped a rubber band around her hair, and snatched her purse off the counter.

She wasn't wearing a bra, but the look of urgency on their faces had her deciding to save the time it would take to run back and put one on. Her tank top had a built-in bra that would have to suffice.

Striker held the medical supplies tucked under one tattooed arm, and was tapping his fingers against it as he paced in front of the door. He jerked it open and ushered her out before relieving her of the keys and locking the door behind them. Jester led the group down the concrete driveway toward the bikes that sat at the end, near the dark and deserted road.

"I'll follow you in my car," she said.

"No, we'll take my bike. It's faster, and then there is no risk of your car being seen anywhere it shouldn't be."

As he spoke he strapped her first aid kit quickly to the back of the bike, and pulled her purse from her shoulder, stowing it in his saddlebag. Lila hesitated at his declaration. What the hell was she getting herself into?

Striker didn't give her any time to try and answer her own question. With a grin, he thrust a glossy black helmet her way. "Ever ridden before?"

"No, never." She didn't bother to tell him they called them donor cycles at the hospital. She was able to remain calm at the idea of walking into an unknown medical emergency, she did it all the time, but her heart rate kicked up at the idea of riding on a motorcycle.

"Just hold on tight and relax, try to lean with me if you can, though the holding on tight is the key. I'm gonna be going pretty fast." He winked as he secured his own helmet.

Lila nodded and shoved the helmet down over her hair. She reached for the clasp only to have her hands brushed away. Striker was so close to her that Lila smelled him with each breath, leather, cigar smoke, and...man. It was an intoxicating combination, and she wished she could lean in, press her nose to his neck, and inhale him.

The strap was too long and he had to adjust it to fit her face. "Thank you for this, Lila," he said, as he worked to shorten the strap. "I'm sure this isn't how you wanted to spend your night, but I trust you and your skill more than anyone." Once the length was correct, Striker worked fast to secure the helmet snugly under her chin.

She was touched by his heartfelt words. When their eyes met, Lila was spellbound by the flare of desire she encountered. He leaned in and kissed her, hard and quick, ending it before it began.

The swiftness of it did nothing to detract from the heat that blasted through her. Thankfully Jester wasn't paying attention to them. She didn't even have time to react before Striker turned away, and threw his jean-covered leg over the bike. "Climb on behind me and wrap your arms around my waist."

Lila did as he commanded. Her front pressed flush against his back, and his firm body was cradled between her thighs as she slid her arms around his middle. She rested her cheek against the cool leather covering the muscular plain of his upper back. An unsteady breath escaped her lungs as Striker gunned the engine then shot down the street, Jester hot on his tail. They sped through a few neighborhoods, and onto the local highway where Striker rested one hand on her thigh despite their speed.

There wasn't anything for Lila to do but cling to Striker and stare into the night. She relaxed after the first few minutes, when Striker's mastery of the bike became more than apparent. Plastered against the sexy body of an enticing bad boy, with the endless stars and vastness of the pitch-black desert speeding by, Lila felt free and uninhibited. It would have been remarkable if not for the unknown crisis awaiting her.

The longer they rode, the more the reality of the situation set in. She was almost certainly about to assist in something illegal, and possibly dangerous, with a man who embodied everything she was taught to avoid. All he had to do was ask her for help, and she put her career, her license, and possibly even her life on the line with barely any resistance. There was no way this could lead to anything but trouble.

Chapter Five

Striker sped down the highway, the night's events replaying in his mind. What was supposed to have been routine club business, collecting protection money from a local bar owner, turned into a gutter brawl when a number of Grimm Brothers showed up.

Tension had always run high between the No Prisoners and the Grimm Brothers, yet they'd managed to coexist in relative peace for years. In the past three months though, there was a shift in the dynamic. The Grimms were making some bold moves on Crystal Rock, and an escalation to violence wasn't a surprise. Christ, he hoped it wasn't a mistake bringing Lila in on this, but his options were limited.

Shit. When she stood in the doorway wearing nothing but a few scraps of clothing, he'd nearly forgotten his reason for being there. Striker had to hold himself back from slamming the door in Jester's face, and pressing Lila up against the nearest wall so he could rip what little she was wearing right off her luscious body. Without clothes the woman was even sexier than he'd fantasized, and he had a vivid imagination, particularly when it came to naked women.

Now, she was draped against him like a second skin, and

the heat pouring off her seared into him. Striker made out each of her breasts as they rested against his back, as well as the heat of her sex in the junction of her thighs where it burned into his ass. He wanted nothing more than to pull off the side of the road, drag her onto his lap, and make her scream his name into the quiet night.

Instead, they rushed toward an abandoned warehouse where he was about to ask her to sew up a hole in his prospect's side, most likely without the proper equipment, and definitely without alerting anyone. He curled one hand around her thigh to anchor her even closer, and knew he'd have to be satisfied with that for now.

After a few more miles, Striker slowed, removed his hand from Lila's leg and veered off at an exit. Three turns later, they rolled into the parking lot of the warehouse. Both he and Lila jumped off the bike as soon as it stopped, and once he had the first aid kit unstrapped, he propelled her toward the building. He watched Lila glance over her shoulder at Jester who had also dismounted but stayed where he was, turning to survey the area.

"He's on watch," Striker said.

She nodded as they approached the dinged and rusty metal door. Striker halted her with a hand on her shoulder before he turned and pinned her with a hard look. "Not a fucking word of this gets breathed to anyone, for any reason. If that's a problem, you don't take one fucking step through that door."

"Your lecture would have been more effective before I got on the bike. I get it. This never happened." Lila crossed her arms and shook off his hand.

Lila appeared calm and in control. Only the drumming of her fingers against her side under her crossed arms gave away her nerves. Her hair was flattened from the helmet and her pupils were dilated, but if he wasn't mistaken there was a gleam of excitement in her gaze. Well, well, the little doctor might turn out to be even more fun than he'd anticipated.

"Okay. Some business went bad tonight, and one of our prospects was stabbed in the side. That's all you get."

"A stab wound? Jesus, Striker! He could have damage to an organ or a major artery. He'll have to go to a hospital if that's the case."

"Let's hope nothing major was affected. We can't have this on anyone's radar."

Striker ushered her through the door and toward a couch where the prospect was lying. Rock, another brother, held a towel firmly against the right side of his flank. His muscles bulged with the force of the pressure he exerted on the prospect's wound.

"Okay, I get why you want to avoid the hospital. You boys keep your fingers crossed that this is a superficial injury. There's nothing in my kit to numb him up, so I'd get some liquor down him fast if I were you," she instructed, her tone all business as she looked at the men gathered around.

"One step ahead of you, Stitch," Gumby said as he held up a bottle of amber brown liquid. "Prospect here is well into a bottle of Jack, and probably wouldn't even realize if you stabbed him a second time."

"I doubt that, but I appreciate the effort." She winked at the prospect who did, in fact, have the glazed look of someone who'd enjoyed more than their share of alcohol. "They call you anything besides prospect?" Striker loved how she made the effort to connect with the prospect. Her relaxed attitude would help keep him calm, and no doubt make her job easier.

"Kwenny," he slurred. His face was devoid of color and perspiration shone across his brow.

She raised a questioning eyebrow at Striker.

He laughed. "His name is Kenny."

"Ah. Well, hopefully taking a knife to the gut will push you from prospect status to full member." Lila smiled at Kenny, and Striker couldn't help but admire her grace under pressure.

"How long ago did this happen?" she asked the room.

"About an hour ago," Striker answered.

"It's great that you have pressure on the wound now. Do you know how long it bled before you were able to plug it up?"

Striker looked to Gumby. He'd been with the prospect the entire time. Striker left to fetch Lila seconds after it happened.

"Not long. I used his T-shirt at first and we've been taking turns holding pressure on it the whole time, using that towel."

"Good work guys. The fact that he's still conscious is good and leads me to believe he doesn't have any internal bleeding. Of course there could be a slow bleed that we aren't aware of, but I won't be able to tell without imaging." She stopped talking and looked around the room. "Is there somewhere I can wash my hands?"

Striker pointed toward the back corner of the warehouse. "Use the men's room. There's nothing in the women's."

She nodded and jogged toward the restroom. As soon as Lila was out of earshot, Striker turned toward his brothers. "I called Pres, and he set up a meet for tomorrow with the Grimm's president. We have to shut this shit down."

Gumby nodded. "This must be drug related. They hate that they can't use our territory to meet with the cartel."

"Tough shit. This ain't their turf, bottom line. Jesus, fastest way to get the cops breathing down our necks would be to run drugs through Crystal Rock." That and the fastest way to rack up hefty prison sentences.

"For real, we may have half the department in our pocket, but no amount of money would be enough to keep them from investigating international drug trafficking."

The No Prisoners weren't saints by any means, and they had their hands in numerous less-than-legal activities, but they had always steered away from drugs, because of the attention trafficking attracted. It also invariably led to club members using, and could self-destruct a club faster than a whore could undress.

The slap of Lila's feet as she jogged back toward them echoed through the empty space and conversation halted. She slipped her hands into some gloves and rejoined them near the couch.

Lila turned her assessing gaze to the bald, stout man taking a turn holding pressure on Kenny's wound. "What's your name?"

"Rock."

"Thanks. Rock, you can move that towel now, but stay close, I may need you to wipe some blood away."

Striker observed Lila as she assessed the wound, not exactly sure what she was looking for, but she muttered to herself a few times, and smiled before addressing the group. "Looks like he was extremely lucky. The wound is more of a slash then a true stab. It's deep enough to require a lot of stitching, but doesn't appear to have pierced any organs or nicked any major blood vessels. I don't believe there was a life-threatening amount of blood loss, either.

"I'll close him up, and this will be as clean as possible considering the circumstances, but in no way sterile. My kit has a few antibiotic pills, but not an adequate supply for the long haul. I can't believe I'm about to suggest this, but I see no other way. Gumby, you come back to the ER on Tuesday when I'm working to have your hand assessed for possible infection. I'll make sure I'm the only one to look at it, and I'll write you a script for antibiotics and pain meds. You can give them to Kenny here and we won't have to worry about his insides rotting from my warehouse surgery. Sound good?"

Striker and the others stared at her. He couldn't see the looks on their faces, but he imagined their expressions matched the admiration and pride on his. "Shit, Doc, looks like you just might be hiding some outlaw under that white coat."

Lila smirked at him before her face turned serious. "Let's get this over with. You three." She pointed at three men standing around the couch. "Help me hold him down. I don't care how much alcohol he has in him, this is going to hurt like a son of a bitch."

The three did as she ordered, and Lila went to work. Striker watched a look of concentration come over her face as she morphed into doctor mode. Rock had been appointed her assistant, and every so often she asked him to hand her something from that insane box she called a first aid kit.

Lila's steady hands worked at a rapid pace, her experience evident in the even stitching and confident way she issued orders. Kenny howled, and struggled against the three men holding him down as she drove the needle through his raw skin over and over. Toward the end he passed out, most likely from the combination of the booze and the pain.

Striker was impressed by Lila. He had no right to feel this way, but he felt extremely proud of her. From the way she calmly handled the situation, he would have thought this was an everyday occurrence for her. Part of it was—maintaining her cool in the face of a medical emergency—but illegal activities in the dead of night wasn't. Or at least he didn't think she was used to it; he really didn't know her at all.

Striker wondered if she would freak out on the way back home once the gravity of the situation kicked in. He'd straight up told her they didn't want this on any police records, and she went to work as though it wasn't a big deal.

On a side note, Lila also looked like a walking wet dream, bent over Kenny with her ass-hugging jeans and form fitting sweater, which did nothing to disguise the fact she wasn't wearing a bra. Fuck, had it only been a few days since he'd gotten laid? Felt like months, based on the way his dick reacted every time she was nearby.

After a few more minutes, Lila pulled off her gloves, and glanced around. "What should I do with these? I'm guessing you don't want his blood, and I sure don't want my prints hanging around this place when we leave."

"Just leave them on the table. Two prospects are on clean up, and will wipe the place down. There won't be a trace of you or any of this here."

"Any of what where?" She smirked at him.

"Good girl. Okay, boys I'm going to take the doc home. Get Kenny back to the clubhouse so he can rest, and I'll meet you there as soon as I'm done."

Striker walked Lila out of the warehouse and back to his bike.

"All good?" Jester asked from his guard post, his focus on the road leading to the warehouse.

"Yeah, it's done. Go help them get Kenny into the van. I'm going to take Lila home."

Jester nodded and left them alone with the bikes.

"Remember, Lila, not a fucking word," Striker cautioned, purposefully hardening his voice.

She huffed out a breath. "Striker, I know, believe me. I'd be in just as much trouble as any of you if I ran my mouth."

"No, you wouldn't, babe. You're a doctor, well respected in the community. All you'd have to do is bat those gorgeous eyes, and tell them how we forced you out of your house in the middle of the night. You'd have the cops eating out of your palm in seconds."

She jammed her hands on her hips and rolled her eyes at him. "I'm not going to do that."

"Good." He nodded. He believed her. He stepped in close enough to see her pupils dilate at his nearness. "You okay with all this shit? I gotta say, babe, you surprised me in there."

Lila shrugged. "I think I surprised myself, but yeah, I'm fine."

They stared at each other for a moment, and she shivered. He attributed it to the rapidly dropping temperature and the adrenaline dump. Despite the scorching heat of the day, nights in the desert could be bitter cold, and she was only wearing a thin sweater.

Striker broke their connection to pull a sweatshirt out of his saddlebag. He tossed it to Lila, and she drew it over her head with muffled thank you. He climbed on the bike and glanced at her just as she grabbed a handful of the sweatshirt fabric and inhaled with her eyes closed. Her eyes drifted open, and he met her gaze as a red blush crept across her gorgeous face.

With a groan, Striker motioned for her to climb on behind him. "I do like knowing I'm leaving my scent on you, babe, but knowing you like it too is going to make for one uncomfortable ride home, if you catch my drift."

Lila's eyes widened for just a second, and then she shocked him more than she had all night. "I like it too. I just wish I didn't have anything between your shirt and my skin."

And with that bomb, Lila pulled her helmet on, climbed

behind him, and wrapped her arms around him. His cock hardened even further, and he shifted in an attempt to keep from strangling it against the bike.

~ ~ ~ ~

What the hell was she thinking? Did she really tell him she wished his sweatshirt was against her naked skin? Lila couldn't believe she had flirted with him so blatantly.

Actually she couldn't believe how she acted the entire night, starting with opening the door to her house in her underwear. None of this seemed real, almost as though she was watching a movie of herself instead of participating in her life.

The potential repercussions of the evening were staggering. She could be suspended from the hospital, or even lose her medical license, and she could be sued for everything she was worth if Kenny died of an infection. She almost laughed at the thought of the school board's reaction if they were to find out.

At the moment she allowed her attraction to Striker to distract her from the real issue, that she'd conducted an illegal medical procedure in a warehouse, in the dead of night, for an outlaw biker gang.

She needed to watch her mouth. Striker was obviously way out of her league when it came to playing games with the opposite sex. True, she was wildly attracted to him; he was smoking hot, after all. That did not mean she could handle him. Striker was one hundred percent alpha male, dominant and demanding, and he'd probably eat her alive.

A warm feeling had traveled through her when he called her babe. Ridiculous. He used the endearment on just about anything with breasts, but still, it felt more intimate than Doc or Stitch, or even her name.

Striker rode slower than he had on the way out, and Lila

was able to appreciate the trip. She tried to ignore the way the muscles of his back rippled under her breasts, and the heat from where her sex was molded to his backside, but it was fruitless.

Without city lights to provide a glow, the desert night was ink black. They were cocooned by the stars and blanket of darkness that surrounded them. She couldn't tell where the sky ended and land began. The result was an impression of limitless oblivion.

Riding a Harley through the desert after dark was something she could imagine herself becoming addicted to, leaving the stress of the day far behind, and reveling in the peace of the quiet night. Of course, she would require the hard male body between her legs to top off the experience. She frowned as she realized her thoughts had done a complete three-sixty, leading her right back to her attraction to Striker.

Before she knew it they turned onto her sleepy street, and coasted to a stop in her driveway. Disappointment surged through her at the realization that she may never have this opportunity again.

Lila tugged her helmet off, shook out her hair, and clambered down from the bike as Striker killed the engine. He made no move beyond removing his own helmet, so she reached down to pull his sweatshirt over her head. Striker stopped her with a hand on her arm, and hauled her toward his big body. With his legs still straddling the bike, his torso was angled toward her, and he pressed his mouth up to her ear.

"Thanks for saving my prospect tonight, Doc. You amaze me every time I watch you work." He skimmed his lips over her ear and she shivered in response.

"I'm glad I could help."

Striker rubbed one large hand up and down the center of her back, directly over her spine, and Lila wanted to purr like a contented cat. Her back was a little sore from hunching over the couch to close Kenny's wound.

"I don't want you to go inside and stress about this all night. There isn't a soul who knows, beyond the guys who were there, and they would die before ratting. I wouldn't have involved you if I couldn't protect you. Your reputation is too important."

His lips still brushed the sensitive skin of her ear with every movement, but the words themselves touched something deeper.

"Keep the sweatshirt. Wear it to bed. I want to go to sleep tonight knowing your skin smells like me."

Just like that, Lila's panties grew damp. She'd never had such a strong physical reaction to a man. But Striker was no ordinary man; he was sex and sin personified, and apparently that did it for her. She turned her head so their lips were just a breath away. "I'll be sure to get rid of the extra layers then."

Striker growled, literally growled, and clamped a hand around the back of her head holding her in place for his lips to claim hers. Desire shot through her as the taste of him flooded her senses. She tasted smoke, a hint of the whisky he snagged from Kenny, and danger. It was a powerful combination she was helpless to resist.

When she opened her mouth to him, a moan escaped, and his tongue tangled with hers. His kiss made her dizzy, and she gripped the leather of his cut with both hands to ground herself as they devoured each other. After a quick nip to her lower lip, he pulled back with a curse. Her head spun as she pulled in air.

"You need to get inside before someone sees us, and I need

to get back to the clubhouse to deal with all this," Striker said, his hand never leaving her back.

Lila blew out a breath and nodded, not trusting herself to speak at the moment. After he fired up his bike, he turned, winked at her, and roared down the street, probably waking half the neighborhood.

Lila rolled her eyes as she made her way up the driveway. She couldn't help the grin that broke across her face as she mouthed *holy fuck*. She had no idea what had happened, but she wanted to know when it could happen again, because one taste of Striker was definitely not enough.

Just as she reached her door Lila heard her phone chime. Excitement shot through her at the thought it might be Striker. Shaking her head, she dug it out of her bag. She needed to give herself a firm talking to before she crashed into major disappointment.

A text message notification lit up the phone, the number unfamiliar to her. Lila swiped it open to read it, and a chill ran up her spine. She quickly scanned her surroundings to see if anyone was lurking on the street. Her block was dark and soundless, illuminated only by the floodlights outside a neighbor's home.

Feeling exposed and vulnerable, Lila darted into the house and threw the lock on the door almost before it closed. After taking a few cleansing breaths, she glanced back down to reread the text.

Really Doctor? Spending your free time with the No Prisoners?

Chapter Six

"I'd like to conclude with a quick story about why this is such an important topic." Lila clicked a button on the remote control and a picture of a smiling high school boy appeared on the projection screen. "This is Kyle. Before I continue, I'll let you know I have written permission from Kyle's parents to share his story with you."

Lila looked up at the crowd, pleased that those in attendance had their eyes riveted to the screen. "Kyle was a high school senior. A straight A student, popular with the girls, and captain of his football team. After graduation, he planned to attend Notre Dame on a football scholarship. They offered him a full ride. He was going to major in computer engineering. Typical kid who had the world at his feet, and endless possibilities."

Her eyes drifted to the clock. Eight twenty-five. She'd timed it perfectly.

"Kyle took a nasty hit during the school's homecoming game. He told his coach he remained conscious, but had a quick flash of black when he hit the ground. They called a time out while Kyle was attended to. He had a mild headache, but otherwise seemed completely normal to his coach and teammates, so they put him back in play. He made it through the rest of the game and his headache got worse. But he wanted to be there for his team, or so he told his girlfriend later, so he toughed it out and didn't speak up."

Lila took a deep breath before she continued. This story always had the power to bring her to tears. Such useless waste of a promising young life. "That night, after the homecoming dance, he was driving his girlfriend home. They were on the highway, going about sixty, when, according to her, he yelled out that his vision was spotty and he couldn't see. The car veered across the yellow line and he was killed on impact. His girlfriend survived, but she'll require the use of a wheelchair for the rest of her life.

"This tragedy was born of a lack of education by the coaches, parents, and students themselves. I aim to change that by providing the proper safety information to ensure something like this doesn't happen here in Crystal Rock. I want to educate coaches on the correct way to assess for a concussion, and provide them with an algorithm for action. Thank you so much for giving me your time this evening. I'll stick around for a while, should anyone have any questions."

The people in attendance, mostly parents and teachers, stood and clapped. She felt the weight of this task float off her shoulders the moment the applause began. Lila walked down the steps of the pop-up stage, and John Heath, the school board president, took the place she had vacated at the podium.

"I'd like to thank Dr. Emerson for the time and effort she put into this presentation. Typically, we meet and deliberate before we take a formal vote, but in this case it's not necessary. Each member of the board is eager and excited to move forward with this project as soon as possible. So, it is with great pleasure I officially tell you your project has been approved, doctor. We look forward to working with you to ensure the safety of our younger generations."

Triumph surged at his words, and an enormous smile broke out across her face. This was why she'd moved away from home, this opportunity to own her life. To create something and nurture it from its inception without always wondering if it only succeeded because of her family's name or deep pockets.

The board president descended the steps, and walked straight toward Lila with his hand held out. "Congratulations, Dr. Emerson. Yours was one of the best proposals we've had in many years."

She accepted his handshake with a smile. "Thank you, Mr. Heath. I'm very passionate about this project and can't wait to begin."

"We have a small budget to award you, but you'll probably need to do some fundraising as well to increase your spendable capital."

She had to bite her lip to distract herself from the desire to jump up and down with giddy delight. No sense in sabotaging the project before it began by acting unprofessional. "I'm going to assemble a committee of people from the community, and begin working as soon as possible.

"Excellent," he said and he held his hand out again. "Will you stay and join us for coffee?"

She shook his hand again. "Thank you for the offer, Mr. Heath, but I didn't get much sleep last night and I have to be at the hospital by six tomorrow, so I need to take a pass on this one."

"Well then, you have a wonderful night."

"Thank you, you as well." Lila bent down and gathered her purse off the floor before she turned to leave the high school gymnasium. A number of people, some she'd met before at the hospital, shook her hand and complimented her as she passed by. After another fifteen minutes of small talk, she walked out into the cool night air.

The sun had set, and the parking lot was cast in shadows. Lila glanced around as a prickle of unease worked its way up her spine. This presentation had taken so much of her mental energy that she'd shoved the worry over the unnerving text message into the back recesses of her mind. Now she stood alone and vulnerable in a darkened parking lot. Maybe she should have taken it a bit more seriously.

The chirp of a car being unlocked sounded through the quiet night, and Lila jumped with a gasp. "Shit," she muttered as her keys fell from her hands. Damn whoever sent that text. By the time she reached her car, she was furious over the fact that someone had scared her. She prided herself on having taken control of her life; she wasn't going to allow some punk make her fearful of every bump in the night.

For a moment last night, she had wondered if she should tell Striker, and now the idea flashed through her mind again. She let it marinate for a moment, then dismissed it. It was probably just someone messing with her; no point in making a big deal about it until it became one.

~ ~ ~ ~

Striker rubbed a hand across the back of his neck, trying to relieve the tension in the muscles. It didn't work, and he rested the palm of his hand on his gun as the door to Black's opened and three Grimm Brothers walked into the bar. Each man held their arms out for Jester to pat them down. They knew the drill, and had left any weapons outside.

Striker turned and caught the eye of the bartender. He gave the man a nod. With a quick glance at the three men who made their way to Striker's table, the bartender headed into an office at the back of the room and closed the door with an audible thud. They'd given the man a grand to shut the bar down for one hour. More than enough to compensate for any lost business.

Really, the bar owner had no choice. What could one man do against five No Prisoners who needed private use of his bar? But they had a good relationship with him, and there wasn't any point in fucking that up, so they paid him off.

Striker turned his attention back to the scarred wood table as Jackal, the Grimm's president, slid into the booth opposite him and his president, Shiv. Striker didn't recognize the man who took the seat next to Jackal. He wasn't the Grimm's vice president. The third man remained by the door, near Jester.

"Shiv, Striker." Jackal nodded at them. This wasn't the type of encounter where you shook hands and asked about each other's families. They'd be civil for the sake of business and the preservation of both their clubs, but there was no love lost between the men.

"Where's Snake?" Striker asked of the Grimm's VP.

Something that looked a lot like fear clouded Jackal's eyes. "He's taking care of some other business."

Striker didn't buy it. Something wasn't right, but it was too late to back out now.

"We need you out of Crystal Rock." Shiv didn't waste any time or breath on pleasantries. "I get that it's a pain in the ass for you to transport your shit around our town, but it's just too damn bad. It's always been that way, and that's the way it's gotta stay to avoid bloodshed."

Shiv paused, and Striker jumped in. "Cops in our town know we don't deal in Smack or Molly or whatever shit you're pushing these days. They're getting wind of product coming through our town, and are starting to sniff around. We have a handle on them for the most part, but it's only a

52

matter of time before a do-gooder cop gets tired of it and calls in the Feds. We're both fucked if that happens.

"You need to move your shit through Scorpions Trail like always and keep out of Crystal Rock. I know you don't want a war any more than we do, and if the Feds show up, I promise we'll steer them right to your door." Scorpion's Trail was a path through the mountains the Grimms had been using for years to transport drugs. It was difficult traveling, but the mountainous terrain kept them off the grid, and made it very difficult for the cops to set up a sting. The Grimms typically hired illegals to run the drugs from Mexico through the mountains with the promise of a place to stay.

In a surprisingly vulnerable move, Jackal ran his hands over his face. On closer inspection, the man looked weary and haggard. His long hair had grayed and deep wrinkles were set in his thin face. Jackal was only forty-seven, but he had the look of a man who'd lived his life hard and wild.

Jackal turned to the man on his left and jerked his head toward the door. The man stood and walked to stand by Jester and the other Grimm, near the door, leaving Jackal alone at the table with Shiv and Striker.

"I'm having some trouble with a few of my members," he said while he stared at Shiv.

"Snake?" asked Striker.

Jackal gave one nod but didn't elaborate.

Was he for real? Striker couldn't believe what he was admitting to them. It was time for Jackal to stand down as president. Clearly he didn't have control of his club anymore.

Shiv appeared just as unimpressed as Striker. "You need to handle your shit, Jackal. It's not my problem that you can't keep your little boys in line. Get your club under control. We've got plenty of contacts down in Mexico ourselves, wouldn't take much to mess with your supply from that end. No more popping in our bars after a run, no more surprise visits to our hospital. Keep your men out of our territory. Stick to Scorpion's Trail or I make some calls."

That was the threat that would be most effective. The majority of the Grimm's money came from running drugs. It was a bit of a stretch to let Jackal believe they could fuck up their supply with just a few phone calls, but it was true they had plenty of MC contacts down in Mexico, and with some effort could probably damage the Grimm's imports.

Jackal nodded and stood. "Consider it done." He motioned to his men and left the bar.

Shiv looked at Striker. "This shit stinks worse than a six-week-old wank sock."

Striker grimaced at the image, and swallowed down the last of his whisky. "I hear you, Pres. There is definitely some shit in that cesspool. We did what we could for tonight. I think the threat of lost money will keep them in line."

Striker wasn't so sure he believed his own words. His gut wasn't happy with this entire situation. "Jester," he called out. "Let Black know we're done and he can reopen."

With a nod, Jester jogged to the back of the room and pounded on the office door. Black emerged a few seconds later.

"Thanks, man. Appreciate your flexibility," Striker said as he handed him an envelope full of cash.

"No problem, Striker."

Striker rose from his seat and stretched. He was relieved this meeting was over, even if he wasn't thrilled with the outcome. He pulled his phone from the pocket of his pants and glanced at the time. Almost nine. Lila should be done with her presentation to the school board by now. Two thoughts assaulted him at the same time. He hoped it went well and they approved her project. And why the fuck did he remember what time her presentation was?

Chapter Seven

Lila sighed as she bent down and tied her running shoes. Clearing her mind today would require an extra-long run. She was an avid runner, using the exercise to destress and process her thoughts.

It was Saturday morning, almost a week after the night that she now referred to as *temporary insanity night* in her head. Work had been busier than usual this week with multiple meetings and a higher than normal patient flow, leaving her little time to wrap her head around the events of the previous Sunday.

There hadn't been any more strange text messages, and as the week went on, she became more confident it was an isolated incident. Someone who had seen Striker at her house and disapproved of their association, maybe a neighbor? Still, she kept her doors and windows locked at all times, and was a little jumpier than usual once night fell.

Lila caught sight of Striker's sweatshirt lying on the top of a clothes pile on her bed. She hadn't washed it, and had worn it every night. A huge part of her knew it was beyond stupid, but the smell of him wrapped around her as she drifted off to sleep was too enticing to pass up. She shook her head, frustrated with her inability to put the man out of her mind. Thoughts of him were dangerous and wouldn't lead anywhere productive.

After a couple quick stretches, Lila chose the playlist on her phone that usually lasted long enough for her to complete a seven to eight mile run. As she jogged down her steps, an older model dirty green car captured her attention. It sat parked in front of her neighbor's house, and Lila made a mental note to check in on the woman later. She was elderly, never left the house, and as far as Lila knew, hadn't had any visitors since Lila moved in.

She enjoyed the push and pull of her laboring muscles until about three miles in, when she realized she wasn't on her usual route. Unintentionally, she'd turned down the street where the No Prisoners' clubhouse and auto garage were located. She'd never been inside the clubhouse, and hadn't needed any work done on her car since she'd been living in Crystal Rock, so she'd never been on the premises.

That didn't prevent her from knowing exactly where it was located, just a few blocks from the small downtown area of Crystal Rock. Everyone in town knew where the clubhouse was. It was a short street with no other businesses or houses on it, but it connected to another road with housing. Well, she was here. What could it hurt to take a little jog past and peek at the building?

Lila glanced over her shoulder as she crossed the quiet street and noticed a car slowly rolling down the road. It looked an awful lot like the car she'd seen parked in front of her neighbor's. It was the same unattractive shade of murky green and the license plate was covered in mud and unreadable.

A nervous flutter in her stomach had her picking up the pace as she ran past the No Prisoners' clubhouse, all thoughts of scoping the place out gone from her mind. Was the driver following her or was she being paranoid?

She continued on, turning down a few random streets without a pattern. If the car stayed with her, it would be obvious that it was following her. None of the streets had sidewalks and Lila felt vulnerable and exposed. Every few seconds, she snuck a glance over her shoulder. Sure enough, the car remained with her for every turn. The driver maintained a fair distance, but didn't really attempt to hide the fact that they were shadowing her.

The rush of Lila's blood pounded in her ears, a combination of the exercise and mounting anxiety, and she found herself running at full speed. She forced her legs to slow down, and not give away the fact that she was aware she was being followed. She switched off the music to better listen for the car.

Suddenly the rumble of an engine grew louder, and she turned in time to see the car barreling down the street straight for her. It swerved at the last second, and shot down the block with the roar of its engine. Lila doubled over gasping for breath as she stared at the retreating taillights.

It had all happened in an instant; one second they were at the end of the road and in the next, the vehicle had been inches away from her. It was apparent the driver was intent on scaring her. Had they meant to hit her, they would have; she wouldn't have stood a chance.

She glanced up from her stooped position, hands on her knees, and watched the car swing a U-turn at the end of the street. Fuck! That first drive-by had been a warning, but was the driver planning to play with her some more, or did they mean to hit her this time?

Lila spun around and sprinted, pushing her muscles to their maximum capacity. Her legs burned. She forced her muscles to near failure, and her heart slammed against her ribs as she hauled ass along the pavement. Dizziness swamped her, a combination of fear and hyperventilation. She was dying to know how close the car was, but refrained from peeking over her shoulder as fear of losing speed swamped her.

The clubhouse was within her sights, just around the upcoming corner. Would they help her if she could make it there before being mowed down? It was the only place she knew in this neighborhood, so she had to chance it. Just as she rounded the corner, the revving of an engine overshadowed the roar in her ears, and Lila prayed her legs would hold out until she got to the garage.

~ ~ ~ ~

Striker's thoughts were with the Grimm Brothers as he loosened the cable clutch on a bike and checked out the ball-and-cam gizzer. Sure enough, there was too much pressure, and it needed to be adjusted. Easy fix, and one Striker could do in his sleep, or while his mind was replaying the meeting with Jackal. Nearly a week later, he had an itch at the back of his neck that demanded its due.

He tightened the locknut and forced himself to think of anything else. The rest of the guys in the garage were conducting a post mortem of last night's party. Striker went, and had two or three opportunities to take a warm and willing woman up to his room, but something had stopped him.

Who was he kidding? He knew exactly what had stopped him. For some screwed up reason, every time he thought of fucking a woman this past week, Lila's face popped into his head. She starred in every fantasy he had while jerking off in the shower, and he felt like a teenager with too many hormones and nowhere to stick his dick.

"So, you see her?" Jester's question knocked him out of his own head.

"See who?"

"That piece Acer snagged last night." Jester put down the airbrush he'd been working with and spun on his stool.

"She was something," Acer broke in with a grin. "My dick is actually sore today."

"Not that we don't all love hearing about your dick, but that bitch you went home with, that was Brandi, right?" Gumby's voice floated up from under the hood of an old beater.

"Yeah, why? You hit that?" Acer asked.

"I think we've all hit that. Good lay, but she is one crazy-ass chick. Broke a mirror in my apartment when I told her to go before the sun came up. Jesus, this engine is practically held together with chewing gum and spit." Gumby sounded disgusted.

Striker barked out a laugh. "Gumb, ever think it may just be you?" He knew Brandi. In fact, he'd been on that ride once himself, and while he enjoyed busting Gumby's balls, the man had a point. That chick was bad news. She'd gone off on him as well when he'd moved on after one night of fun. If she kept that dramatic shit up, the club would have to run her ass off.

"Wait, why haven't I seen her around? Shit, can't believe I'm missing out on some prime pussy." Jester looked around. "Everyone had a shot at her?" He turned and walked toward the exit of the garage bay muttering something about being left out of the pussy loop. Turning back toward the garage he announced, "I'm going to grab a beer. No one talk about any new broads while I'm gone. I can't afford to miss out, I've got a rep to uphold."

The men cracked up, and Jester took a few steps backward

out of the garage flipping them the bird with both hands. As he watched, Striker caught sight of a woman sprinting full out, on a direct course for the garage. She threw a quick glance over her shoulder as Jester stepped out of the garage.

"Whoa there, darlin'." Jester reached out a hand and steadied the woman who nearly collided with him at full speed. "Stitch?" he queried, his voice full of surprise.

Lila sank to her knees, hands splayed on the ground in front of her as she sucked in great gulps of air. "Car... followed...shit...need...air." She was panting so hard she could barely form words.

"Hey, Doc, I'm not one to discourage a gorgeous woman on her knees at my feet, but you may want to tone it down a notch if you're not gonna be able to stand at the end of your run. Hey, you okay?" His voice changed from teasing to concerned as Lila started to tremble at his feet.

Striker wiped his grease-stained hands on his jeans before he walked over and crouched down beside Lila, and placed a hand on her heaving back. Her head dropped forward, and sweat dripped from a long ponytail onto the ground as it dangled over her shoulder. Her entire body heaved, and she gulped in air. Jesus, was something seriously wrong with her? "Lila, what the hell is going on? What are you doing here?"

After a few moments, her breathing finally calmed enough for her to answer his question. She sat back on her heels, and scrubbed her hands over her sweat-dampened face. "I'm sorry, I know I shouldn't be here." She paused to take a few breaths. "I was out for my morning run...and noticed a car...on my street." Still winded, it took a while to get her point across. "After a few miles...I saw it again. Thought it might be tailing me." She took three deep breaths in a row. It seemed to do the trick and she was able to continue. "I turned down a bunch of streets to see if I could lose it or if it really was following me, and it stayed with me until about three blocks that way." She gestured with her hand, her breathing still audible. "Then it tried to run me down. I was close to here, and it's the only place I know in this area, so I just ran as fast as possible until I got here."

"Fuck! You sure it was gunning for you, and not just a shitty driver?" Striker asked, still on the ground with her.

"I'm sure. Like I said, he stayed with me despite multiple random turns."

"Running, huh? No wonder your ass is so tight, Doc." Jester bobbed his eyebrows at her.

Leave it to Jester to spew out a ridiculous comment at such an inappropriate time.

Lila burst out laughing. "Thanks, Jester, I needed that."

"Hey, Striker." Jester tilted his head toward the street where an old model green Buick with muddy plates was slowly rolling past.

"That the car, babe?"

Lila's head popped up and her eyes went wide. "What? He's here?" She scrambled to her feet like she was preparing to bolt.

"Gumby," he called out. "Follow him. See where the fucker goes." Gumby sprinted to his bike and shot off after the car that sped up after it passed the clubhouse.

Striker slid his hands up Lila's arms to her shoulders, and turned her to face him. "Hey, babe. Lila, look at me."

She faced him, and the frightened look in her eyes caused an unfamiliar surge of protectiveness in Striker. He felt a gut-wrenching need to ensure her safety, similar to the night he shielded her from the Grimm Brothers. "There is no fuckin' way he'd drive in here. Not unless he had a death wish."

Jester raised a brow at Striker's forcefully spoken words. Striker wasn't usually one to rush to a woman's defense, but the statement seemed to be what Lila needed to hear.

Striker watched her gather herself, take a deep breath and nod at him. It was then he noticed what she was wearing, or rather how little she was wearing. He trailed his eyes down her body, and dropped his hands from her damp shoulders, clenching them into fists at his sides. It was either that or reach out and palm her tight ass encased in tiny spandex shorts. On top she wore a neon yellow, stretchy tank top that ended just above her belly button, and left an expanse of creamy skin he wanted to lick. He forced himself to wrench his eyes back up to her face.

"Let's go into the clubhouse and get you a drink. Anyone you know have it in for you?"

"I don't know. I don't think so." She shook her head as she answered, but a thoughtful look crossed her face.

Striker placed a hand on her lower back and steered her toward the clubhouse with Jester trailing behind. He enjoyed the feel of her satiny skin under his callused hands. Unable to stop himself, his thumb caressed a circle on her soft flesh, and he heard her emit a small gasp at the intimate contact. When they reached the heavy metal door, he held it open for her.

"Ladies first."

Lila turned. "Jester." She motioned him forward with a snarky grin.

Jester hooted out a laugh and slung an arm around Lila's shoulders. The action pulled her away from Striker, and Jester propelled her through the door. "Girl, you are gonna be some trouble, aren't you?"

Striker was glad her sass was coming back so quickly. Seeing her so unnerved had caused a twist of fury in him. He followed them through the door with a shake of his head. Lila was already trouble, just not the kind that Jester was referring to.

Chapter Eight

Lila's eyes took a minute to adjust to the dim lighting after being out in the blinding Arizona sun. She blinked the space into focus, and scanned the room. She never expected to be in here and couldn't keep her wild curiosity at bay. The main room was large, and her interest was drawn to a well-stocked, carved wooden bar running along the entire left wall. A handful of four-person square tables rested to the right with their chairs flipped on top. The center was open, allowing people to pass through toward the rear of the room.

A long staircase at the back of the room led to the second level. License plates, street signs, motorcycle prints, and a fair number of pictures of almost naked woman littered the walls, giving the place an eclectic, masculine Americana style. She had to admit it wasn't what she'd been expecting. In her mind she pictured the place as a dirty, smelly frat house of sorts, and was pleasantly surprised by the cleanliness and order of the clubhouse. She could even get behind the masculine biker decor, except for all the nude women plastered on the walls, but men will be men.

Jester uncurled his arm from around her shoulders as they reached the bar. "What's your poison, darlin'?"

"Oh, um, I'll just have whatever you have I guess. Isn't it a little early for a drink?"

"Nope," Striker answered. "Rule is, if you've nearly been run down before noon, all bets are off."

"Hey, prospect, let's get a couple of Bourbons over here." Jester rapped a meaty fist against the bar and took a seat next to Lila.

Striker slid onto the barstool on the opposite side of Lila. "Make it three."

She twisted on her seat to get a better look at Striker. God, he was hot. He wore a plain, dark gray T-shirt that stretched across his wide chest and muscular arms. Slightly dirty from working on motorcycles in the garage, it only enhanced his manly appeal. She hoped the prospect would bring the drinks soon so she had something to occupy her hands. Otherwise she was likely to reach out and stroke them over Striker's sinewy body.

"You all right, Lila?" Striker asked.

Lila blew out a breath. Her hands still trembled, but at least she could breathe and speak now. "I think so. God, I've never been that scared. For a few minutes I thought he'd catch me." Resigned to the fact that lightning didn't strike twice in one place, she decided to be forthright with them. "I received a disturbing text message last weekend, after I got home Sunday night from...you know."

Striker's attention was fully focused on her. "It's fine, babe. You're okay to speak freely in here."

"Right. Well then, after I helped with Kenny Sunday night, immediately after, before I even got in my house, I received a text. I dismissed it as a harmless prank, but after today I'm not so sure."

"What'd it say?" His voice had dropped to a menacingly low tone.

"It said, 'Really, doctor? Spending your free time with the No Prisoners?'" She didn't bother to check her phone for accuracy. The veiled threat was burned into her brain.

"Shit, Stitch! You should have said something right away." Jester frowned at her from the barstool on her other side.

Lila swung her gaze in Jester's direction. "I figured it was just someone being an ass."

She caught Jester and Striker exchanging a look. "What? What are you thinking?"

"You should have told me, Lila. We could have checked it out." Striker shook his head. His lips pressed into a thin line.

"I didn't realize the MC did much in the way of personal security work," she shot back. She took a sip of her bourbon. They were right, but the fact that they scolded her made her feel embarrassed and had frustration tightening her stomach.

Jester chuckled. "That we don't, Doc. We do, however, take care of our own, and we owe you one. Not to mention this threat seems to be a direct result of you helping us out."

"Jester, can you go brief Shiv on all this shit?"

"Who?" She looked between the men.

"He's the club's president," Striker told her.

Once he said that, the name rang a bell. If rumors were to be believed, his nickname came about after he survived a prison stabbing meant to end his life.

Before Jester could respond, Lila's phone chimed. Striker's hands brushed the bare skin of her bicep as he slipped the phone out of the band on her arm, and handed it to her. The now familiar tremor of arousal that began under his fingertip traveled straight to her core. She peered down at the screen, and didn't bother to disguise the gasp of surprise that escaped. "Shit." Her stomach sank and her blood chilled in her veins.

Striker plucked the phone from her unsteady fingers, and

frowned at the screen. She watched his face harden as he read the text. *Scared, doctor? I see you ran right to the No Prisoners, literally.* He tossed the phone to Jester who read it, abruptly turned, and strode with purpose toward a set of double doors at the back of the room.

"Listen, Lila, I shouldn't say anything to you, but I know you can keep your mouth shut, and you appear to be ass-deep in this, so I'm gonna give it to you straight. There's a high chance this is the Grimm Brothers."

His admission worsened her distress. "The MC from last week in the ER?"

He nodded, and a muscle ticked in his jaw. "We're trying to sort our shit out with their president, but something's going on in that club. It's starting to get ugly, as you can guess, since you witnessed what happened to Kenny. We're handling it, but it's going to take some time. They saw you last Friday. Noticed me jump in to shield you, and screwing with you may be one more way of fucking with us. If it is the Grimm Brothers, you're not safe. You're going to need some protection. The kind of protection only the club can provide, you get me?"

"Let me guess, that means no cops?"

"No cops." He nodded, and trailed a hand up her arm. Warmth followed the movement, and continued through her body even when his hand settled, strong and sure on her shoulder.

"But wouldn't it be better just to let the cops handle it? Then you can stay uninvolved."

He shrugged. "Doesn't work that way. It's not how the club handles things. We're already involved. The police would initiate an investigation into every aspect of the club, and we can't allow that."

Striker was taking this very seriously, and that fact didn't do anything to ease her worry. It had to be bad if Striker was concerned. "So what do I do?"

"I'm not sure yet," he said as he gave her shoulder a gentle squeeze. "We'll discuss it as a club, come up with a plan. Ultimately it will be Shiv's decision, but, like Jester said, you've helped us out and we owe you."

She appreciated his honestly. Lila had never encountered Shiv, but she assumed he didn't go around protecting people out of the goodness of his heart. This was an outlaw MC after all, and they weren't known for their charitable works. Striker and Jester had both claimed the club owed her, but she'd done them only one favor. How much weight would that one act hold with the club?

"Hey, VP!" Jester's thundering voice rang out from between the doors he'd disappeared through a few moments before.

"Yeah?" He turned his head toward Jester.

"Shiv wants to talk to the Doc." Jester's large body filled doorway as he held the doors open, waiting for them.

Striker stood, and reached a hand out for Lila. She hesitated for a second before she took his hand and allowed him to draw her to her feet. Her stomach fluttered with nerves, and her heart pounded in her chest. Striker's hand came to rest on her lower back, right on the bare skin where her shirt left off. Goosebumps ran up her spine when his fingers slid across her sensitive skin, making her anxious for an entirely different reason.

"Cold?"

"No."

A slow, smug smile spread across his face, and he winked at her. It was obvious he could tell he was getting to her. She wasn't very adept at hiding her feelings, and hadn't been this attracted to a man probably ever, so she didn't have the skills or experience to fool him.

As a unit, they moved toward the doors, and Lila forced herself to breath in and out and not give into the nerves threatening to overtake her. When they reached the doorway, Striker slid his hand around her waist and gave her a gentle squeeze. She appreciated the silent gesture of support.

"Wait here for one second, babe."

Striker and Jester disappeared behind the heavy wooden doors while Lila took a few cleansing breaths to calm her nerves. After a moment, Striker reopened the door, and waved her in. As she passed through the doorway his hand once again found her, this time resting on the back of her neck, a move she found to be surprisingly protective. The door closed behind them with a thud, the sound causing her already on-edge nerves to jump.

A large, square, industrial steel table filled the majority of the room. It was eclectic and looked like a handmade work of art. Shiv was perched on the edge of a chair at the head of the table that had about ten other chairs around it; maybe another ten were around the edge of the room.

A jagged scar ran from the corner of Shiv's mouth, straight across to his ear and made him an intimidating presence. Lila knew exactly what was required to leave a scar of that magnitude.

She took a moment to study him, guessing his age to be somewhere around forty-five to fifty. His deep-chocolate-colored hair hung well past his shoulders and a long dark beard adorned his face. Two narrowed eyes, which were nearly the same color as his hair, pierced her with a look she couldn't decipher. In his hand, a thick cigar emitted a pungent aroma, while a swirling pattern of smoke drifted up into the air.

Lila's eyes darted around, noticing there were about ten

other club members in the room, some at the table and others scattered in the chairs around the perimeter. She swung her gaze back to Shiv, and held still while he took the time to visually inspect her as well. All of a sudden, she felt like a small rabbit being hunted by a ruthless predator, and was grateful for the measure of support Striker's hand on her neck provided.

Shiv must have noticed that hand as well because he slowly raised one eyebrow at Striker. As though he had all the time in the world, he placed the cigar between his lips, and slowly puffed. A plume of smoke filled the space between them, swirling up toward the ceiling. "Everybody out. I'd like to speak to the good doctor alone."

Lila stiffened. Be alone with this fearsome outlaw? As his men shuffled out, a few that she'd encountered in the emergency room acknowledged her, while others stared her down. Striker was the last to exit, and he gave her neck a light squeeze before he departed the room. The instant his hand left her body, she became fully aware of being alone with Shiv, and felt exceedingly vulnerable.

She swallowed down her apprehension, and maintained eye contact with Shiv. It didn't matter if she was quaking on the inside. She'd put on a good show and hide her fear.

"Doc, I've heard good things about you from some of my men you've patched up. They tell me you're discrete, thorough, and don't ask too many questions. Combine that with your nice ass and rack, and my boys just may start falling down the stairs on purpose."

This was all part of a game she needed to win. It was obvious he goaded her with that last comment for one reason: to see how she would react. Would she storm out in outrage and offense? Would she get teary with embarrassment? Luckily she found his comment amusing, and huffed out a laugh, deciding to go with sass. "Wouldn't be the first time."

He laughed and seemed to warm to her just a bit. "Seriously though, I appreciate your willingness to help the prospect last week. I know the circumstances were unusual, but Striker told me you were impressive, and handled yourself quite well with this rough crowd. Jester was just filling me in on the texts you received as well as what happened with the car this morning. It seems as though we landed you right in the middle of a shit storm, and may need to extend you some protection."

Lila weighed his words carefully. Odds were this man wasn't going to offer his resources without some kind of a catch. Unsure of how to respond, she remained quiet. He had the floor, and she'd let him have his say before she spoke.

"I'm willing to work with you, Doc. We have enough manpower to keep an eye on you until we sort out this mess. We protect our own. This is nothing new to us."

She sensed he wasn't going to play all his cards, and she would have to be the one to concede. "But I'm nothing to you. I assisted you once, and now you're telling me you're willing to protect me for an unspecified amount of time, until you clear up your problems with the Grimm Brothers?"

If Shiv was surprised she knew so much, he didn't let it show, his face remained impassive, and she couldn't get a read on his thoughts. After a brief pause, he leaned forward in his chair and docked both elbows on the table. He steepled his fingers and rested his chin atop them, studying her carefully before he spoke. "Cutting right to the chase, Doc, huh? You're right. I'm not offering my services free of charge. What I'd like, is to use your medical expertise when necessary."

Damn. She had a feeling it would be something like this.

"You'll need to be more specific."

Shiv rotated his cigar between his thumb and forefinger, his eyes on the dancing smoke that floated from the charred tip. "Shit happens. My guys get injured. This problem with the Grimms may exacerbate that. Often times it's something we don't want reported, or even made public. Having a physician we could depend on as needed would be invaluable."

The weight of the offer sank in. In exchange for protection he wanted her to serve as private physician for the club. It would, without a doubt, involve more incidents like the one on Sunday night. Injuries the club couldn't risk being reported to the police because an investigation would be harmful to their wellbeing.

Could she do that? Did she really need protection, or was this all an overreaction? Striker seemed to think it was warranted, and surprisingly, she trusted him. He'd been up front with her thus far.

If word were to leak of this deal she'd lose her medical license at the very least, serve jail time at worst. But the club was discrete, they'd die before ratting out *one of their own*, as Shiv called it. And this would make her one of them, but it wasn't a decision she could make in ten seconds.

"We're talking about a lot of risk to me, personally and professionally. You can't expect me to agree to this without some serious thought. I need time."

"I like you, Doc. You're a no bullshit kinda broad, and around here that's pretty rare. Most of the girls that hang with the club are easy on the eyes, and know a hundred ways to get a man off, but brains aren't their strong suit. You're quite the combination. Something I see hasn't gone unnoticed by one of my men in particular."

She blushed at the reference to the chemistry brewing

between her and Striker. "You didn't answer my question."

His mouth turned up in a sardonic smile, and she shivered. She walked a fine line; this was not a man she wanted to cross. He'd make a very unwelcome enemy. But, despite his cold look he said, "Ok Doc, let's try this. Since you helped us out with Kenny, in a gesture of good faith, I'll give you five days to decide. In those five days I'll extend you our protection, no strings. You agree to the terms, and it will continue. If not, we part ways and wish each other well. Deal?"

After a moment, she nodded. Five days seemed a reasonable amount of time to give this some serious thought. "Okay, five days."

Shiv sighed, and scratched his chin. "Okay good, but this has to be a club decision. I'll call everyone in and we'll vote on it. Then we'll decide what needs to be done to keep you safe. Go have a drink at the bar. This shouldn't take too long."

Lila placed both hands on the cold steel table and stood. She nodded once at Shiv then turned to exit. The double doors were heavy, and she needed both hands to force them open. Relieved to be in the presence of additional people, she veered toward the bar.

Shiv's loud voice resounded behind her, and she flinched. "Meeting in two minutes, I have a proposition to vote on."

One of the prospects ran out in the direction of the garage bays, Lila assumed to let the brothers still working out there know they were needed. Those that were scattered around the clubhouse started to make their way toward the meeting room. Most gave her curious stares as they passed, a few looks were blatantly sexual, and some were just plain scary.

She felt eyes on her, and turned toward the bar where she

met Striker's heated gaze. He knocked back the rest of his drink, and slowly walked straight toward her, not breaking eye contact. Lila was mesmerized by the power that radiated from his shifting muscles as he stalked toward her. When he reached her, he raised an eyebrow, and brought his lips to her ear.

"You okay?" He breathed against her skin.

She was powerless to stop the surge of desire his warm breath ignited. "I'm good." It came out as a whisper.

"I'm looking forward to hearing what you two came up with."

Lila gave him an uneasy smile. "I think I'm in over my head," she said in a low voice that betrayed her ambiguity about this entire situation.

"Don't worry so much, babe." He took her ear lobe between his teeth and gave a quick tug. When he pulled back, he pressed a quick kiss to her forehead and joined his brothers.

The feel of his teeth nearly brought her to her knees. Jesus, what would happen if he ever got that mouth on more of her body? She wasn't sure she'd survive it, but it would be worth it to find out.

Could she take Shiv up on his offer of protection for medical care? How would that even work? She'd just received the go ahead to begin the concussion program at the high school, and imagined the school board wouldn't be thrilled if she had bikers tailing her everywhere she went. She flat out refused to postpone the first committee meeting, which was scheduled for a week from Wednesday.

And how would she pull off the details of working with them? What if they needed her help when she was already at work in the ER? Where would she get the supplies she needed? Countless questions bounced around her head. She had a disturbing vision of herself sitting in a jail cell for stealing medical supplies from the hospital. This could never work.

"I'm gonna need you to make it a double," she told the prospect, and dropped her head to her hands as she sank onto a barstool.

Chapter Nine

"One last thing before we vote on this," Shiv said.

Striker raised an eyebrow at him. "And that would be?"

"Between us, keeping Doc Emerson safe, and her keeping us alive and healthy, we'll be seeing a lot of her around here. This deal makes her family. She ain't like the rest of the skanks who come around here looking to bag a biker. This is business, plain and simple. You treat her like you'd treat an ol' lady. If one of you wants to make her your ol' lady that's one thing." Shiv looked directly at Striker with a smirk. "Otherwise it's hands and dicks off. I don't want this deal fucked up because one of you couldn't keep your pecker in your pants."

The men nodded though someone muttered something about it being a shame to waste a pair of tits. Striker had to grit his teeth not to snap at them for talking about Lila that way. What the hell was wrong with him when it came to her? Any other woman and he'd be joining in the talk.

"I vote yea," Shiv announced, kicking off the vote.

Striker couldn't honestly say he was in favor of this deal. Lila was too good for them, and bringing her into the fold would only drag her down. On the flipside, he was the one who set this whole mess in motion when he went to her for help with Kenny. Plus, he wanted to be the one to protect her. Shit. He really had no choice but to vote it in, and deal with the consequences later. One by one they went around the room, each voting yea until it got to Striker who closed out the unanimous vote.

"Okay, that was easy. Now——" Shiv was interrupted when Gumby burst into the room.

Striker hopped up from his chair. "How far did you tail him?"

"Got as far as the town border. I turned back when he drove into Sandy Springs. With my cut on, and no backup, I didn't want to risk chasing him through Grimm country." Gumby sat in the empty seat at the table.

"Thanks, Gumby. At least this points in the direction we were thinking. It's gotta be the Grimms. Fucking Jackal. What the hell is going on in his club?" Striker had hoped this threat to Lila was independent of the Grimm Brothers, even though he'd suspected that's exactly who it was.

"I don't know, brother, but we'll figure it out. What did I miss?" Gumby asked.

Shiv gave him a quick rundown of the vote. "Sorry we didn't wait for you. You good with this?"

"Of course," said Gumby, as he nodded. "I think the Doc's great. I'm all for having her work with us, and for keeping her safe. My vote would have been yea."

"Good." Shiv leaned back in his chair. "Now, let's come up with a plan to keep the Doc alive so she can keep us alive."

~ ~ ~ ~

Thirty minutes after the meeting began, Lila glanced at the clock on the wall for what felt like the millionth time. Was it usual for a vote to take this long? She cut herself off at two drinks, figuring the last thing she needed was to be plastered in this place in the middle of the day. Just when she felt the fingers of panic reaching for her, the doors to the meeting room burst open, and the men spilled out.

Lila didn't know what was expected of her so she stayed put on her stool and waited for some direction. Shiv and Striker were the last to exit. They came through the doors together, making a formidable pair. It would not be wise to get on their bad side.

They hugged in that manly fashion, slapping each other's backs before they separated. Shiv nodded in her direction and started up the stairs while Striker aimed straight for her. His face was a blank mask and gave nothing away. Did they agree to what Shiv proposed? Would they respect the five-day grace period he consented to? Lila rubbed her clammy palms on her thighs and waited.

"Vote passed. You've got five days to make a decision," Striker said as he reached her. "That was not what I was expecting."

The breath she'd been holding whooshed out, and Lila sagged in relief. "What were you expecting?"

Striker shrugged and ran a hand through his hair, mussing it. "I expected you to throw some money at the problem."

"Throw some money at the problem?" Lila frowned. "I feel like I should be offended by that."

"None intended. I thought Shiv would offer you protection for some cash. Come on, you're on my bike." He took her hand and tugged her off the barstool.

"Are you taking me home?"

"I'm taking you to your house to get your things." He towed her along toward the parking lot, and she followed dutifully.

"My things? Come on Striker, this is like talking to a wall.

More details needed."

He smirked at her over his shoulder. "Well, babe, we're going to my house. You're going to be staying with me until we figure this mess out."

Holy shit! That was not what she had agreed to. Nor was it a smart idea. She could not take time out of her life to play house with Striker. She had a hectic work schedule that was about to get busier with her new initiative for the high school.

Not to mention she wasn't sure she could keep her hands off him if they were sleeping under the same roof, if he was only a door or two away. Did he have a girlfriend? She didn't think so based on the way he kissed her the other night, but that didn't necessarily prove anything.

When she didn't reply Striker halted, and faced her, a grin on his face. "That okay by you, darlin?"

She should not get a warm rush every time he used an endearment, but she couldn't help it. That did not mean she should be staying at the man's house, with him. Lila stopped walking. "I'm not sure this is a good idea. It's probably overkill anyway. You don't think they'd come to my house, do you?"

The amused expression fell from Striker's handsome face. "Lila, they already came by your house, twice. Someone saw you leave with me and the car was there this morning. This is some nasty shit, and I don't think it's worth taking chances. I truly think you'll be safer at my house."

Lila gave him a small nod. "You're right. Sorry, I'm just freaking out about how this will mess up my life."

"You on board?" He watched her while he waited for her answer.

Closing her eyes, she swallowed and jumped off the ledge. "Yes."

"Then let's roll, babe."

Lila hurried to follow him outside. It appeared the discussion was over.

It came as no surprise to Lila that the day had grown blisteringly hot. The desert sun scorched the ground and caused her eyes to narrow in protest. Lila's brain swirled with the events of the past few hours. At some point all of it would sink in. There was a good chance she'd lament these hasty decisions at that time, but for now she decided to just go with it. Seeing how they took the threat against her seriously made her even more certain she needed assistance.

When she reached the bike, she grabbed for the helmet Striker offered her, but he held it captive.

"I'm sorry you got caught up in this shit, Lila. I'm going to be straight with you, I'm not sure this deal is entirely in your best interest, but my hands are tied. If you decide to go through with this I will do everything I can to protect you, from the Grimms, and from whatever else may crop up in the future. You do realize this will tie you to the club for the long term. It's not something you can decide to do today and change your mind a month from now. You'll know too much. Shiv won't let that happen."

He said Shiv wouldn't let it happen, as though Striker himself would be willing to let her walk in the future. The look on his face was more concern than warning.

Lila nodded, moved by the possibility that he may care for her, at least a little bit. There was an intense chemistry between them and she wondered how long it could be ignored. Probably not too long if they were going to be sharing a roof. "Thank you, Striker, you're a good man."

Striker grunted. "No, I'm not, babe. That's one thing you'll damn sure find out soon enough."

He released the helmet to her, and she climbed on behind

him, after securing the clasp with a snap. In the course of a few hours her life had spun out of control and she wasn't sure she could set it on a straight path again.

~ ~ ~ ~

Lila thought he was a good man. Hell, if she knew even a quarter of the shit he'd done in his lifetime she wouldn't want to be in the same town, maybe not the same state as him. There was no way a woman like her, who saved lives for a living could reconcile the type of life he lived. He was an outlaw who frequently danced over the line of the law. He was a fighter who could kill a man with his bare hands— could and had. True, he knew the meaning of loyalty and brotherhood, and he'd do anything for his club family, but she was mistaking that for goodness. He'd never deserve someone like her. Unfortunately that didn't stop him from wanting her like a drug.

They stopped at her house, and she grabbed enough clothes to last a few days. One of the prospects could take her back during the week to get more if necessary. For now, Striker just wanted to get her under his roof and away from whoever was targeting her, especially if it was the Grimm Brothers.

They stood in her driveway and he strapped her overnight bag to his bike. He felt the tension coming off her in waves as she frequently scanned their surroundings. "It's okay, Lila, we weren't followed and no one is on the street. You can relax."

She gave him a smile and stopped watching the street, but replaced the action with the tapping of her foot against the driveway. "Where do you live?"

"I have a room at the club that I stay at sometimes, but my house is about a half hour out of town, on the lake. You'll be much more comfortable there than at the clubhouse." He stepped close to her as he spoke.

"Sounds great. I promise I'll stay out of your way when you're home. I'm working the day shift for a while, the hospital hired a physician who wanted to work nights, which is great for me. By the way, how will I get to work? I'm not going to stay home. And now I'll have committee meetings for the concussion program too."

"I'm not asking you to barricade yourself in the house. But you will have someone following you and staying with you wherever you go. That's not negotiable. And I'm not worried about you being in my space, Lila."

"You may change your mind when I take over your bathroom," she teased.

He could tell it was important for her to maintain some control over her life by keeping a normal work schedule. "I think I'm man enough to handle it, darlin'." He stroked a finger down her smooth cheek.

Their eyes locked, and Striker ached for another taste of her. He wasn't used to denying himself when it came to sex, but he respected her in a way that was unfamiliar to him. She was going to be living with him. It was pretty much inevitable that this attraction between them would ignite, but for the first time, he cared beyond getting her into bed.

Striker cupped the back of her neck and drew her toward him. When she was just a breath away, he paused. "Just a quick taste," he whispered.

He watched her eyes flare with desire, and before she had a chance to respond, he slid his hand from her neck, up to fist in her hair. In one swift move, he tilted her head back, and crashed his lips down on hers.

She opened her mouth, and melted against him, which only served to amp up his need. He knew if he fell in too deep, he wouldn't be able to make himself stop for hours, but he slipped his tongue in her mouth and swirled it around hers anyway. She let out a low moan, and clung to the leather of his cut, pulling him closer. He hardened instantly, and pressed against the softness of her belly.

"Shit." He gasped. Before he got completely lost in her intoxicating flavor, he wrenched away. One of his hands held her hips anchored to him while the other was still tangled in her hair, keeping her head tipped back. "You better get on the bike, babe, before I give your neighbors the show of their lives."

He released her and mounted the bike after he slid on his shades. From the shelter of the darkened sunglasses, he was able to watch her reaction to his kiss. Swollen lips and mussed hair gave her a sexy rumpled look. Lila hadn't spoken yet, but as he watched, her tongue came out to trace along her bottom lip as though trying to recapture his taste. He gave a low groan. "Bike, babe, now."

"Oh, yeah, right, get on the bike," she muttered. Lila hustled the few steps to the motorcycle, and scrambled on behind him. She wobbled a bit, and he smirked at the knowledge that he was the reason for her unsteady movements. This time when her arms snaked around him she didn't hang onto his waist but placed a palm on each of his thighs in an intimate hold. His dick twitched and he rolled his eyes heavenward to say a quick prayer that he'd make it home without crashing or getting a ticket for driving while lusting.

Chapter Ten

"Wow! Striker, this place is fantastic. I have to admit it's not at all what I was expecting." Lila said as she stepped across the threshold into Striker's single story Spanish style house. If she wasn't mistaken, the house sat directly on the lakefront. The view from the back must be breathtaking. She was pleasantly surprised. Add another layer to the many that seemed to make up the man.

After he followed her through the door, Striker shot her an amused look. "And what were you expecting?"

"Oh I don't know, a biker bachelor den of sin perhaps."

Striker cracked up at that. "Well, babe, you are officially the first female not related to me, or married to a friend, to step foot into this house."

"Seriously?"

"Death and taxes."

"So you've never taken a girl here for…whatever?" Lila wasn't sure if she believed him.

Rumors ran rampant around town about him and his women. It was no secret that he flew through them. Most of the MC members were known for bed hopping. Ha! Bed hopping may be too tame a term; *fuck and forget* was probably more appropriate. She would never admit this out loud, but instead of being disgusted by the knowledge that Striker had been with many, many women, she was curious to know what it was like to be on the receiving end of all that experience.

"No, Lila, I've never brought a woman here for a meal, for a chat, or for a fuck." He sounded agitated. Had she offended him?

"I'm sorry, Striker. It's just...well, it's no secret around town that you attract a lot of female interest, so I guess I just assumed..." She wasn't entirely sure how to avoid digging the hole deeper.

Luckily, he snorted out a rough laugh. "I'm certainly not a monk, Lila, I just don't bring them here. This is my home, my sanctuary."

"So why are you letting me stay here?" Her voice had dropped, and she whispered the question she was both dying and dreading to hear him answer.

"Because from the moment the club decided it wouldn't be safe for you to stay at your own house, I couldn't picture you anywhere but here with me." The heat in his eyes backed up his words.

"Oh." That shut her up.

"Come on, babe."

As she followed him through the foyer, Lila absorbed her surroundings. The entryway was sparsely decorated, but very comfortable, and masculine in a way that didn't scream swinging bachelor. A cozy-looking leather couch took up the majority of the living room. Motorcycle magazines were scattered on a coffee table in front of the sofa, and a large flat screen TV dominated the wall. Shades of beige and peach paint covered the walls, fitting well with the Spanish style of the home.

The living room flowed into the kitchen, giving the place an open and inviting feel. While the kitchen was small, it was equipped with state of the art appliances and had a modern look.

"Do you cook?' she asked.

"Some. I won't win any awards, but I won't kill anyone either. You?"

"Love to. I find it a great way to de-stress, although I haven't done too much since I've lived here. Not so much fun cooking for one. That and the fact that I'm at work all the time."

"Well, feel free to go to town in the kitchen. In fact, I insist."

Lila chuckled at that.

"The house has two bedrooms, one bath, so, sorry, but we have to share. I know it's small, but the lot is big, and I bought it thinking it would be perfect to expand on one day."

"It's fantastic." She meant it.

"You haven't seen the best part. Follow me." He opened the fridge, reached in and snagged a couple bottles of beer. After he bumped the fridge closed with his hip, he turned toward the sliding glass doors and exited the kitchen onto the deck. Lila followed him out to the backyard. Her mouth dropped in surprised delight when she took in the view.

The backyard was enormous, and all sand, opening right up to the lake, which was about eighty feet back. A huge wooden deck with a fancy, stone encased stainless steel grill ran along the entire length of the back of the house, and extended well into the yard. Near the grill, a picnic style table with bench seats sat waiting for a barbecue. On the opposite side of the deck, two chaise loungers called to her, perfect for watching the sun set over the water.

Striker held a beer out to her. "Pick a chair. We can sit for a while then grill up some dinner. Sunset is killer back here."

Lila took the offered beer, and plopped down in a lounge chair. The view was spectacular, the beer was cold, and the company, like the air, was hot. She smiled to herself as she leaned back, and relaxed for the first time that day.

Striker was right to call this place his sanctuary. The peaceful quiet of the open lake soothed her nerves and eased some of her fears. She felt safe here, away from the bustle of town. Lila let herself breathe and allowed some of the worry over the morning's events to dissolve away. Whether it was strictly the location that relaxed her, or the man who owned it, she couldn't say.

Neither spoke for several minutes, lost in thought. The quiet was welcome after the stress of the morning. Lila closed her eyes and had almost drifted off when Striker's voice startled her back. "What was it that brought you all the way out to this bum fuck town from DC?"

"I just needed a change." It was her standard answer whenever someone asked her about the topic that invoked so many negative emotions.

"That's a very simple answer. I'm gonna have to call bullshit on that one."

"Excuse me?' Lila narrowed her eyes at him as her hackles rose. It was easier to get cranky then think about the things that haunted her. "Fine then, I'll change my answer to none of your damn business."

"I like it when you're snarky, babe, but don't get pissed. Sounds like I may have stomped on a nerve. It wasn't my intention. I'm just trying to get to know you better." He shrugged, and finished his beer.

"And is turnabout fair?"

"You bet."

Lila took a long pull of her frosty beer, and stared out at

the lake considering whether she wanted to open up to him. She must have paused for too long because he changed tactics. "Come here," he said. He encased her hand in his larger one, and pulled her up from her chaise, over to his.

Lila sat down between his spread legs, and he arranged her so her back was pressed up against his chest with his arms resting around her midsection, just below her breasts. He plucked the beer out of her hands and brought it to his lips before returning it to her.

"What are you doing?" She sat tense against him, not exactly sure how to react.

"I'm enjoying the feel of you. You've been wrapped all around me on my bike a couple of times now, and I thought I'd reverse the position. Turnabout being fair and all that."

As the warmth and strength of his body seeped into her, Lila closed her eyes and let the tension ooze out. Each of the many sides to this man fascinated her. He was a criminal, a badass biker that intimidated people pretty much for a living, yet he was also a protector, a serious flirt, and now apparently he was angling to be her confidant. Not ready to open her eyes despite the picturesque scene before her, Lila kept them closed and enjoyed the wonderful sensation of being held by this fascinating man.

When she was relaxed once again, with her head pooled against his shoulder, she decided to jump in with both feet. In the six months since leaving DC, there wasn't anyone she'd shared her story with, not a single person who knew the real her, and the loneliness was becoming stifling. It would be nice to have someone know her beyond the surface, and know what drove her. "My father is Howard Dewitt."

"Hmm, sounds familiar. Should I know the name?"

"He's been in the news a bit lately," she replied, unable to keep the disdain out of her voice. "He owns Eagle Bank."

Striker stayed silent for a few seconds. "The one that's about to be taken over by that other major bank?"

"Bank of the States, yes. Got it in one."

"Holy fucking shit, babe."

Lila laughed at his reaction, and absently stroked her fingers over his forearm where it crossed under her breasts. "I started using my mother's maiden name when I came out here in hope of maintaining some anonymity, and so far I've been successful."

"Jesus, Lila, your father is a billionaire, and wields a ton of power politically. Do your parents know where you are?"

She waived away the beer when Striker offered it. "You can finish it. And, yes they know where I am. There was no point in trying to hide it from them. With their connections they would have known where I was going before I did. Anyway, as you figured out, I grew up with money. Lots of old money. An obscene amount of money, really. And if I'm being honest, I have to say I had a wonderful childhood. I never wanted for anything material, and while my parents weren't overly warm or involved in my day to day upbringing, I had amazing experiences that most would envy."

Striker snorted at that, and polished off Lila's beer. The bottle clanked as he set it down on the deck.

"I know what you're probably thinking. This is going to turn into a 'poor little rich girl' story, and I suppose in a way it is, but money is just one part of what makes up someone's life. It can certainly open doors, but it does not mean a flawless, problem free life. People always expect those with money to feel like they are so lucky and their lives are just wonderful." She paused to gather herself before she got too worked up. "Sorry, I'm rambling. Talking about this always has the power to get under my skin, and I don't want you to view me as a stuck up rich bitch."

"Whoa, babe, I'm not judging you, not at all. I see how hard you work. Never would I think you're stuck up or a bitch." Striker lowered his head, and nuzzled the side of her neck. The contact soothed her. "Tell me the rest. I want to know more about you," he said, and then dropped a gentle kiss where her neck met her shoulder.

Lila shivered when his lips brushed her skin. "By the time I was halfway through my teenage years, it became apparent that my purpose in life was to marry a man who would further advance my father's career and financial assets. I had to dress a certain way, wasn't allowed friends outside our social circle, and my mother constantly reminded me that my worth would be measured by the wealth and status of the man I married." Lila shook her head and sighed.

"Damn, baby, that's cold." Striker continued to rub his lips along her neck, not kissing her but stroking her flesh with his mouth. It felt amazing, and the delicious physical sensations helped override the negative emotional ones.

"Anyway, for most of my life I went along with their plans. They are my parents, and it was all I knew. I played the good little daughter, never got in any trouble, told the media what they wanted, attended political functions with a smile, dated who they picked out for me, dressed in what they chose, those kind of things. But let me tell you, that person is not who I am inside, and I've felt like an actor in a play my whole life. When I broached the idea of going to medical school, I thought they would disown me. College was allowed so I wouldn't appear uneducated, but then I was supposed to marry the man of my parent's choosing, who would promote my father's business interests."

"Why did you decide to become a doctor? Like helping people and saving lives?"

She laughed. "Yes, there's that. I suppose that's always a factor when someone chooses to go into medicine. But I also just like the work. I enjoy the physical act of doctoring along with the puzzle of figuring out what is wrong with someone. Does that make any sense?"

"Absolutely." He stopped nuzzling her neck, and interlaced the fingers of one hand with hers.

Lila enjoyed his touch more than she should. If she looked too deeply into the meaning, he might stop, so she continued to talk in the hope of prolonging the moment. "Throughout medical school I continued to date the men my parents chose for me. At the time, I had decided that I'd pick one who was tolerable, marry him out of duty, and derive enjoyment from the professional part of my life if not the personal. I didn't have enough backbone to stand up to my parents. Plus, I felt I owed them for not ruining my plans to go to medical school. Problem was, I just couldn't imagine myself spending my life with any of the men they chose, even in a platonic sense."

"No backbone?" Striker interrupted. "I'm having a hard time imagining that, darlin'. You faced down a one percenter president without blinking an eye today."

His comment brought a smile to her face. "I've grown a sturdy one since then, though I was a nervous wreck talking to Shiv. Glad I hid it well."

"So, what was the tipping point?"

The sunset was amazing, the giant orange orb inched closer and closer to the shimmering water as each minute passed. "I fell for one of the guys they set me up with."

Striker tensed behind her, his voice a harsh rasp. "Is there some asshole back in DC that thinks he can claim you as his?"

He sounded jealous. Could he be jealous? The thought

was thrilling, and Lila squeezed the hand laced with hers. "No. Not just no, but hell no! Aaron and I seemed perfect for each other, complimented each other in every way. He got me, understood my feelings about the world we grew up in, and said all the right things all the time. Looking back on it now I should have suspected something was off by the way it all seemed so effortless." She paused. The rest of the story was embarrassing. She'd been naïve, and beyond mortified when it all fell apart.

"So what happened?" Striker's words were spoken softly. He must have realized this part of the tale was difficult for her.

After a fortifying breath, she plowed on. "One day I overheard my father on the phone. Turns out, my boyfriend was the son of Bank of the States' CEO. He'd been trying to acquire my father's bank for years. My father expressed interest in running for Governor of Maryland. He decided it was time to sell so he could put all his efforts into the gubernatorial race. This deal will make him tens of billions. He agreed to sell if the CEO agreed to have his son, Aaron, marry me. Can't run for governor with an unmarried daughter near thirty. How would that look?" She laughed, a mirthless sound. "I was heartbroken and humiliated. Everything about our relationship was a lie, a business deal."

"Are you fucking serious?" Striker spat out behind her. "What a bunch of fucking motherfuckers."

Striker's outrage on her behalf made her laugh, especially the deterioration in his language, which was vulgar on a good day. "I'm very serious. I couldn't bear to stay, so I tucked my tail between my legs, looked for a job in an off the grid town, and left without a backward glance. They controlled the first part of my life, no way were they taking the rest."

"I'm surprised your parents haven't tried to drag your gorgeous ass back to DC."

Lila flushed at the compliment. "I may have threatened to go to the media if they didn't let me leave, and promise to stay away."

"Devious, babe. Think you might need to give me this shithead's address though."

She snorted out a laugh. "No way. I can't afford to have you arrested for murdering him. I do not want to get stuck staying with Jester or Gumby."

"I have one question you're not going to like," he said.

She turned her head up to look at him. The sun had dipped close to the horizon, and the warmth of the day was quickly giving way to the chill of the night. Striker's strong jaw ticked, hinting at his anger on her behalf. "I already thought about it," she said, knowing what he was going to ask before he voiced the words. "My parents aren't above using underhanded tricks to get me back in their web, especially now that the bank merger is basically a done deal. My father will want his picture perfect family intact when he throws his name in the governors' race. It's possible they didn't believe I'd really go to the media, but I was serious, and will do it to protect my independence. Tomorrow I'll call my father to feel out the situation."

"I'm ninety-nine percent sure it's the Grimms, but it wouldn't hurt to cover all the bases."

It was becoming difficult to remain unaffected while she sat snuggled between Striker's muscular thighs. The hand that wasn't holding hers had slipped down to caress the skin of her belly between the end of the shirt and top of her low-rise jeans. Her nipples pebbled against her bra, and a heavy, achy feeling settled low in her stomach. She hoped Striker's eyes were closed, and he couldn't see the affect he was having on her.

Chapter Eleven

Striker felt the moment Lila changed from relaxed and liquid to tense and rigid. He couldn't prevent his body's reaction to her. She attracted him on so many levels. The first few times he'd encountered her it was strictly physical, but the more he learned about the independent, compassionate, and intelligent woman who rested between his legs, the stronger the attraction grew.

"Um, Striker—"

"Yeah, I know, hon, just ignore him."

"Not easy to ignore a baseball bat poking at you," she muttered under her breath.

He chuckled. "You might as well get used to it, he's never far away when you're around."

Lila tilted her chin, and he looked down at her beautiful face. He wouldn't have blamed her if she moved back to her own chair, but for some reason she stayed. "Guess we'll have to get your mind on something else then," she said. "Your turn to spill all your secrets."

"What do you want to know?" Striker asked. He stopped moving his hand, and rested it on her stomach, palm down. The silky smooth skin felt warm and soothing under his rough, callused hand.

"Well, to be honest, I'm very curious about how you got involved in the MC. You have to know all the rumors about you guys, and the reputations of clubs like yours are sketchy at best. I guess I just wonder what the draw is for you."

"You go right for the tough questions, don't you?" Like her, there were things in his past he preferred not to think about.

"I'm sorry. You don't have to answer if it's too personal."

He lifted the hand that had been holding hers, and tugged at her ponytail. The action brought her face back into a position where he could make eye contact. "No, I promised you I'd open up if you did." He let out a deep sigh and held her gaze. "I think the story is similar for many of us, at least the abbreviated version. Shitty childhood, not big on following the rules, rebellious, and of course an obsession with motorcycles."

Lila placed her hand over the one of his that still rested, palm down, against her stomach. She intertwined their fingers and gave a small squeeze. "How shitty?"

"My childhood?" He turned his palm up and linked their fingers once again. It was sweet of her to return the reassuring gesture while he talked. "Less shitty than some, more than most. Grew up in a trailer park, here in town. My old man went to prison when I was ten. He plowed his car through the kitchen of a house somewhere near Vegas after about ten drinks. Killed three of the four people in the family. A few years back I got word he died in prison."

Lila remained quiet, but tightened her hand in his.

"My mom was a junkie. After the old man went inside, she started disappearing for days, sometimes weeks at a time." Long buried feelings of abandonment and fear sneaked to the surface. "Went on that way until I was eighteen, then one time she never came back."

"God, Striker. I'm so sorry. Here I am complaining about my petty problems." She shook her head. "How did you survive?"

"Lila, just because our issues are different, doesn't make yours any less important than mine were." It didn't surprise him one bit that she'd try to downplay her own feelings to validate his.

"I had this neighbor, a crotchety old bastard who worked on bikes right there at his trailer." He laughed as he recalled the redneck garage set up the man had. "He'd give me tasks, let me eat with him when I was done, and threw me a few bucks at the end of each project."

Lila huffed. "I have a feeling you're leaving a lot out."

Striker smiled at her insight. She didn't need to know how bad things got at times. How desperate he'd been for food or how he'd steal drugs from his mom's stash and sell them to have money for the next time she split. Pity was the last thing he needed from her.

"So obviously you developed a love of motorcycles. Then what? How'd you get involved with the No Prisoners?"

"Well, there was no way to grow up around here and not be aware of the MC." Striker paused. He wasn't used to laying himself bare before anyone, especially a woman. It made him feel vulnerable in a way he didn't expect, and wasn't quite sure how to handle.

Accustomed to comforting people, Lila must have sensed his unease. "You can trust me with your story, Striker. I'd never betray your trust by judging what you share with me. And I'd never dream of telling anyone."

He knew that, but hearing the sincerity of her softly spoken words made him more than willing to share with her. It made him want to share. "The draw was the brotherhood, the family. I think it's that way for most of us. A lot of the guys are misfits in society, men without roots or kin who are looking for a connection to similar people."

He quieted and let Lila mull over his words. "I can understand that," she stated. "I left my family because I didn't fit, and I wasn't understood. But after being here for six months, alone, I feel a gap in my life. Until you spoke of your connection to the MC, I hadn't realized what was lacking for me. But that's what it is, connection to people, a family. Not that I ever had a strong one, but it was still something. I can see the draw for you. The desire to form bonds with similar people who have similar experiences and values is a strong one. You're lucky you have people who play that role in your life."

Striker rested his head back on the lounge chair, and closed his eyes as her words brought him peace. He shouldn't have been surprised that she understood him. "They are my life. The bond with my brothers is unbreakable. It's the driving force for all of us."

He felt her head move against his skin as she nodded, her hair tickled under his chin. "Close your eyes and relax, Lila. Today's been a crazy day, and I want to take a nap with you here like this while the sun sets."

Something had shifted between them this evening. Lila was as attracted to him as he was to her. It wasn't something she hid well. The best thing he could do for both of them would be to stand up and retire to his room, but in this moment he'd rather ride his Harley through a field of broken whisky bottles than walk away from her. Striker felt Lila's body soften as she dozed off. He opened his eyes in time to see the sun dip below the horizon before he allowed them to drift closed again. Sleep was not far behind.

~ ~ ~ ~

The next morning, after a night of tossing and turning, wondering what Striker was doing in the room across the hall, Lila sat on the bed and stared at her phone. She'd plotted out multiple iterations of what she planned to say to her father, and finally felt prepared to make the call.

She and Striker had dozed on the deck, wrapped up in each other, for about an hour before waking up chilled and hungry. Striker grilled some steaks, and Lila had fixed a salad and potatoes. Since the evening had cooled considerably, they ate inside. The meal was eaten in companionable silence, but once it was finished Lila grew nervous and uncertain of what to do next. It was the coward's way out, but she had fled to her room, pleading fatigue.

Now she sat and stared at the phone as though it was rattlesnake poised to attack. Striker was at the garage working on a custom build. He'd offered to take her along, but she declined, needing to take care of this call. Striker promised he would only be away a few hours, and a prospect watching TV in the living room was assigned the boring task of babysitting.

Okay, enough stalling. Lila rolled her eyes at her own spinelessness, picked up the phone and located her father's cell number in her contacts.

He answered on the third ring.

"Lila. Have you come to your senses yet?"

Well hello to you too, Dad. Lila held the phone away from her ear, and stuck her tongue out at it. The childish gesture made her feel marginally better. "Hi, Dad. How are you? How's mom?" There wasn't any point in engaging in a battle right from the start. The decision to move away from home had been difficult for Lila's mother to accept, and while she was just as guilty as the wannabe governor in Lila's eyes, she had a bit of a softer spot for her mother.

"We are fine, Lila. I assume there is a purpose for this unexpected phone call beyond your inquiry into our wellbeing. I know you have a busy schedule, what with all the riding on backs of motorcycles you've been doing lately, so let's skip the small talk."

He knew. Lila's stomach sank. Could he be responsible for the text messages and the incident yesterday? Would he stoop so low as to hire a thug to frighten his daughter into running back to the fold? "You're having me watched?" She worked to keep her voice level, and free from anger.

"Of course I'm keeping track of you, Lila. You made a lot of angry threats during your tantrum before you left, and I have too much at stake right now to leave loose ends."

She ignored his digs. Telling her she threw a tantrum and calling her a loose end was his method of goading an outraged response from her. There was no way she would give him the satisfaction of an emotional outburst. "Is that all you're doing?"

"What do you mean?" he sighed, the sound full of frustration and impatience.

Here's where it got tricky. She couldn't admit to the texts and car incident or he would flip out and probably send in the National Guard. Not in a concerned parent way, but because he couldn't have any unfinished business so close to the merger, as he said. She chose her words with care. "You admitted you have someone keeping tabs on me, are they assigned to pressure me into returning to Washington as well? Should I expect some subtle maneuvering in that direction? Because I believe I made myself perfectly clear before I left. I have no qualms about going to the media with the Aaron incident, and can add to my list of grievances if necessary."

Her father chuckled, and Lila clenched her teeth to hold

the nasty words inside her mouth. "No, Lila, contrary to what you might think, I quite believed you when you made your threat. You are very much like me in that respect; you'll do whatever is necessary to get your way. I have someone keeping me updated as to your goings on every so often and that's all. I need to be certain you haven't engaged in anything that will sabotage this deal and my campaign for governor. But really, Lila, bikers? Is this some kind of post adolescent rebellion?"

"Call off your dog," she spat out. "If I wanted you to know details of my life I'd give them to you myself. Since this is the first call in six months, you should be catching on that I don't want you to know those specifics. I'll stay away from your campaign if you stay out of my life. That's been the arrangement all along."

"Be careful, Lila," he warned, his voice so cold she was surprised her phone still felt warm in her hand. "A few well-placed calls to the FBI, and I can have your new *friend's* whole world turned upside down."

She gripped the phone until her knuckles turned white as resentment surged. In that instant, she was certain her father wasn't responsible for the threat against her. It wasn't his style. He was much more likely to make a call to the FBI, and have the No Prisoners investigated from now until kingdom come, something Lila refused to allow. "You be careful as well," she said, her voice equally icy. "I can destroy your chance to be governor with just one well-timed interview."

There was silence on the other end. Good. Let him chew on that for a while.

"I trust by your silence you are aware that I'm serious, and this isn't an idle threat. I believe we have an understanding. Call off your man, immediately."

"You don't give me orders, child. You'll come crawling

back on your own once your new biker friend fucks you over, until then I need to be sure your foolishness won't harm the family."

With that parting shot he ended the call, and left Lila fuming on the bed. Damn him, having to get the last word. Her hands trembled as she dropped the phone to the bed. Well, she'd set out to discover if he was the one behind the texts, and was confident he wasn't, which was a relief. Although, that meant it was most certainly the Grimm Brothers, and that was not a comforting thought.

Chapter Twelve

"Fucking piece of shit. How the hell am I supposed to get this garbage looking like new when the owner obviously didn't take care of it, and it's in worse goddam shape than they told me?" Striker slammed the wrench he'd been working with into a toolbox, as he complained to no one in particular.

"Hey, Striker, how's that custom rebuild coming along?" Jester asked him, his tone overly cheerful.

"Eat shit, asshole."

They guys in the garage cracked up. Striker was in a piss poor mood. Lila had been living under his roof for three days, and his dick had been rock hard since she stepped foot in his house. He was going out of his mind, and something had to give soon. His hand wasn't cutting it anymore. Last night, he'd gone so far as to agree to go with his brothers to Black's for an afterhours party, complete with strippers. One of the girls there would have taken care of him, but he'd begged off at the last minute. It seemed his dick wasn't going to be happy until it found its way inside Lila.

"What the hell is going on with you, Striker?" Acer asked. "You've been a miserable son of a bitch the last few days.

With that sexy piece you got staying at your house, we figured you'd be all relaxed and spouting poetry. What's wrong? She not wanting to play doctor with you?"

In a move so fast none of them saw it coming, Striker slammed Acer against the wall with a forearm across his throat. Acer's eyes widened as he gasped for breath, but he didn't fight back. They were brothers, closer than most biological family, but that didn't mean they couldn't throw down when it was warranted. Usually most of the guys avoided getting physical with Striker because he was a fierce and skilled fighter. He had the nickname for a reason.

"What did Pres say, huh? She's family now, treat her with some fucking respect." Striker's chest heaved as he tried to control his anger.

"So it's like that, is it?" Jester asked cracking up. "Oh this is good."

Striker turned his menacing gaze toward Jester who raised his hands in surrender. "Hey, I mean no disrespect, brother, just making conversation." His lips were turned up and his shoulders shook slightly with the effort to hold in his laughter.

Striker removed the pressure from Acer's throat, and turned back toward his work. From over Striker's shoulder, Acer braved his wrath again. "Seriously, Striker, she's gorgeous, smart, and classy. None of us are going to judge you for wanting more than a roll with her. Hell, half the guys will be pissed you got there first." Leave it to Acer to notice a classy woman. No matter how much ink the guy got, or how much leather he wore, he still reeked of the wealthy background he came from.

Striker sighed, and admitted defeat. "Yeah, well, she's driving me fucking crazy. She gets home from work and puts on these little tank tops and tiny shorts that she calls pajamas, my whole house fucking smells like her, and last night she took a bath."

"That bitch!" laughed Acer.

"I know you like 'em dirty and all, but personal hygiene is not a bad thing. In fact, most women do insist on being clean," Jester piped in with a smirk.

Gumby rolled the creeper he was lying on out from under an old mustang to add his two cents. "Don't think it's the soap he has a problem with. More likely the sexy broad hanging out naked in his tub. How's your dick feeling these days, Striker?"

Shiv picked that moment to walk into the garage. "This what you dumbasses do in here all day? Talk about each other's dicks?"

Everyone in the garage busted up at that. Striker loved the banter and camaraderie he shared with his brothers, but it wasn't quite as amusing when he was on the receiving end of their taunts.

"Nah," said Jester. "Striker was just telling us about the joys of unfulfilled lust."

"You mean you ain't hittin' that?" asked Shiv, which elicited another round of laughter.

"Fuck you all."

"Any word from Jackal?" Jester asked the question that killed the lighthearted mood in the garage.

Shiv frowned and rubbed the back of his neck as he always did when he was frustrated. "No. I've tried to contact him multiple times and haven't heard anything in reply."

Striker picked the wrench up again, and renewed his efforts to loosen a bolt that had rusted over. "It's gotta be Snake. That asshole is power hungry. I wouldn't be surprised if he was putting pressure on Jackal to tell us to fuck off."

"Would it work? Would Jackal cave if Snake pushed hard enough?" Gumby was back under the car, but he always paid close attention.

Everyone looked at Striker. He'd had the most dealings with Snake in the past, but Shiv knew Jackal better, so Striker couldn't say. He spun the wrench in his hand while he thought. "I'm actually more concerned that Snake will try to take Jackal out of the equation entirely. He's not the type for subtle manipulation. Shooting Jackal in the head would be more his style."

"Shit," Shiv sounded disgusted. "Maybe Jackal's off the radar because he's taking care of the Snake problem."

Striker didn't think so, but he kept that opinion to himself. If Jackal had a handle on Snake he'd have reached out to Shiv or Striker. Lila hadn't received any more texts, but he wasn't in anyway convinced it was over.

On his way back to the clubhouse, Shiv stopped by the bike Striker was dismantling. "Everything going okay, VP? Any trouble with your houseguest?"

"No trouble as far as threats against her, no more texts."

"Just the trouble of having a woman underfoot?"

"Something like that." He grunted in satisfaction as the bolt finally gave way.

"You know, Striker, having an ol' lady can be a real nice thing sometimes." Shiv had been married to his third wife for about five years, although she regularly threw him out, and made him sleep at the clubhouse at least three times a month.

Striker snorted. "You sure you're the authority on marital bliss?"

"Never claimed to be. Just saying it can be nice."

"I'll keep that in mind." Striker's phone rang, and he pulled a dingy rag out of his back pocket to wipe the grease off his hands before checking the screen. It was Bobby Kiderman, or Kid to the MC, the prospect he'd assigned to follow Lila to work today. When he couldn't be with her, the club was having a prospect tail her. Striker brought her to her house to pick up her car two days ago. The assigned prospect followed her to work, then hung around during her shift, switching out every few hours. "Hey, Kid, what's up?"

"You need to get down here, VP, Right away. Got some shit going on with your girl."

If the Kid hadn't sounded so serious, Striker would have pointed out that she wasn't his girl. "Shit, what's happening? Is Lila okay?"

"I'm not sure. I'm out in the parking lot. They've barricaded the entrance, and won't let anyone in or out. Cops are here and shit's crazy."

Fuck. Protective urges Striker wasn't aware he possessed flared to life. The need to be with Lila was so strong, it felt like a physical punch to the solar plexus. "On my way." He ended the call and immediately placed another one to Lila. When she didn't answer, deep concern for her safety rose up in a tidal wave of fear.

"Jester, Gumby, Acer, let's roll. Trouble at the hospital." Striker took off at full speed toward his motorcycle.

They all dropped what they were doing and raced to their bikes.

"Grimm Brothers?" Jester was the first to say what they were all thinking.

"No details yet. Kid said cops blocked off the entrance to the hospital. No one in or out."

"How you plan to get in, VP?" asked Gumby.

"I'll break the damn door down if I have to. No way they're keeping me out."

"Hell you could probably use your unsatisfied dick as a battering ram," Jester yelled over the roar of their engines, successfully easing some of the tension they were all feeling.

Striker flipped him off as he gunned it and flew through the open gate.

~ ~ ~ ~

Lila sat on a plinth in one of the ER treatment rooms, her head spinning from the past hour's events. She had obviously recognized she was in some level of danger. That's why she was staying with Striker and considering Shiv's offer, but this incident really drove it home. Now she was officially scared out of her mind. This was the push she needed to make a decision. She would let Striker know when she saw him that she'd take the deal Shiv offered, and handle whatever consequences arose later. There was also no doubt in her mind that it was the Grimm Brothers who were hassling her.

A colleague examined her, and determined that she didn't suffer anything worse than a few bruises, at least physically. If she was ever able to step foot in her office again without having a panic attack, it would be a miracle. Her head pounded as though a drumline marched in one ear and got stuck on their way out, and her throat ached from where the attacker had grabbed her neck. On her left breast, he'd left a row of humiliating finger shaped bruises. Lila shuddered as she recalled the fear of further violation.

A sharp rap on the door caused her to jolt. "Yes?"

A man's head poked through the cracked door. "Dr. Emerson? I'm Detective Marks. Is it all right if I ask you a few questions?"

"Yes of course, please come in."

The detective stepped in the room, and left the door open behind him, correctly guessing she wouldn't want to be closed in with a man she didn't know at the moment. "How are you holding up?" he asked as he reached forward to shake her hand.

"I'm pretty damn freaked out if you really want to know."

His handshake was firm and quick.

"I'm sure you are." After he released her hand, he drew a small notepad out of the inside pocket of his jacket. "Think you can walk me through what happened here today?"

Lila studied him for a moment before she spoke. He looked to be in his late forties, and was tall and lean, wearing a suit instead of a uniform. He still had a full head of hair, and the salt and pepper color gave him a distinguished look. "Sure. Um, let's see." Her voice shook as she struggled to organize her thoughts. "I'm sorry, my head is spinning in a million directions."

"Please take your time, doctor." His eyes were kind, but Lila had no doubt that was only because she was the victim. He had an air about him that suggested he could be hard and unyielding if necessary.

"I had just finished treating a patient, and there wasn't anyone in the waiting room, so I came to my office to—"

Angry shouts sounded from the entrance to the ER. "I don't give a fuck what your protocol is. If you don't let me back to see Lila, I'll knock your fucking teeth out, and bust down the door."

"Look, Striker, I really don't want to have to arrest you today, but I sure as hell will if you don't back off right now." The irritated voices could were clearly heard from the treatment room Lila occupied. It was closest to the entrance.

As soon as she heard Striker's voice, relief poured over her. They had connected on his deck a few nights ago and she needed that connection now. "Please, Detective Marks, can you let Striker come sit with me?"

"You in tight with the MC?" One eyebrow rose with his inquiry.

"I've treated them a number of times and have just become friendly with Striker," Lila answered, knowing that she had to tread carefully. She wanted Striker with her for two reasons. One, because she knew his presence would comfort her and make it easier to tell the story, and she wanted him to know exactly what she did and did not tell the police.

Detective Marks observed her for an instant before he nodded. With a resigned sigh, he poked his head out of the room and called toward the entrance. "Officer Diaz, please allow Striker, and *only* Striker through. Dr. Emerson would like him with her."

Lila exhaled a huge breath the moment Striker entered the room. He rushed toward her and gently cradled her face between his hands. "Damn, baby," he said as he tipped her chin up to inspect her bruised throat.

Their eyes collided. His had darkened, and worry mixed with fury radiated from the normally ice blue gaze. "I'm okay, Striker. I was just about to tell Detective Marks what happened. He said you could be in here with me, if that's all right with you."

Before he released her face he leaned in and placed a chaste kiss on her forehead. Lila wanted him to kiss her for real, to make her forget about what happened for just a few minutes, but it would have to wait for later, if it happened at all. She smiled at him, and took his hand, gripping it tight as she turned her focus back to Detective Marks who watched their interaction with undisguised curiosity.

Lila ignored his expression. "So, as I said, I was heading to my office to do some paperwork. I stepped in and closed the door, but my back was to it the whole time. He must have been hiding behind the door because the second it closed he was on me."

"You sure it was a he?" asked the detective.

The question surprised her, but she didn't have to think

about it for long. "It was a deep voice, and he was taller than I was. And stronger. I'm confident it was a man."

Waves of anger were radiating from Striker, so she squeezed his hand. "He grabbed the back of my neck, and slammed me face first against the wall. His hand was large, and reached almost all the way around my neck which is why I have bruises on the front." She absently ran her free hand over her bruised throat. "Anyway, he held me there and told me he'd been watching me. I don't remember screaming, but I must have because Dr. Knox rushed in to check on me. The man released me immediately, shoved Dr. Knox out of the way, and took off."

"You never saw his face, correct?"

"I didn't. I wasn't ever face to face with him, but I heard a few people say they saw a man in a ski mask run out of here. After he left, a number of staff members rushed in, and someone called nine-one-one."

Marks studied her for a few seconds before he shifted his attention to Striker. Lila could practically see the accusations forming in his head, but all he said was, "Thank you for your cooperation, Dr. Emerson. I'm glad you're mostly unharmed. We will be in touch with you soon, let me know if you think of anything else. Sometimes additional details come to you once you've had time to process. My card." He handed her a business card.

She stuck the card into her pocket as he turned to exit the room. "Thank you for your help, Detective."

The detective turned back to her, nodded once then left them alone. Striker stepped in front of her, and captured her face in his hands once again. She sensed a battle waging in him between his immense fury and concern for her. With a gentle touch, he drew her face toward his own, and captured her lips in a kiss designed to soothe rather than arouse. Lila felt the emotion he poured into the kiss, and her heart stuttered in her chest. This man was quickly becoming vital to her, and she wasn't sure what to do about it.

Striker pulled back and rested his forehead against hers, sliding one hand around the back of her neck as the other stroked down her spine. "Scared me, baby."

Lila didn't respond, the moment felt so intimate and emotionally charged, she was afraid she'd break down. Somehow she'd managed to hold it together this far. At some point the tears would come, but she wanted to be away from the hospital before she gave into them.

Striker shifted his head so his lips were against her ear. "Someone may be outside that door listening, so the second we get home, you're telling me the rest of that story. Don't think I couldn't tell you were holding out on that detective."

"I have no plans to keep anything from you. I just knew you wouldn't want the cops to hear it all. By the way, I'm in. Tell Shiv I'll take the deal. I need the protection," she whispered back.

He nodded, helped her down from the plinth, and guided her out of the building to where his brothers waited. She watched his tense face as they walked outside. What was between them would certainly end in heartache, but Lila was through suppressing the desire she had for Striker. Over the past few days they'd begun to form an emotional bond as well as their physical attraction, and she was eager to see where it would lead.

Chapter Thirteen

Striker was grateful for the thirty-minute trip to his house, it gave him time to get himself in check. A white-hot rage had coursed through him the moment he glimpsed the purple bruising around the delicate skin of Lila's throat. Her neck had been so soft and enticing the day he held her on his deck, he hadn't been able to resist brushing his lips all over it. The thought of someone squeezing that supple flesh until it bruised had him ready to kill.

The club needed to get serious about eliminating the threat against her. Jester informed him Shiv had called a meeting for the following morning, knowing Striker would want to be there for Lila tonight.

Now, he sat in his house with Lila, Jester, and Acer. Gumby went back to the clubhouse to provide Shiv with details they hadn't wanted to talk about over the phone. Lila was resting on one end of the couch with Acer on the other, while Striker paced in front of the television, full of agitated energy.

Jester emerged from the kitchen with a glass in his hand. He plopped his large frame down on the coffee table directly in front of Lila, so close their knees collided, and handed her the glass. "Here, baby doll, this will help."

"What is it?"

"Whisky."

Lila took a healthy sip, and coughed as the liquid took a fiery trip down to her stomach. "Whoa, not used to that."

Not in the mood to indulge them, Striker stopped pacing and cut right to it. "I want the rest of the story, now."

Lila nodded at him and didn't mince words. "It was a Grimm Brother."

"You sure about that, Stitch? You need to be very certain, because there will be fallout." Jester leaned in to rest his hands on her knees as he spoke to her.

Lila's gaze shifted between Striker and Jester. "I'm as sure as I can be. I saw one of his hands, it had a tattoo that said Grimm, one letter on each knuckle." As she spoke she absently rubbed at her neck as though remembering his hands on her. The gesture ignited the anger in Striker once again.

Acer, who had remained silent through most of this, spoke up from his spot at the opposite end of the couch. "That's them, they all have that tat. Shit, this is gonna get ugly."

Striker walked over and shoved between Lila and Jester, whose hands still rested on her knees. "Get your fucking hands off her, brother."

Jester straightened, a smirk on his face, and he raised his hands in mock surrender, while Lila bit her bottom lip and shook with the force of her suppressed laughter.

"These two are about to leave so you can rest and relax for the rest of the day." He knew he was being a dick, but seeing her finger those bruises pissed him off. Striker had a feeling there was still some detail Lila was holding back. He needed to get it out of her, and hoped she'd open up once they were alone.

"Guess that's our cue." Acer rose from the couch, and circled behind it to make his way toward the door for the door with Jester right on his heels. Striker's eyes narrowed as Acer dropped a kiss on Lila's head as he passed by. "You're made of tough stuff, honey."

Lila looked up and smiled at them as they exited. "Thank you both for being there today."

The second the door closed behind his brothers, Striker sunk down on the couch next to Lila, then turned and assessed her. She was so beautiful, even bruised and scared. "Okay, babe, time to come out with the rest of it."

"What do you mean?" Lila looked everywhere but at him.

"I know there's something you're not telling me."

She rose from the couch to bring her now empty glass into the kitchen, and he followed. When he got there he found her standing at the sink staring out the window at the shimmering lake. Striker slid behind her, and gently boxed her in, his hands resting on the edge of the sink on either side of her body. After the ordeal she had today, he was worried about startling her so he kept his voice soft, and didn't touch her. "I need you to tell me the rest, Lila. None of this is on you, but I have to know what we are dealing with, so I can keep you safe."

She turned and faced him, placing her hands on his chest. Striker took it as an invitation to close his arms around her and hold her. Her body quivered slightly in his embrace. With a gentle squeeze, he rested his forehead against hers. "Please tell me, baby."

"Okay." He watched her close her eyes as though it would be easier to say behind a curtain of darkness. "When he had me against the wall with his hand on my throat his other hand came around and under my shirt. Then he, well, he touched me." She paused as her voice caught, and took a

116

deep breath as though inhaling the courage to continue. "He stuck his hand in my bra and squeezed my breast, hard. I was so scared he was going to do more. If Dr. Knox hadn't heard me scream…"

Striker didn't know what was worse, hearing her words or watching tears track down her cheeks as she let the sentence hang. He felt more than just protective of her, he felt possessive, and the feeling had risen fast and with intensity. He had no right to think this way, but the thought of another man touching this woman was unacceptable. He needed all his strength to prevent his own hands from trembling with fury. "Did he leave a mark on you?" His voice sounded tight, even to his own ears.

Lila nodded and opened her eyes, which were red with tears. "I have a few bruises."

That statement was his breaking point. He stared at her with cold, furious eyes. "He's a fucking dead man." The need to know she was truly unharmed was stronger than his need to breathe, and he grabbed for the hem of her scrub top, attempting to lift it over her breasts.

"Striker! What are you doing?" Lila slapped at his hands, and tried to wrestle her shirt away from him. "Stop it. Are you crazy?"

"I need to see, I need to make sure you aren't hurt, see for myself." He couldn't keep the frantic need out of his voice.

"Hey." Lila put her hands on his face, and forced him to look at her. "I'm ok, I'm a doctor, and I'm fine. Plus, I do not want the first time you see me naked to be because you are checking out my bruises."

Her assertion brought some sanity back, and he chuckled softly as he stroked his hands up and down her back. "Point taken, gorgeous. Why don't you go take a long, hot shower while I make us something to eat?"

In a move that floored him, Lila grabbed the edges of his cut and pulled him closer to her. "Why don't you take one with me?"

The air in the room thickened at Lila's request. Striker, who had been semi erect just standing near her, hardened in a nearly painful rush. There was nothing he wanted more than to follow her into that shower, bury himself in her wet heat, and make them both forget the stress of the day. He'd been dreaming of running his hands over her soapy body, and listening to her moan as he pleasured her. But something stronger than sex alone was happening between them, and, for the first time in his adult life, he cared about a woman beyond the physical. Dragging her farther into his world would be a mistake that could destroy them both.

With a gentle hold, he removed her hands from his cut. "I can't believe I'm about to say this, but I'm not sure if this is a good idea, Lila." As he stared at her eyes, which no longer had tears, but were bright with desire, he wasn't sure he'd be able to resist what she offered.

"I've already gone over all the reasons this is a bad idea in my head, a thousand times." She shook her head and let out a small huff. "But I haven't found one that trumps how much I want you." Her voice was breathless with need, but steady and she tried to reach for him again.

"Wait, let me finish. I gotta lay it all out for you first, I need you to know who I am." He let go and took a step away from her. It wouldn't be possible to say what he needed to say while he was touching her, especially if she decided she couldn't be with him.

"All right, but, Striker, I know who you are."

"You may think you do, but I need to be sure. This life I live is rough, babe, it's raw and dangerous at times. And you'll be meshing into my world; I can't leave mine for yours.

Not trying to be an ass, but that's just the MC way. It's who I am, it's in my bones, and will be until I'm six feet under. I can guarantee I'm not like any preppy DC guy you've dated in the past. You need to be good with that, and good with me. I'm not one to hold your hand while we stroll down the street and window shop. I won't sweetly make love to you like you're made of glass. I've got too much need for you to be gentle. If we do this I'm going to fuck you until you're screaming, until you can't walk tomorrow. I like it hard, and fast, and I like to be in control."

He tried to scare her away, give her one last out because he knew he did not have the strength to walk away from her at this point. She was too decent for his world, but he was a selfish bastard, and if she didn't want this she would have to be the one to end it, to leave. He wasn't going anywhere.

Chapter Fourteen

Lila saw right through him. Striker was stepping back to distance himself, trying to scare her away. His words should have done just that; he was right, his world was so far beyond her experience she should run in the opposite direction. Striker had stated his intent. He wanted more than tonight, he wanted her in his bed and in his life. This would be the last straw for her family, they'd disown her for sure, but that was the least of the potential troubles on the horizon.

It may be insanity, but Lila craved him, and instead of driving her away, his promises aroused her. She wanted exactly what he was offering, wanted to explore the intense passion brewing between them. Even if it ended in disaster, at least she'd have the memories of what it felt like to be desired by a man like Striker. His brand of alpha male was something she'd never experienced in her high society conservative life. She'd be a fool to pass it up. "Striker, I want you. I want you more than I've wanted anything, ever. I want everything you have to give me any way you want to give it to me."

The last word barely left her mouth before he slammed his lips on hers in a kiss meant to fry her brain. There was no teasing, no warm up, only intensity. Lila opened her mouth to him and she tangled her tongue with his as her hands slid up into his hair, to keep him exactly where she wanted him. Her nipples hardened, and her panties flooded with need. As promised, he wasn't gentle. His arms wrapped around her body in a crushing embrace as his mouth kissed her senseless.

Time stood still as Lila moved her hands down his back. The wide expanse of firm muscle shifted beneath her hands and she marveled at the powerful male animal under her fingertips. As suddenly as it began, he ripped his mouth away, and dragged her toward the bathroom.

Without breaking contact, Striker shoved the shower door open, reached in and turned on the spray. As Lila stood there, a flutter of nerves bloomed in her stomach, and she was suddenly very aware of the disparity in their experience levels. "Striker, I haven't been—"

He stepped closer, and placed a finger over her lips. "I didn't ask for a resume, Lila. I want you so bad I've jerked off more times since you've been in my house than I have in the last five years combined. Besides, I told you I like to be in control, so I have no problem running the show."

He reached for the hem of her shirt, and this time she gladly let him draw it over her head. She had on a simple black bra, nothing overly sexy since she had been at work, but the way his eyes dilated told her he thought differently. "I've been dying to see you like this."

The room warmed and filled with steam, adding to the seductive ambiance. Nerves that had been present seconds ago fled when Striker reassured her of his desire. Lila reached back and unhooked her bra, and extended her arms to let it tumble to the floor.

With a greedy gleam, Striker did a slow perusal of her body until he caught sight of the bruises. His jaw clenched and his face clouded with an emotion she couldn't read. Striker dipped his head and pressed his lips to the side of Lila's breast, directly over one of the marks. The kiss was so light, she barely felt the brush of his lips against her fevered skin.

Lila gazed down at the dominant man showering her with gentle care, and her heart stuttered in her chest while her throat thickened. She sifted a hand through the soft strands of his hair, wanting to return some of the tenderness. "Striker," she whispered. "I'm okay. Really, I am."

"I hate that some man touched you like this, intending to hurt you." His words were spoken in the same quiet tone she'd used. "I promise you, he will not get away with it."

He repeated the kiss over the other two round purple marks on her skin, even though it was more soothing than sexual, Lila's nipples puckered with need. "Let's not make this about him right now. I don't want to think about it anymore."

"I've been dreaming about seeing and tasting your tits for weeks. And they're beautiful by the way. I'll do my best to keep my mind on the task at hand for now, and worry about trouble later."

In a move that stunned her, Striker dropped to his knees at her feet and yanked her pants down. Lila didn't know what to do with herself so she just stared, mesmerized by the powerful man on the floor in front of her. He shifted his gaze upward and their eyes met as he hooked his fingers in the sides of her silky black bikini panties, and began to draw them down her legs.

When he reached her ankles, he rasped, "Step out." His voice was strained, almost hoarse.

Lila obeyed immediately, and watched as his gaze left her face to travel down her body. Every inch of skin he looked at tingled as though he'd caressed her with his hands. He rubbed her legs with his strong palms, gliding them from her calves up to her hips. Her skin felt seared by his long fingers where they gripped her flesh. She had to touch him, and the only place she could reach was his head so she slid her fingers through his hair, and scored her nails over his scalp.

Striker's lids drifted closed, and Lila knew he enjoyed her touch when a gruff sound of pleasure escaped his lips. One hand slowly traveled from her hip across her body to her center and dipped into her. Sensation rocked through her, driving a gasp from her lips, and her hands automatically tightened in his hair. His eyes lifted back to hers as he lightly stroked her. "You're so wet baby." He groaned.

Slightly embarrassed to be under his intense, up close and personal scrutiny, she ducked her head.

Without warning, Striker stood, and Lila whimpered at the loss of his touch. "Get in the shower."

His voice was tense with arousal, and the knowledge that she wasn't the only one affected served to excite her even more. Lila obeyed, and stepped her shaky legs into the shower.

When the warm spray ran down her body, Lila sighed in contentment, and turned so she faced him. She was sore, but hadn't wanted to alarm him further by admitting it, and the heat of the shower felt amazing on her abused body.

Lila found his appreciative gaze on her once again. Her nipples were beyond hard and aching as they pointed outward, as though beckoning him. She was so turned on and sensitive that the feel of the water running down her breasts was enough to draw a moan from her.

Striker noticed and a sexy smirk formed on his handsome face. "Everything okay, baby? I bet those pretty nipples would feel even better with my mouth on them. You want that?"

"God, yes." Lila didn't trust herself to speak beyond that.

Striker was still clothed, and standing outside the shower, a situation she decided needed to change. She wanted to make him as crazy as he was making her. With a grin of her own, she skimmed her hands up her body toward her breasts, anxious to provide some relief for her straining nipples.

Striker shot a hand into the shower and gripped her wrist with a gentle but unbreakable hold. "Uh uh. Those are mine. Hands at your sides or I'll make you wait even longer."

Lila's body was on fire and she didn't think she could wait another minute. Never had a lover spoken to her like this. Never had one played with her, and aroused her with words alone. Admittedly, her experience was limited; she'd only slept with two men in the past. She wasn't sure how much more she could take, but she did as he asked and dropped her hands.

"Good girl."

Striker shrugged out of his cut, and tossed it on the counter, next to the sink. When he reached down for his T-shirt and pulled it over his head, her eyes widened and her jaw fell open. "Holy shit."

"Like what you see, baby?"

"Striker, you're gorgeous." And he was. His chest was broad and thick around with solid muscle. The words *Take No Prisoners* were tattooed across his broad right pectoral muscle and multiple tattoos decorated his arms. When he'd placed his cut on the counter, she'd noticed his entire back was tattooed as well, but he'd turned around too fast for her to take it in. Lila would love to explore them further, find out what each one symbolized, but it would have to wait. As her eyes continued their journey she took in his abs, which could have been crafted by a sculptor. Every inch of him was hard, toned and masculine, and for the time being, hers to enjoy.

Her eyes locked on his hand as he moved to the zipper of his pants. He tortured her, lowering the zipper one tooth at a time until he had enough room to slide his pants and boxers to the floor.

Captivated, Lila watched his impressive cock spring from its confines. It rose proudly from his body as though seeking her out. More cream eased from her body at the thought of how good it would feel when he finally pressed inside her. Lila was so wet she was grateful for the shower; otherwise, she would have been embarrassed by her body's blatant expression of need.

She held her breath as Striker joined her in the shower. He didn't waste any time getting his hands on her body. The feel of them, work-roughened and firm, as they glided over flesh made Lila tremble. She wrapped her smaller fingers around his biceps, or at least as far around as she could grasp, needing something solid to hold on to. Lila felt the hard length of his erection trapped against her stomach, and she pulled him even closer.

Striker slid his hands around to close over her breasts. Her nipples pressed into his palms and she groaned. The sensation was wonderful, but she needed more, needed something greater to ease the burning need. He nudged her until her back made contact with the tile wall. The contrast between the warm hands and water on her, and the cool tile hitting back made her jump.

"Easy, baby," he whispered as he bent his head so his mouth lingered an inch from hers. "Tell me what you need. You want my mouth on these pretty tits?"

"Please, Striker." Her voice was thick with longing.

"Please what, Lila? Tell me what you want, say the words, baby. I'll give you everything you ask for." As he spoke he continued to caress and squeeze her breasts. It felt amazing, but he was right, she needed his mouth.

She'd never participated in any kind of dirty talk, never asked a man for what she wanted, but she found herself excited by the concept. "I want your mouth on me Striker."

"Where? Here?" he asked as he nipped at her ear.

"No, well yes, I like that but, I need your mouth on my nipples." It became difficult to keep her eyes open, so she let the lids drift closed.

Half his mouth quirked up in a grin. "Sounds like a good place to start. Then maybe I'll move on down to your soft belly." His fingers moved to the area he spoke of and shivers raced across her skin. "Then finally I'll get a taste of your pussy. I've been dreaming about tasting you for weeks, Lila."

"Oh, God." Dirty talk did it for her, as it turned out, and she was grateful for the wall supporting her back.

She hadn't opened her eyes yet so she couldn't see what was coming, wasn't prepared when his mouth latched onto her nipple and he sucked her with strong pulls.

"Striker," she cried loudly. Her fingers dove into his hair to hold him to her.

As he licked a path to the other breast, his fingers replaced his mouth so neither was neglected. Lila's back arched and her body strained toward him; she couldn't get close enough.

Each tug of his fiery mouth and pluck of his fingers sent a lightning shot of pleasure from her nipples to her clit. His mouth journeyed down her body and she moaned, letting her head fall back against the wall. Her fists clenched in his hair and tugged at the strands, and he let out a low groan, telling her he enjoyed her rough treatment of him.

She felt him kiss, nip, and lick a path down her stomach, and pleasure overwhelmed all her senses. Her breasts still tingled from his attention, her stomach quivered with each bite and suck, her pussy clenched in anticipation of what she knew was to come, while warm water flowed over her whole body. It was almost too much. Her brain couldn't keep up with the onslaught of sensation well enough to process everything.

"Striker," she pleaded. "It's—"

"Shhh, I know baby," he answered as though he could read her mind, sense her churning emotions. "Turn that smart brain off, and just feel what I'm doing to you. I promise you'll love it all."

She managed to huff out a laugh at the understatement. "I already do."

He sunk to his knees once again, and wrapped a hand around one of her thighs. "Lift for me beautiful."

She did as he asked. He spread her wide and hooked her thigh over his shoulder. Fingers splayed, her hands hit the shower wall in an attempt to stay grounded. She stared down at him in awe of the erotic scene she was a part of. Her leg was draped over him and his hand was on the wall, which afforded her an excellent view of the muscles in his shoulder at work. With his head slightly bent, he stared at her center, and she had a perfect snapshot of his back and ass. She couldn't wait until it was her turn to explore his hard body.

"You are so fucking sexy, Lila."

He leaned forward and ran his tongue along her slit. A shock of pleasure tore through her system. His tongue continued upward to circle her clit. She moaned and thrust her pelvis toward his face. His hands moved to her hips, steadying her as his tongue flicked her clit over and over. Somehow he managed to hold her still and keep her leg over his shoulder.

She felt one hand leave her hip and seconds later he drove a finger up into her, curling it forward to hit the spot designed to drive her crazy. Lila locked her knee praying she wouldn't collapse before he was finished. Nothing in her limited experience prepared her for this assault on her senses. Again and again, he tongued her clit, and rubbed his finger inside of her until she thought she'd die from the sensations. Unable to keep quiet, her moans and whimpers filled the shower stall, and her hips pumped, riding his finger.

Striker was relentless in his goal of giving her the ultimate pleasure, and when his lips surrounded her clit and sucked she went over the edge into the strongest orgasm of her life. Her body shook and she cried out at the rush of feelings that overtook her.

Striker stayed with her, his finger gentling as his mouth placed soft kisses on her inner thighs until she came down from the high. "Thank you," she whispered, choked up. The physical she could handle, almost, but the emotion slayed her. She probably sounded like an idiot, but she wanted him to know how much that meant to her.

"Believe me baby, it was my pleasure." He gave her a genuine smile as he rose to his feet and placed a gentle kiss on her lips. Lila tasted herself when his mouth met hers. A first for her, and it made the moment seem even more intimate.

"Speaking of," she said, reaching for him.

He stilled her hands with his own and snatched up a bottle of body wash. "We came in here for a reason."

"But—"

"Lila, it's early, we have all night to make each other scream. Let's wash up then I want you to sleep for a while."

She took the soap from him, and rose up on her toes to kiss him thoroughly. They enjoyed the rest of the shower caressing each other as they washed, kissed, and explored. When they were both cleaner than they had ever been,

Striker turned off the cooling water, and led Lila out of the shower. He dried them both then steered her toward the bed.

"Climb in babe," he instructed after he threw back the comforter.

Now that the high of her orgasm had faded, she felt self-conscious with her nudity. "I'm going to run to my room and grab a shirt."

Striker gave her a grin as he shook his head. "I don't think so."

"What?" she squeaked.

He strode over to where she was standing awkwardly, unsure what to do with her arms so they hung at her sides. When he was close enough to touch her, he dipped his head without warning and sucked a nipple into his mouth.

"Oh," she cried out. The renewed flare of desire was instant.

"Today was intense and terrifying for you. You need to catch a few hours of sleep, and I want to feel your whole body against mine while you rest, no clothes between us. It will reassure me that you're okay. Then, when I can't stand it anymore, I'll wake you up so I can slide into you and give us what we're both dying for."

Lila gave him a shaky smile, and climbed into the bed. Striker joined her and rolled her so her back was spooned against his front. She fell asleep in seconds, wrapped in Striker's protective embrace, relaxed for the first time all day.

Chapter Fifteen

Striker woke a few hours later still curled around Lila's sleeping form. The even rise and fall of her chest against his torso was reassuring, and he was glad she'd been able to sleep.

The moment he registered the feel of her bottom snuggled against his cock, he hardened in a rush. He slid one palm over her silky smooth thigh and he savored the feel of her in his arms. Something was happening here, something beyond sex, and he felt powerless to stop it. More than his fair share of women had rotated through his bed, being VP of the MC attracted them in droves. He always assumed he would have an ol' lady someday, and in so many ways Lila seemed his perfect match. Unfortunately, any relationship between them was doomed to fail. She was far too good for him, and at some point he would have to find the strength to end it.

Striker pressed his lips to Lila's neck, and kissed his way across her jaw while his hand snuck around the front and he slipped a finger into her core. As he let his fingers and mouth play, he felt her grow soft and wet.

"Mmmm." She moaned. "I could get used to this wake up call."

"That's the plan, babe. Are you on the pill?" He asked, his mouth against her ear.

Her body convulsed when his lips brushed her ear as he spoke, and she nodded.

"I always use a condom, and I got tested last week. I'm clean. Can I take you bare?" He dipped his tongue into her ear swirling it around.

"You got tested?" The last word came out as a moan.

"We've been dancing around each other for a while, Lila. This was bound to happen, and you're a doctor. I figured you wouldn't let me near you without proof I was clean. You want to see the paper?"

"Thank you, Striker. And no. I don't need to see the paper. I trust you."

He trapped her ear lobe between his teeth and gave a tug. "So is that a yes to bareback?" Goosebumps erupted along Lila's neck, and Striker ran his tongue across the ridges.

"Yes. No condom, and please hurry."

"Fuck, you're going to feel incredible."

While they talked, he lightly rimmed her entrance with one finger. Teasing her, feeling her rear squirm against his length was a form of self-torture. When, with a feminine sound of need, Lila reached back, and clenched his ass to anchor him to her as she ground her backside against him, the teasing wasn't enough anymore. He couldn't wait any longer; his body was screaming for her. To possess her. Own her.

Striker flipped her over, and settled between her thighs. One elbow rested on each side of her head while he fused his mouth to hers. Her arms came around him, and her velvety hands stroked the taut muscles of his back. "I need you now, baby, you ready for me?" he asked between biting kisses.

"God, yes. I'm beyond ready for you."

"I can't go slow. I can't be easy right now. I'm too close to the edge. Can you handle me, Lila?" he asked through gritted teeth as he tensed with the effort to hold back. He didn't want to attack her like an animal.

She reached between them, closed her soft hand around his cock, and gave him a firm squeeze. His breath hissed out as she pumped him once, twice, then swiped her thumb over the sensitive head. "I don't want slow. I don't want easy, Striker. I want hard, and I want fast." She positioned him at her opening.

Her words were the catalyst he needed. With one fierce stroke, he slammed into her, and a smile lit his face as she to arched up and cried out in pleasure. Despite Lila's bold talk, he knew it had been a while for her, and the last thing he wanted was to hurt her.

Shit! She was so hot and tight around him he thought he might come just from holding still inside her. He fought the urge to move, and peered down at her. Christ, she was beautiful. Skin flushed, neck arched, she squirmed slightly to adjust to his thick penetration.

"Don't hold back. Fuck me, Striker," she cried.

The last thread of his control broke. He found both of her hands, and flung them roughly over her head, linking their fingers as he pressed them to the mattress. He drew out, and groaned as her body clenched as though trying to pull him back in. With a feral cry, he hammered into her. There wasn't any finesse as he thrust fiercely, over and over. Lila wrapped her legs around his waist and met him stroke for stroke.

"Christ, Lila, what are you doing to me?"

"I don't know." She panted. "But you do the same thing to me. Oh, God, Striker, It's never been like this."

Her uninhibited admission fueled him even further, and, if

possible, his hips moved faster, harder.

He'd never been with a woman whose body and mind pleasured him in equal measure. Emotions he hadn't felt in over a decade made him feel vulnerable while also enhancing the pleasure.

Lila felt like heaven around him, hotter than the desert sun, and so tight it was an effort to pump in and out of her despite how wet desire made her. Striker always used a condom, and the silken warmth of her pussy gripping him made his eyes roll back in his head. She had better stay on that damn pill forever. Now that he'd had a taste of perfection, he would never tolerate a barrier between them.

The walls of her channel fluttered around him, and he knew she was close. Lila seemed mindless with pleasure. Whimpers escaped her with each thrust, and she clawed at his back as though she was trying to climb inside him. Their mouths ate at each other until suddenly she pulled away and emitted a loud shout of release. Her slim body shook under him, squeezing his cock, and sent him over the edge with her. He shuddered as waves of pleasure assaulted him. With one final kiss, he collapsed on top of her.

"I'll move in a minute," he whispered, around his heaving breath.

"You don't need to," she answered as she stroked her hands up and down his back.

After a few minutes, Striker lifted his head and looked in her eyes. He found them slumberous and contented. "Never been that good, baby." He rolled over, and slid out of her. Not finished enjoying the feel of her, he tucked her into the curve of his body. After he drew the blankets up to cocoon them, he wrapped his arms around her midsection. "Sleep, Lila."

Chapter Sixteen

Lila woke to the morning sun streaming through the windows. She felt fantastic, last night was one of the best of her life. They had slept for a few hours after the first round of earth shattering sex. Striker had woken her again in the night to have her a second time. At some point, they stumbled to the kitchen for some cold pizza before falling back into bed. He'd proven to be a demanding lover, who definitely liked to be in control, and she found she loved it. Who knew badass alpha bikers were her type?

Striker's heavy arm lay across her stomach, trapping her to his side. One of his legs was wedged between hers and there was something resembling a pipe prodding at her back. "I see I'm not the only one who's up."

Striker barked out a laugh and nipped at her shoulder. "Sassy," he said. "And while I'd give anything to sink back into you, we slept in, and I have to be at the clubhouse for church soon."

"I'm sorry. You have to go where?"

Striker chuckled. "Church."

"Oh...okay."

"What babe? Didn't think I was the religious type? That's

a little offensive you know."

Lila felt her face heat. He was right. It was judgmental and offensive of her. "I'm so sorry. You're right. It is horribly offensive of me."

Striker burst out laughing, and she turned in his arms with a frown. "I'm just messing with you, babe. Church is not church as you're thinking. It's what we call a meeting in the club."

Even more embarrassed to be caught in her ignorance, Lila slugged him in the arm. "Not funny. You had me feeling like a bitch."

He gave her a quick, hard kiss. "Sorry, I couldn't resist."

She rolled her eyes at him. "I guess I'll just hang here today."

"What do you mean? Don't you have to be at the hospital?"

"Oh shit," she said as she slapped a palm to her head. "I forgot to tell you. I suppose I was distracted." She gave him a sassy grin, and ran her hand over his stubble-covered jaw. "Since yesterday's drama made such a spectacle at work, they asked me to take a few weeks off until we clear everything up."

Striker nodded. "It's a good idea. The more contained we can keep you until this is all over, the safer you'll be. If fact, we should probably limit the places you go to here and the clubhouse until we get this all sorted out."

"Oh, no." There was no way she was going to be under house arrest while they worked to keep her protected. Striker exuded confidence, which often crossed the line into arrogance, and gave off a vibe that commanded respect and obedience. She bet he didn't hear the word *no* too often, from his brothers or from women. But this was too important.

"That's not going to work for me at all, Striker. I get why

they don't want me at the hospital, and to be honest, I can use the time off to focus on my concussion project, but there is no way I'm putting that on hold."

"Lila—"

She covered his mouth with her palm as she shook her head. "No. I have my first committee meeting this Wednesday, and I will be there. I don't care if you send ten men along, but I will not postpone this. As soon as I do, another project will hit their radar and take precedence. Then, before I know it, they'll take my allocated funds and distribute them elsewhere and my program will die. So, I'll follow your rules and do what you ask to stay safe, but I will not delay this project."

"Yes, ma'am," Striker said with a grin. "I kinda like it when you boss me around."

"Striker," she growled. "I'm very serious about this."

"I know you are, babe. And I'll work something out with the guys. I promise we'll figure out a way to get you to the meeting and keep you safe. You can't tell anyone about what's going on, though. We'll have to think of a reason my guys will be with you. And for today, I want you at the clubhouse with me."

"Thank you." Lila leaned forward and placed a kiss on his chest, right above his heart. She was relieved she wouldn't have to be alone so soon after the attack. "I'll be glad to be close to you today, and I can bring my laptop to work on while you do your thing."

She started to turn, planning on some coffee before a quick shower, when Striker's leg clamped across her waist. He clasped her face between both hands, and gave her a deep, drugging kiss that had her blood humming with lust. "Sorry, babe, should have done that first thing."

Charmed, Lila smiled at him and climbed out of bed,

reaching for a shirt on the floor. It was Striker's, and probably dirty, but she had to take a shower anyway so it really didn't matter. Striker sat on the opposite side of the bed with his feet on the floor, and Lila turned to ask him when they had to be at the clubhouse, but the words died in her throat. "Oh my God! Striker, your back!" There were a number of angry red scratches on his upper back between his shoulder blades.

Striker looked at her over his shoulder and cracked a grin. "I know."

"What happened, Striker? How did you get those?"

He stood up and came toward her with a loud laugh. "What do you mean what happened? You happened, babe."

"What?" She grabbed his shoulders and tried to turn him around so she could examine his back. "I didn't do that, there is no way I did that to you. Let me see them."

"Well you were the only one in bed with me last night." He bent forward as his body shook with the growing force of his mirth.

"Don't laugh. It's not funny! I hurt you, and I don't even remember doing it." She felt awful and embarrassed for having lost control like that.

He pulled her to him. "It didn't hurt then, and it doesn't now. In fact, I'm thinking of going to the meeting shirtless today."

"Shirtless!" Lila was almost shrieking now. "Why on earth would you want anyone to see that?"

"Are you kidding me? I had you so out of your mind with pleasure last night that you didn't even realize you were clawing my back like a wild animal. Fuck yeah, I want everyone to see that."

Lila shoved him away playfully and finally laughed. "So this is about your overinflated male ego?"

"I like to think of it more as a testament to my amazing skills." He strolled past her, and gave her a quick slap on the ass. "Better get moving, Doc, we leave in fifteen minutes."

"Fifteen minutes?" This time she did shriek as she scrambled toward the bathroom.

Chapter Seventeen

An hour later, they rolled up to the clubhouse, and Striker helped her off the bike. She'd taken twenty-five minutes to shower and dress, and had to listen to the typical male grumbling about how long it takes women to get ready. It was strange to participate in such a normal morning routine right before Striker attended a meeting about how to stop a lunatic from harming her.

Striker reached for the clasp on her helmet, and unstrapped it before pulling it off her head, and giving her a quick kiss. She loved how attentive he was being today. There wasn't any morning-after awkwardness. At some point they'd have to talk about what they were doing, but it could wait.

He grabbed her hand, and tugged her toward the door. "We'll have to stop at the bike shop to pick up a better fitting helmet, and maybe some riding boots."

"Oooh I'd love that! I think I'll get a hot pink one," she said, knowing exactly what his reaction would be.

Sure enough, Striker scowled at her. "No way am I riding with a chick wearing a hot pink helmet. Sorry, babe, not happening." He held the door for her, and placed his hand on her back, guiding her through. "You okay to hang at the bar?"

She tapped the computer case she'd pulled out of his saddlebag. "Sure. As long as I have a flat surface for my laptop, I'm good."

They made their way to the bar where a pretty woman with long blonde hair stood washing out some glasses. Dressed in a tight black tank top and ass-hugging jean shorts, she bopped her head to whatever music was flowing from her ear buds. Written in cursive across the front of her shirt was the words *Take No*, and Lila assumed *Prisoners* was scrawled across the back.

When she caught site of them, she pulled her headphones out and waved. "Hey, Striker, church is about ready to start, you better get in there."

"Thanks, Marcie. Hey, this is Lila. She's going to hang here while I'm in the meeting. Lila this is Marcie, Hook's ol' lady. I don't think you met him yet. He's been out of town the last week on club business. Keep her out of trouble, Marce," he said with a wink.

Striker turned to Lila, and slid one hand around the back of her neck, tugging her into his space for a lingering kiss. His other hand gripped her ass and held her flush against him. Their tongues tangled, and her knees grew weak. This was the first time she'd been involved in such a public display of anything physical, and she should have been embarrassed, but Striker ravaged her mouth so thoroughly, all thoughts of her surroundings slipped away.

"Oh, motherfucker!"

Lila jumped as the frustrated expletive cut through the spell of Striker's kiss.

"Hey watch your mouth asshole, there are ladies in here." She recognized Jester's voice, but not the one who'd spoken first.

Striker broke away from her, and they both turned toward the noise in time to see Gumby slap some money in a grinning Jester's palm with a look of disgust. What was going on? She glanced at Striker for clarification, but he just shrugged.

"What are you to morons rambling on about?" Striker asked with a droll tone.

"You just cost me fifty dollars, VP," muttered Gumby.

Jester sauntered over, and hauled Lila from Striker's embrace to sling a heavy arm across her shoulders. "I prefer to think of it as the lovely Doc here won me fifty bucks," he announced with a smile.

"Come on, Striker, you said she was freaked out after the attack yesterday." Gumby scowled at him.

"Well, dumbass, that's exactly when a woman is likely to put out. You act all sensitive and shit, and she'll shed her clothes like they're covered in fire ants. Tell me I'm right, Striker."

"What you are is a dipshit," Striker answered.

Lila's gaze bounced between the three men. "Wait, you bet on how I handled being attacked yesterday?"

Jester gave her shoulders a squeeze and shot her an arrogant smirk. "No, doll, we bet on whether or not Striker would finally be getting into your scrubs last night. I for one would like to thank you for giving it up." He rubbed his new fifty between his thumb and forefinger.

"Wow, you guys really are a bunch of pricks. And what did I tell you yesterday about putting your hands on her?" Striker faced Jester, his eyes narrowed and teeth clenched. It looked a bit like he was ready to attack.

Lila burst out laughing. "How on earth did you even know you won?"

Jester tightened his arm around Lila causing Striker to

scowl further. "Well he kissed you in that *I wish we had a bed instead of a meeting* way." Jester shrugged as though it was an obvious conclusion.

Still laughing, Lila held out her hand to Jester. "Well, you gonna give me half? It's only fair since I did win it for you. Though I have to say, my performance was definitely worth more than fifty dollars."

There was a chorus of howls and whoops from the guys, even Marcie got in on it, with a shrill whistle from her position behind the bar. Striker snickered, and lost the murderous look on his face. He took Lila's hand and rescued her out from under Jester's tree trunk of an arm, before he planted a kiss on her forehead. "Damn straight it was, baby."

"Let's go. Church, now." Shiv's voice boomed through the clubhouse.

"You good to stay here, babe?" Striker asked in a low voice.

"I'm great," she answered with a smile, the banter having put her in a light mood.

"I'm glad you can laugh at those idiots. I was worried you'd be offended by their bet."

"Are you kidding? I love how ridiculous you all are with each other. I don't mind at all. I can handle myself, Striker."

"Mmm, you sure can." He reached around her, and grabbed an ass cheek in each hand, pulling her close for a quick kiss before he winked and sauntered after his brothers into the meeting.

"Striker!" Lila gasped, as she felt her face flame. When she turned back to the bar she gave Marcie a slightly sheepish smile. "I'd ask if they were always like that, but I don't think I need to."

"You don't know the half of it. They're all crazy." Marcie's smile was genuine, and Lila immediately liked the woman.

"Do you mind if I work on my computer while I wait?" Lila asked Marcie. "I don't want to be antisocial, but I have a long list of tasks to get through."

"Nah, girl. Go ahead. Anything I can help you with?" Marcie bustled around behind the bar with speed and efficiency as she stocked the now dry glasses on a shelf.

Lila paused a second before she denied the need for assistance. "Actually, maybe there is." She filled Marcie in on her plans for the concussion program. "I've been given a small budget from the school board, but I'd really like to update the safety equipment for the football team, and that's going to take a lot more money than we were granted. Which means I'll need to organize a fundraiser. Any ideas of something that might bring in the big bucks?"

"Hmm." Marcie rested her hip against the bar as she absently swirled a towel around the inside of a glass. "What about a casino night? That usually has a big draw."

"That was my first thought as well, but I'd like it to be teenager friendly so the players and their friends can participate. Some parents may not approve of gambling, even if it is for a good cause."

Marcie nodded and set the glass down on the shelf. "What about a silent auction? The club held one about a year ago to raise money for the widow of one of our guys. We had quite a few donations from stores and restaurants in town. The garage donated a free oil change and tire rotation. We ended up raising quite a bit more than our goal."

Excitement bubbled up at idea. "Marcie, that's perfect! I love it! We can try to get some smaller items donated as well so the students can participate and bid."

"Glad I could help. Actually, I helped plan ours when we had it and I'd be more than happy to help you out if you need any extra people."

Marcie's face reflected nothing but the sincere desire to assist, and Lila was touched. "Thank you, Marcie. I can use all the help I can get. The first planning meeting is Wednesday at seven, right at the high school. Think you can make it?"

"Absolutely! This will be fun. Striker and Hook are closer than most brothers. We all grew up together, so I can't wait to get to know you better. It's about time Striker found himself a good woman."

All of the excitement that had risen while they talked about the fundraiser deflated faster than a balloon stuck by a pin. "Oh, I'm not Striker's woman. I'm not really his anything. He just got saddled with me while the club helps me out with a problem."

Marcie laughed so hard tears tracked down her face and Lila frowned. She wasn't sure why the other woman found her statement so funny, but she didn't really appreciate it.

"I'm sorry, Lila, but maybe I should have taken a video of that kiss Striker just gave you. You do not kiss a woman like that if she means nothing to you. You kiss a woman like that if you want to tie her to your bed and never let her leave."

Lila felt her face flame at Marcie's description. "I'm pretty sure we're looking for different things from the opposite sex, not to mention I'm in a little over my head with the whole biker scene."

Marcie stared at her, and Lila had the distinct impression her worth was being sized up.

"Can I give you some advice? Well, I guess it's more like insight into this life."

"Please do." Lila closed her laptop and gave Marcie her full attention.

"These guys live fast and wild for a time, some never settle, but, as it turns out, even most crazy bikers eventually want someone to come home to. I've known Striker for a very long time, and can tell you with certainty that he's a really good man. Now, I'm not going to bullshit you, he's sampled quite a few of the skanks that come around the club. Hang arounds who are looking to party and hook up with a biker. It's all a part of the game. But lately I've gotten the impression that the game's getting old, and he may be ready for something lasting. Don't sell him short, he just may surprise you."

"Thank you for telling me that. We haven't even had a conversation about what's happening between us, but it's more powerful than I expected and stronger than I've experienced before." She just wasn't sure that was anything to build a foundation on. She had a career to consider, goals to accomplish, and, bottom line, she wanted a family someday. Despite Marcie's reassurances, she wasn't convinced Striker wanted to go that route.

Marcie smiled. "I've wanted him to meet someone special for so long." Marcie jogged around the bar, and gave Lila a quick hug.

Lila smiled and returned the embrace. Marcie's friendly and open nature was refreshing.

"Oh shit, here comes the bitch," Marcie muttered as she released Lila, and walked back behind the bar.

Lila turned to see whom Marcie was talking about. "Who's a bitch?"

"Whatever happens next, don't get into it with her."

"Don't get into what with whom?" Lila looked around confused. "You mean don't get in a fight? I would never. That is not my style."

Marcie shifted her gaze back to Lila. "You do seem too classy for that, but then Brandi has a way of making you forget yourself. I keep hoping they are going to run her ass off." That last part was muttered half under her breath.

"Oookay…" Lila wasn't sure how to respond.

"Hi, Marcie, who's the new girl?"

A woman approach the bar. She was gorgeous, with long, platinum, probably from a bottle, blonde hair, huge breasts, and a tiny waist. Her face, however, was heavily made up and she was dressed like a tramp.

A skimpy, black halter-top with a deep V showed more of her breasts than it covered, and her denim shorts were so tiny, Lila wondered if she bought them in the children's section. Her feet were encased in what could only be called *fuck me heels*. Lovely. What was she, twenty-two at the oldest? Who was this woman? Lila had a feeling she was about to find out, and she didn't think she was going to enjoy it.

Marcie resumed drying glasses, and didn't bother to look up, making her distaste for the younger woman, girl really, quite obvious. "This is Lila, she's *with* Striker." The emphasis on *with* was not lost on either of them.

Lila wasn't entirely certain she was with Striker in the way Marcie meant, but she was feeling a bit possessive at the moment, and decided that what they'd shared last night, and the fact that she was staying at his house, gave her the rights to him for at least that day. She assumed a smile that no doubt looked phony, and decided to have a little fun. "Hey, Brandi, are you the daughter of one of these guys?"

Marcie covered her mouth and coughed as she attempted, in vain, to disguise a laugh. With a nasty sneer in Marcie's direction, Brandi answered Lila. "Oh no. I most certainly am not. I'm… close to many of the guys here."

"That's true. You've spread through the club faster than a virus."

Brandi took a seat on the barstool next to Lila and ignored Marcie. "Striker, huh?" She gave a dramatic shiver. "*Goood* man. In fact I still have some beard burn on my thighs from him."

The urge to slap the smug grin off this girl's caked on face was overwhelming, and Lila now understood why Marcie had warned her not to engage. She turned toward Marcie with a raised eyebrow, and Marcie shrugged at her as if to say, "Told you she was a huge bitch."

Before she could fire back, Brandi continued. "You don't really look like you hang out in biker bars too often, Lila. You should probably run along, and I can tell Striker you had somewhere to be when I see him later tonight."

Marcie smacked the glass she was drying on the bar with a loud clank, and let out a harsh laugh. "Oh man, did you just make a huge mistake. I did tell you she was with Striker right? As in *with*. As in you are trying to run off the VP's woman."

Warmth rushed to Lila's cheeks. She was grateful Marcie hadn't said ol' lady, because that would have been too much of a stretch, though she was sure Brandi noticed the word choice as well. She felt stupid just sitting there not saying anything, while these two woman exchanged words around her, but she was out of her element. This kind of interaction was not familiar to her, and she truly had no idea what Striker thought of their relationship, or what his relationship was with Brandi. It caused her to hesitate in defending herself.

Sounds from the back of the room caught their attention, and all three ladies turned as the meeting room doors were flung open. Striker was first to emerge, looking fierce. They must have come up with a plan to eliminate the threat from the Grimm Brothers. His eyes lit for a second when they landed on her, then narrowed in displeasure when he shifted them to the woman sitting next to her. Brandi's huge smile faltered a bit under his dissatisfied glare, and Lila knew her own uncomfortable look had registered with him.

She assumed they were working up to an unpleasant scene, when Marcie gasped and ran around the bar. "Hook! Oh my God, what happened? Someone help me with him."

All heads turned toward the entrance in time to see Hook stumble into the clubhouse. He was hunched over and his face was bleeding. It looked like he'd suffered a serious beating. Without hesitation, Lila sprang into action, and dashed toward him.

Chapter Eighteen

When Striker stepped out of church, his blood was pumping and his muscles were primed for action. After witnessing the bruises on Lila's breasts, he was more than eager to shed a little Grimm blood. He could almost feel the satisfaction of his fists pummeling the man who had placed his hands on Lila. This was a payback he was eager to dish out.

He'd hoped to sneak her up to his room where he could burn off pent up energy. He smiled when he spotted her at the bar, but the tense look on her face alerted him to the fact that she was not pleased about something. Striker shifted his gaze to the adjacent barstool. Fuck. Brandi sat next to Lila, her greedy gaze on him like he was some kind of prize she won at the fair.

That damn girl was trouble plain and simple.

"Stupid bitch," Jester muttered under his breath. "This is what happens when you let them take their mouths off your dicks. They start causing trouble with them."

Striker ran a frustrated hand through his hair and started toward the bar. Marcie suddenly cried out in shock and ran toward the door. He twisted in her direction, and saw a bloodied Hook nearly collapse on the floor. He dashed over and wrapped his arm around Hook, who grimaced at the contact. Marcie was on his other side, and helped support him as well.

Lila reached them seconds later, and barked orders like a seasoned drill sergeant. "Take him somewhere he can lie down so I can see what we're dealing with."

Striker nodded and pointed to a hallway. "There's a room down the hall for guests, it has a few beds. That work?"

"That's perfect. Can someone grab the supply kit I stashed in your room? I'm going to need it."

"Marce, hand him off to Jester so we can help him to the room. He's too heavy for you," Striker instructed, shouldering as much of Hook's virtually limp weight as possible to take the load off Marcie.

Tears streamed down Marcie's face, but to her credit, she didn't freak out. She whispered in Hook's ear, telling him he'd be okay, before she gently transferred his arm from her shoulders to Jester's. She winced along with Hook when Striker shifted some of his weight to Jester. Hook tried to smile at her, but it turned into a grimace when the muscles in his bruised face contracted.

When they reached the room, Striker and Jester turned sideways to maneuver Hook through the door without jarring him. The room was large, though pretty sparse, with half a dozen bunks and a few chairs. They were used when brothers from other chapters were visiting, or if someone needed a place to crash, usually with a chick. No one was utilizing the room currently, so they carried Hook to the nearest bunk. After they set him on the edge of the mattress, Striker helped lower his shoulders to the pillow while Jester hefted his feet onto the bed as gently as possible.

When he stepped back, Striker got a good view of Hook for the first time. The left side of his face was grossly swollen and bruised in a gruesome display of colors. Blood trailed from his nose and mouth, and had run down to soak the white fabric of the T-shirt Hook wore under his cut. Striker also noticed some long, horizontal tears in his shirt, and wondered if they'd slashed him with a knife. It seemed to be their weapon of choice. Christ, Hook could really be in a bad way. Thank God Lila was here to see to him right away.

As he thought of her, Lila slipped in next to him, and whispered in his ear. "I'll do what I can, but I obviously can't X-ray here and I'm not a surgeon, so he still may need a hospital."

He nodded, and peeked at Marcie who sat perched on the edge of the bed whispering to Hook while she stroked a hand over his hair.

"I'm also going to need to know what happened. I get you don't want me to know club business, but I'm going to need details about what they did to him so I can get a better feel for his injuries. Not sure if you want Marcie to hear all that."

Striker spared a second to admire how level headed Lila was, particularly during a crisis. He gave her a swift kiss on the mouth, smiled at her usual embarrassed blush, and turned to Marcie. "Hey, Marce—" he began.

Hook, who must have guessed where this was going, spoke to his wife at the same time. "Baby, I'm all right. I need you to wait outside for a bit while I talk to the guys, okay?"

Marcie, tears still tracking down her pretty face, looked like she wanted to protest, but she nodded and turned to Lila. "Take good care of him, please."

Lila gave her a quick hug. "Of course I will."

Marcie turned back to Hook with a stern voice. "Don't be a hero, tell her when it hurts."

Hook chuckled then clutched his side as though the movement was too much. "Ow, oh fuck, you know me too well, gorgeous."

Jester threw an arm across Marcie's shoulders, and propelled her out into the hallway, while Lila got right to work. She dug around in the massive first aid kit until she found some gloves and a pair of scissors.

"Okay, Hook, sorry we had to meet this way but I'm Lila, MC doctor extraordinaire." She winked at him as she sat on the edge of the bed. The effortless way she connected with her patients and put them at ease never failed to impress Striker. "I'm guessing it would be quite painful for us to try and take your shirt off over your head, so I'm going to cut it down the middle to get a better look at you. While I'm doing that I want you to tell me what happened."

Striker met Hook's gaze, and gave him a quick nod to let him know it was okay to speak openly in front of Lila.

Hook spoke while she cut down the front of his shirt. "I finished up business early, and I got back into town about an hour and a half ago. Hadn't said anything to Marce yet. I was going to surprise her. Anyway, I stopped at—oh shit that hurts, Doc." He grimaced when Lila prodded around his ribs.

"Sorry, I'll try to be more gentle. Keep talking, it will help distract you."

"I went into that biker gear store at the edge of town to grab something for Marce. Got jumped on the way out. There were three of them, Grimms for sure. Beat the fucking hell out of me."

Lila scooted up toward the head of the bed to examine Hook's face. Striker observed, taking it all in and thinking of what this meant for their plans.

"What did they hit you with?" Lila asked Hook as she felt around his skull. "Hold on, as you talk I'm just going to move your arms and legs around, let me know if anything hurts."

"Everything hurts, Doc," he said with a groan as she shifted on the edge of the bed. "They hit me with fists mostly until one of them knocked me down, then they kicked me with their boots. One of them did pistol whip me which is probably why my face looks so good."

Striker pushed away from his spot by the wall. He walked over, and crouched down by the bed. "What made them stop?"

"Group of guys walking by started shouting about calling the cops. They split pretty quick after that. Somehow, I managed to ride back here without wrecking."

Between the attack on Lila yesterday, and Hook's assault today, Jackal had clearly lost all control over his club. He never would have authorized these sloppy attacks in broad daylight with witnesses. It was only a matter of time before Snake was in control, if he wasn't already. The club needed more information so they could plan an intelligent move.

~ ~ ~ ~

Lila stood and removed her gloves, staring down at Hook. He really did look awful. It was as bad a beating as she'd ever treated, and she trained in a city ER. She looked over at Striker as she tossed her gloves in a nearby trashcan. His face was a closed mask, revealing no emotion, but he had to be infuriated. From what Marcie told her, he and Hook were close; this would hit him hard. She smiled at him, hoping to provide him some reassurance.

After he gifted her with a wink, she returned her attention to Hook. "I'm pretty sure you have a few broken ribs, and that slash on your side will need to be stitched up. You left out the part where they sliced you with a knife. Can you hold this gauze to your side? If you can't hold it with enough pressure, Striker can do it."

"Nah, I got it." Hook placed his hand over the mound of

gauze Lila pressed to the wound in his side.

"Luckily, I don't think you have any facial fractures, but you could use a few stitches there too. I can handle all that here. What I can't do is see inside to know if you have any internal bleeding or know with any certainty what is or isn't broken."

Hook had closed his eyes, but he nodded, indicating he heard her. Striker moved closer while she spoke, and now had his hand on her lower back where he rubbed in small circles. Lila wasn't sure if it was for her or himself, but it comforted all the same. "I'm guessing I'm wasting my breath, but I wouldn't be doing my job if I didn't recommend you go to the hospital for some tests."

Hook didn't bother to open his eyes. "Nah, I'm good, Doc. Just sew me up and give me enough whisky to knock me out. I'll be fine."

Her medical kit rested on the floor. Lila bent down and rummaged through the contents, searching for what she needed to numb, clean, and close his wounds. She pulled out a vile of lidocaine, new gloves, and syringe. With a quick and competent hand, she drew the medication into the syringe and turned back to Hook. One full syringe was plenty to deaden the skin around the lacerations on his face and side.

"That first part I can do," she said after she injected him. Hook's only reaction was a small flinch each time the needle pierced his skin. "No way I'm doing the second. This will take about five minutes to kick in, and then I'll close you up. I want us all to stay here tonight so I can keep an eye on you. If something happens, and you start crashing, you're going to the hospital if I have to drape you over the back of a bike and take you myself. Understood?"

The corner of Hook's mouth that was still recognizable lifted, and the eye that wasn't swollen shut popped opened to peer at Striker. "She's feisty, brother."

"A little too feisty I think. I may have to do something about that, find a way to keep her in line." He took advantage of Lila's preoccupation with her supply kit, reached over, and gave her a sharp crack on the ass.

"Ouch!" she yelped and jumped up at the same time Hook laughed then groaned.

"Oh, shit, man, don't make me laugh. You might kill me."

"Striker! I'm working here, you can't do that now." Lila huffed feeling her face flame. She wasn't sure she would ever get used to his public displays, as she was always concerned with what others thought of her actions. Probably came from constantly having to be aware of the media and public eye while she was growing up.

"This ain't work baby, it's family drama. If I can't discipline my woman in front of my family how are they gonna know I'm doing my job?" He crossed his strong arms over his chest and narrowed his eyes at her in what she guessed was supposed to be an intimidating posture, but the smirk on his face gave away the fact that he teased her.

She'd physically moved across the country to escape the shadow and watchful eyes of her family, now it was time to break some of the mental holds as well. Why shouldn't she be playful and affectionate with him in public? Besides, it wasn't really public; it was family, as Striker said. She was now part of this group of overtly sexual men who, even in a friendly way, always seemed to be touching the women they were around. Time to put on her metaphorical big girl panties and give it a try.

She turned her gaze on him, and lowered her eyes seductively. With two steps forward she pressed her soft body against his rock hard one. She wound her arms around his back, and trailed her fingertips down the soft leather of his cut until she reached his firm, denim encased backside. Then Lila slid her hands into the pockets of his jeans and enjoyed the feel of his firm ass in her hands. "And what exactly am I supposed to do to make sure you behave as I'd like?"

As he grew hard against her stomach, she had to admit she felt a little smug. This man had obviously been with a lot of women, and if Brandi was any indication, they were all young, hot, and probably did things she never even heard of. It made her feel powerful to know she could elicit an instant reaction from this experienced man with just a touch.

He stared at her in mild surprise, his blue eyes hooded with desire. "Baby you can punish me any way you like, anytime you see fit. In fact—" He tossed a glance in Hook's direction before playfully tugging her toward the door. "It doesn't look like he's bleeding too much anymore. We'll be back in a bit, brother."

"Hey, man, no need to leave, I'm not going to be moving too well for a bit here. Least you could do is put on a good show for me, keep me entertained."

Striker raised an eyebrow at her and gave her a sexy grin. "What do you say, baby? I'm game if you are."

Were they crazy? There was no way she was going to have sex with Striker while Hook watched, and he was married for crying out loud. She was about to tell him she might never sleep with him again when she realized they were teasing her. She'd been bested, though she had a sneaking suspicion if she was all for it, Striker wouldn't turn her down.

"Ok you win," she conceded. "I shouldn't try to one up the masters. Hook should be numb by now. Let me get to work so he can rest."

Chapter Nineteen

Ninety minutes and thirty-eight stitches later, Hook dozed with Marcie curled up to his uninjured side. Lila didn't think Marcie was actually asleep, but her eyes were closed so she took a minute to study the couple unnoticed.

They were good together. She could tell the connection they shared was solid and deep just by watching them interact for a few minutes. When Hook's face didn't resemble a punching bag, Lila imagined they made quite a striking couple. What drew her eye to them though, was the peace they seemed to find in each other. For the couple, the day was wrought with drama and stress, yet just being in each other's presence seemed to steady each of them. Witnessing their closeness had Lila smiling despite the tension of the past few hours.

She sensed when Striker approached her from behind, and grinned as he enfolded her in a tight hug. Lila marveled at how it felt to be enveloped in his strength—safe, protected, and just a little bit restless. The warmth of his mouth pressed against the tender skin of her neck, and she rested back against him. Her eyes fluttered closed while a tingle of desire made its way through her system. Unable to prevent it, a soft hum of contentment escaped her lips.

More kisses were pressed to her neck, and she wanted to sink into Striker and forget about danger, rival clubs and anything negative. Striker's lips moved to her ear, and he spoke in a low whisper. "We okay to leave them for a while?"

Lila shivered at the tickle his mouth evoked where it brushed her ear. She nodded. "I told Marcie I'd come back in an hour or so to check on Hook. I made sure she knows what signs of an emergency to look for."

"Then let's go upstairs, and we can rest a bit in my room." Striker snaked an arm around her waist, and led her out into the hallway.

It was still early in the afternoon, and the clubhouse was mostly empty. Striker warned her it would get pretty crazy at Gumby's birthday party, which was planned for Friday night, and she was curious to see this place in action, curious and a bit anxious. Lila wasn't worried anything would happen to her, there was no way Striker would allow that, however, she was nervous to see if she could hack it. But there was no point in worrying about it now, she'd know soon enough.

As they reached the stairs, Striker moved his hand from her waist to interlock it with hers. She held on tight and enjoyed the way he seemed to always want to be physically connected to her. Neither spoke on the way to his room, and Lila wondered what was going through his mind. When they arrived at the room, he unlocked the door, and guided her through before him.

The room was simple, but a comfortable size. In the far corner, a queen-sized bed rested along the wall, with a night table and lamp adjacent. Across the room, a small dresser was pushed against the opposite wall. To her left was the entrance to his personal bathroom, the best feature in her opinion. Posters and pictures of various bikes covered the walls. A fair portion of them included scantily clad women draped over those bikes.

Lila barely had time to take it all in when she heard the lock on the door snick in place behind her. Striker grabbed her around her waist and spun her to face him. Reversing their positions, he backed her against the door and claimed her mouth. She melted, and sighed in pleasure when his tongue found hers. For a long time, he kissed her deeply, stroking his hands along her arms, and up farther until they framed her face.

The kiss was drugging, and Lila lost herself in the passion of it. Surprisingly, Striker kept his hands on her face, and a few inches of space between their bodies. This encounter felt more emotionally charged than sexual. After a few minutes Striker eased away, his large hands still framing her face. Ice blue eyes bored into hers, and she was helpless to do anything but stare at him.

"Dr. Emerson, I think you're fucking amazing."

Lila couldn't prevent the thrill that bubbled up at Striker's sincere words. He was so handsome standing there, gazing at her like she really was amazing. Unsure of what to say she silently stared back at him.

"There's a lot we have to talk about, but I need to get one thing clear first," Striker said, his expression taking on a serious air.

"What's that?"

"Tell me what Brandi said to you."

Oh that. She'd forgotten about Brandi when the excitement with Hook started, and now wished they could just let it go.

"She alluded to you and her being together, quite recently." Lila stared down at her shoes hoping he'd accept her explanation, and wouldn't pursue it further. Her feet looked tiny in her girly sandals compared to his clunky riding boots. Strange thing to notice at the moment, but it made her feel feminine.

"Babe." There was a warning quality to his voice, one that told her he wasn't buying her half-baked explanation.

Lila wanted to sink through the floor. "It's embarrassing for me to say. Look we only just got together so if what she said is true, it's not even any of my business."

"Lila, do I have to go ask Marcie to tell me?"

"No. No! God, that would be even more embarrassing. I'll tell you." She blushed and closed her eyes, unable to look at him as she repeated Brandi's words. "Okay, she said she still had beard burn on her thighs from you. Happy?"

When he didn't say anything for a time, Lila's stomach twisted. . He hadn't moved away, his body was still intimately pressed up against hers. But she wondered what was brewing in his mind, and cracked one eye open.

"She fucking said that?" He looked furious. His jaw ticked, nostrils flared, and his hands tightened on her body.

The other eye flew open. "She did. You can ask Marcie if you want. I'd never make something like that up."

"Oh no, baby, I believe you. I knew she was a bitch. I just didn't realize she was also so stupid."

Lila snorted at that.

"I fucked her once."

She grimaced at his blunt words and wished they were talking about anything else. Lila struggled a bit in attempt to put some distance between them, but he just gripped her shoulders tighter and forced her to look at him.

"No, babe, we're going to have this conversation so it can be over and done, and we never have to visit it again. I fucked her once, six months ago. I had and continue to have no interest in a second go around."

Lila remained silent, but she raised her eyes to search his, finding truth in his words.

"I'm thirty-six Lila, I've lived fast and wild for a long time, but I know how to tell when I have something important. Yes, this is new, but you're in my head in a way I don't think I've ever experienced. You are *not* just another fuck to me. And while whatever this is lasts, I will not screw around on you."

"Striker," she whispered, emotion thickened her voice.

He placed a finger across her lips to quiet her. His words weren't flowery or poetic; they were raw and real, just like the man. But they were romantic in a sense; their sincerity made them so.

Lila knew he was asking her to trust him, to trust in their connection, and trust that he wouldn't hurt her. She did trust him, completely, and needed him to know that. What better way to let him know she had complete faith in him, than to show him?

Lila drew his finger into her mouth and lightly raked her teeth across the pad at the tip, before swirling her tongue around it and sucking lightly. His eyes darkened and smoldered with instant desire, and his impressive erection grew between them, pressing against her stomach. Her provocative act wasn't only affecting him; her nipples pebbled against the satin of her bra. The soft material abraded the sensitive points and made her hungry for more.

Emboldened by Striker's obvious arousal, Lila released his finger, and slid her palms slowly up his chest, under the leather of his cut. With a gentle push, she nudged him backward until his legs bumped the side of the bed. Her hands trembled slightly as she glided them back down to unbutton his jeans. She gave him a sexy half smile and inched the zipper down, slowly so as not to injure the bulge straining to burst free.

"What are you doin', babe?" he asked as her hands slipped into his jeans and around to his ass, working the fabric over his hips and down his legs.

Lila didn't answer. She took the time to maneuver his black boxer briefs over his ass, and down to join the jeans around his ankles. The skin of his taught buttocks was warm and smooth beneath her greedy hands, and she wanted to linger, but had a more important prize in mind. Shifting her eyes downward, she admired the thick erection rising from between his powerful legs as though begging for her touch. Lila wrapped her hand around him and squeezed as she finally replied, "I'm trying to break that control you love so much."

"Fuck," he said on a groan. His eyelids dropped closed and he balled his hands into tight fists at his sides.

Lila took advantage of his distraction, and placed her hands on his chest. With a shove, she sent him down to the bed where he landed with a soft bounce. Striker's eyes flew open as she dropped to her knees and settled in position between his thighs. He was gorgeous, his flesh hard and swollen. Her mouth watered at the thought of tasting him. She also felt a feminine thrill at the fact that she had him at her mercy. She slid one hand over his thigh and gripped his cock with the other. Lila leaned forward to swipe her tongue over the sensitive head. When he grunted, she opened her mouth wide, took him in, and sucked.

~ ~ ~ ~

Striker's head dropped back on his shoulders with a muffled curse, and his hands gripped the edge of the bed so hard he thought he'd poke ten holes straight through the mattress. Holy shit. Lila's mouth was blazingly hot, and when she sucked, the pleasure was so intense it bordered on pain, causing his eyes to roll back in his head.

Thinking was almost impossible when she licked the ultra-sensitive spot under the head, but some small portion of his brain remained aware, and told him he was an asshole. Before he lost all ability to reason, he needed to make sure she didn't think he'd said all that to wrangle a blowjob. God, he hoped she wanted this as much as he did because there was a good chance he'd expire on the spot if she stopped.

"Lila, baby, you don't have to—"

Lila released him with a pop and sat back on her heels, still fully clothed, lips wet and swollen from accommodating his cock. "Striker, I feel everything you're feeling, and I trust you. Let me show you, please."

His mouth dried up, overcome by the alien feelings her words evoked. Until she spoke, he hadn't realized how important it was to know he wasn't alone in wanting something more.

"Besides, I've been wanting to taste you," Lila added with a sexy grin, before she returned to the task of driving him crazy. She took him deep, and sucked him like she loved it. Head bobbing in his lap, her tongue swirled over the tip and occasionally stroked the length of him. Christ, it felt unfuckingbelievable. The heat of her mouth seared him as her hand smoothed up his thigh and dipped in to cup his balls. She gently rolled them while continuing to suck at him like a tasty treat. It took everything in his power not to fist his hands in her hair and take control, but he wanted to show her he trusted her as well.

Striker gazed down at the sexy sight between his legs, and almost came on the spot. Eyes pinched tight as she concentrated on her task, Lila's mouth was open wide, stretching around his girth, lips shiny and wet as they moved along the span of him.

When Lila's body shifted, Striker caught site of her nipples, pebbled and clearly outlined against her shirt. Her legs were closed, knees pressed together, and her lower body rocked back and forth like she was trying to find relief. Small moans of pleasure escaped around his rod as it slid through her slick mouth. Holy fuck, she was turned on. Her mouth was filled to the brim with his dick and she was getting off on it.

With that realization, Striker's control was shot to pieces. He yanked her up from the floor, and ignored her startled protest when he tossed her on the bed and opened her jeans in one motion.

"What—"she began as he frantically yanked her pants off and shoved her thighs wide open so he could kneel his big body between them.

"Your mouth is fucking amazing baby, but I need to be inside you. Now. You good with that?"

"Oh, yeah," she whispered.

"You ready for me, Lila? God, I hope you're ready for me." His voice was hoarse, desire filled.

With one hand he fisted his cock and ran it up the length of her folds, testing her wetness.

"Fuckin' soaked, baby." He groaned when he encountered the slippery warmth. "Do you have any idea what it does to me knowing you got this wet sucking my cock?"

She gifted him a sly smile. "You may have to show me."

"Yes, ma'am." He slammed into her in one stroke burying himself to the hilt, as a loud cry was forced from her throat. In a quick decision, Striker rolled them over maintaining their intimate connection. "I want you to ride me baby."

"Yes, sir," she answered with a flirty smirk, as she leaned forward to place her hands on his chest. She moved up and down on him, slowly, sliding with ease. She looked hot as hell

164

above him. Her breasts swayed with every rise and fall, and her hair flowed around her face. Striker coasted his hands up her body, and paused to spend some time at her breasts. He pinched and rolled her nipples, triumph swelling as her head fell back on her shoulders.

"God, Striker, I love your hands on me." Her hips undulated against him with increasing speed and he knew she was losing control.

Striker looked at where they were joined. The sight of his arousal disappearing into Lila's body again and again was sexy, so sexy he could barely tear his gaze away. Then, suddenly he needed to feel more of her skin against his skin. He surged up and gripped her thighs, wrapping her legs around his waist. He scooted until his back hit the headboard, and her arms flew around him to steady herself. She was essentially sitting in his lap, molded to him from groin to chest. The position didn't allow for great movement, but it surged him deeper into her and fused their entire bodies together.

"Striker." She moaned with her eyes closed. Her pelvis ground against him and she rocked in his lap.

"Tell me, baby." He knew he wouldn't last much longer, and wanted to give her what she needed.

"I've never—I mean, you're so deep, I'm so full." Her voice was heavy with emotion.

"Open your eyes, Lila, look at me," he commanded.

They moved together, eyes locked, the only sounds those of their gasps and whimpers. The position was intimate, and the visual connection prevented either from hiding any emotion behind closed eyelids. All the feelings they'd developed for each other, but were afraid to voice because they both knew the relationship was doomed, passed between them through their intense gaze.

Part of him wanted to tell her how important she was becoming to him. How she made him a better man. How he admired the amazing woman she was, and wanted to be with her twenty-four hours a day. But it would only make him a selfish bastard, so he kept it inside and showed her instead.

Her entire body trembled as her pussy began convulsing, and he knew she was coming. "Stay with me, baby, keep your eyes on me."

Lila cried out with abandon as an orgasm slammed into her, causing her to rhythmically clench around him. Unable to hold back any longer he let out a long groan and shuddered in her arms. It was unbelievably intense, the physical release and the emotional satisfaction he found in her arms.

They held each other, still linked, unable to break their connection, until their bodies calmed and breathing returned to normal. When the quaking slowed, Striker kissed her, maintaining their position and showing her with his mouth how much she meant to him. Eventually he pulled his head back and untangled their bodies to lie them down on the bed.

"That was the hottest thing I've ever experienced," Lila whispered. Her hand ran over his chest in a light caress.

"For me too," he agreed.

Chapter Twenty

Striker lay quiet for a few minutes and enjoyed the afterglow of the powerful sexual encounter. Lila's soft weight cuddled against him while they rested was something he could become addicted to.

"We never got a chance to talk about the meeting. How did it go?" A nervous tremor sounded in her voice, and Striker regretted that the sated moment couldn't last longer.

"I think their VP is going to stage a coup. Fuck, maybe he already has. These sloppy broad daylight attacks, with witnesses present, is not something their president would allow. Snake is much more violent, much more impulsive and power hungry. He doesn't have near the leadership experience Jackal does, but he wants to be in charge. It's a volatile combination." He stroked a hand over the smooth strands of her hair as he spoke to her.

Being with her like this, sharing his burdens in a relaxed and intimate way, was good for his soul. It made him hope he may not be the worst man in the world for her. The feeling only lasted a second, because the topic of conversation was reminder enough of why he was all wrong for her.

"That doesn't sound good at all. What does this mean for

the club, for me?" She linked the fingers of one hand with his where it rested on his stomach.

Striker brought their joined hands up to his lips and pressed a kiss to her knuckles. "Well we need to be sure of what's going on before we make a move. So first step is surveillance."

"Won't that be dangerous? What if you're caught?" Lila lifted her head, and propped her chin on his chest. Fear was evident on her face.

Striker shook his head. "Not for you to worry about, babe. Let the club handle it." He wasn't going to share details about how they planned to stake out the Grimm's clubhouse. "What time were you supposed to check on Hook?"

"Oh my God! I totally forgot! What kind of doctor am I?"

Striker laughed as she shot out of bed as though it was made of hot coals. "The horny kind?"

Lila glared at him while she threw her clothes on and ran out the door. She hadn't bothered to fix herself up, and her tousled hair alone gave the appearance of someone who'd been fucked well and good. Striker laughed out loud imagining her embarrassment at the inevitable teasing she'd receive from Hook when he saw her.

Striker rolled out of the bed, and bent to retrieve his discarded pants. He slipped them on and shrugged into a plain T-shirt and shoes, and headed back downstairs toward the bar. He had some trash to take out.

A few steps from the bottom, he stopped to take in the room and decide how he wanted to play this. Striker needed to have a chat with Brandi, one that ended with her leaving for good, and he needed the rest of the club to know she was no longer welcome. While he wasn't one to air his shit in public, or cause a dramatic scene with a woman, he wanted this witnessed so the crazy bitch couldn't accuse him of anything that would get him in trouble with Lila.

Brandi was seated at the bar. Striker watched her shamelessly flirt with Kenny who moved a bit slow from his injury. The Kid sat next to her and wasn't left out of her little seduction scheme. She batted her painted eyes, and leaned forward so far her tits practically fell out of her top. Both prospect's gazes were glued to her chest, and Striker could have filled a bucket with their drool.

Being VP had a number of perks, obedience being one of them. When he was in earshot of Kid and Kenny he called out to them. "Beat it, prospects. I need to talk to Brandi."

Both men looked surprised but wisely didn't argue. Kenny turned to a task of restocking bottles, and Kid moved a few stools down the bar, no doubt straining his ears to hear every word. He wouldn't have to work too hard. Striker didn't plan to make any of this a secret.

Brandi twisted around on her stool, and gave Striker a sultry smile that left little doubt as to her intentions toward him. "Hey, Striker," she purred. "What happened to your little friend?"

"Lila is no concern of yours." His voice held no warmth, but if Brandi picked up on it, she didn't let it show.

"Whatever you say. Whatever you want." She leaned forward to show off even more of her breasts, if that was possible.

Striker wanted to roll his eyes at her desperate yet ineffective attempt to seduce him. He was over her shit.

"Are you ready to have some fun with a woman who knows what you like?" Brandi batted her eyelashes in a way he assumed she thought was sexy. In reality she looked like she had something in her eye.

Never one to pass up an opportunity for a little fun, Striker smirked. "I am. Actually that's exactly why I'm here."

Brandi's face lit up, and she rose from the stool to take a step toward him. Before she could speak, Striker did. "It's time for you to go, Brandi."

Undeterred, Brandi's heavily made up mouth turned down in a pout. She reached out to run a hand up his chest, but Striker stopped her before she could touch him with a hand around her wrist. It wasn't a gentle hold. "Come on, Striker, don't be like that." Brandi's whiney voice grated on his nerves.

"I didn't think you were an idiot as well as a bitch, Brandi, but this is the second stupid thing you've done today, so apparently I was wrong."

Her gaudy face fell. The come hither look turned to a nasty sneer as he released her wrist. Here comes the vindictive bitch. Striker smiled, glad she would show her true colors in front of the entire club. It would only serve to justify his decision to run her ass out of there. None of these guys were interested in drama or a high maintenance woman.

"Fuck you!" Her high pitched shriek reverberated through the clubhouse. Silence fell as a dozen or so eyes trained on the escalating scene at the bar. "You think you'll get it half as good from that snobby bitch? Say whatever you want now, Striker, but you'll be bored with her ass and come running back to me soon."

Striker had about one minute of tolerance left for this nonsense. "Brandi, I'll say this slow since you seem to need it." Someone snickered across the room. "I fucked you once, six months ago. Since then you've spread your legs for nearly every guy in the club. You're little more than a whore, and you've caused trouble more than once. We let you stay because most of the guys thought you were a pretty good lay. I don't really agree, but what are you gonna do?"

Brandi's hand flew up, and sailed toward his face. Striker

caught it before it had the chance to crack across his cheek. With a fierce grip on her wrist he leaned in close and spoke in a low voice for her ears only. "You have exactly one minute to get the fuck out of here. Try to hit me again, and you may need to be carried out of here. I hear you so much as glance in Lila's direction at any time, and you won't like what happens. You understand me?" His voice was lethal, and he knew by the way her eyes widened and she struggled out of his hold that she was finally taking him seriously.

Brandi yanked her arm free, took a step back, and looked at the floor with a nod, all bravado and flirtation gone. Without moving her focus from the ground, she grabbed her purse and started toward the door. Before she left, Striker called out one last warning. "You are not to step foot in this clubhouse again. Don't test me on that. I promise you won't like the results."

Once she put a few steps of distance between them, her attitude returned, and she flipped Striker off with both hands. When she was halfway to the exit, a low chorus of "Hit the Road Jack" rose up from behind Striker. By the time Brandi had a hand on the door, the entire room had broken out in song to bid Brandi farewell.

The door closed with a slam, and the men went from singing to laughing as they slapped each other's backs and called for more drinks from the prospect. Striker chuckled himself, and turned in the direction of the room that housed Hook. His eyes met Lila's where she stood at the end of the hall, obviously having witnessed the entire exchange.

Curious as to her reaction to this little display, Striker raised an eyebrow in question. Lila shook her head and gave him a stern look. Striker moved toward his woman, and didn't give her a chance to scold him. He dragged her in for a kiss that had him hard and wishing they were alone. He released her, and laughed at the pink blush that bloomed over her face as the room erupted once again, this time in whistles and catcalls.

Chapter Twenty-One

Lila glanced around the classroom at the faces of the volunteers who came out for her first "head banging" committee meeting, as Striker had called it. Marcie was there as promised, and Lila couldn't have been happier to see her new friend. Marcie's bubbly personality would be a huge asset when organizing the fundraiser. Cammie, her RN friend from the hospital, was there as well, and Lila raised a quick hand in greeting.

Nine others sat scattered around the room in the students' desks. Lila recognized a few as parents of athletes from the football team she'd met the night of the school board meeting. The remaining faces were strangers.

"Thank you all so much for coming," she began, unable to keep the grin off her face. "This project has been an aspiration of mine for a while, and your willingness to volunteer your time means the world to me. What I'd like to accomplish tonight, is—"

The sound of the door opening drew the attention of everyone in the room. Lila turned toward the distraction as well. She wanted to bang her head against the black board when Earl White hustled into the room, and scurried to an open seat in the front row of desks. She'd completely forgotten he'd told her he wanted to volunteer.

"I'm sorry, Dr. Emerson. I know I'm late, but I had to wait to leave the house until mother was settled for the evening. I really hope I didn't miss anything important. Well, it's all important, but you know what I mean. You look very nice tonight, doctor."

Lila plastered on a polite smile for the man whose effusive nature was all the more embarrassing when she was supposed to be in a leadership role. "It's fine, Mr. White. Glad you could join us." She almost choked on the words as she imagined how difficult it would be to get anything accomplished with him around.

When she shifted her focus back to the room, she caught Marcie's gaze. The other woman batted her eyelashes, and made a silent kissing motion in Lila's direction. Lila had to press her lips together to keep from laughing out loud. Yes, it was quite obvious that Mr. White had a little crush on her.

"As I was saying," she continued. "I'd like us to go around and introduce ourselves, and maybe let the others know what motivated you to be here tonight. Then I think it would be best if we split into two groups. One group will focus on planning a fundraiser to raise money for new safety equipment and pads. The other group will be making an educational presentation and pamphlets based on the research materials I've received from the Center for Disease Control."

She looked around the room, pleased to see people taking notes and giving her their undivided attention. There wasn't anything worse than people who joined a committee and didn't have any real intention to work. So far, it appeared that her volunteers were all dedicated to the cause.

"How do you want us to divide up?" Cammie asked from

the center of the room.

"I'd like to keep the groups fairly even in number. So if you think your strengths would be better served in one group over the other feel free to join that group. If you could go either way, then please join whichever group needs extra people. Sound good?"

They went around the room and each person gave a little intro speech. Lila jotted down notes, and was glad to have a name to put with each face. She had to cut Earl off when he spoke for over five minutes about how wonderful it was for her to want to prevent injuries in the high school athletes. When they were finished, they split into the two groups, and ended up with two teams of six, exactly as Lila had hoped.

"Great guys. This is perfect. I'll bounce between the groups as much as possible, but in the beginning I'll probably spend most of my time with the education group so I can help with the medical jargon."

Everyone nodded their agreement, and a buzz of conversation filled the room as ideas and plans began to form. Of course, Earl was in the group she'd have to spend most of her time with, but she vowed to treat him like any other committee member and not let him distract her.

Two hours later they wrapped up for the night with plans to meet at the same time and place next week. Each volunteer worked hard, and they accomplished more in one evening than Lila expected. She was nearly bouncing with fulfilled excitement as she crossed multiple items off her to do list.

"Hey girl." Marcie strolled up to Lila and gave her a hug. "This is going to be great. You've really got a solid team here."

"Thanks, Marcie. I think so too," she said as she returned the embrace.

"And I see the president of your fan club is——"

"Excuse me, Dr. Emerson? May I have a word with you? In private." Earl sent a distasteful look in Marcie's direction.

Marcie raised an eyebrow, but didn't comment on Mr. White's rude behavior. "I'll meet you outside, hon, I'm sure the guys are waiting on us." She left the room after Lila nodded at her.

"I wanted to offer to walk you outside. There are about five of those motorcycle hoodlums waiting out in the parking lot, and I wasn't sure if you'd be comfortable walking out to your car alone."

Lila considered him before she spoke. He had to know she was friendly with them. She'd just hugged Marcie, and after the incident at the hospital, most of the town was aware she had some kind of connection to Striker.

"You can walk with me, Earl, but I want you to know that the motorcycle club is no threat to me." She wasn't about to lay claim to Striker, her head was too mixed up about their relationship, but there wasn't any point in hiding the fact they were, at the very least, friends. It was a small town. The cat was already out of that bag. "I'm friends with a number of them, so, while I appreciate your concern, it's not necessary."

They arrived at the parking lot, and Lila spotted Striker chatting with Marcie and Hook. She couldn't believe Hook was able to ride his motorcycle so soon after he was assaulted, and had strongly advised against it, but here he was. Striker told her there was no way he'd let Marcie come without him while there was trouble with the Grimm Brothers.

"I see," Earl told her as Marcie jogged in their direction. Rather than sadness as she had expected, his voice was filled with profound disappointment, as though he'd lost respect

176

for her. "You're too good for those criminals. Everyone knows that, and no one understands why you spend time with him. Mother told me stories about them that would make you think twice about associating with them. I can tell you if you'd like."

Marcie reached them in time to catch Earl's last few sentences. She shot a frown at him before she grabbed Lila's hand. "Come on, girl. We gotta roll. Don't want to be too late for Gumby's birthday bash."

Lila nodded at Earl White, and let Marcie pull her toward the bikes.

"I told Striker I'd come get you so your boyfriend wouldn't get too jealous." Marcie giggled as she towed Lila along.

"Gee thanks, Marcie."

She reached Striker's side, and he pressed a swift kiss to her mouth. "How'd it go, babe?"

Some of the excitement of the successful evening came back to her at his inquiry. "It was amazing. I have a fantastic team, and I think we'll get done ahead of schedule."

Striker smiled at her and handed her the helmet. "I'm proud of you, Lila. You've been working your ass off the past few days to prepare for tonight. I'm glad it went even better than expected." He gave her another kiss. "We'll swing by your house so you can change then head to the clubhouse. Ready to go?"

"You bet." She climbed on behind him and her eyes drifted to Mr. White as Striker pulled out of the lot. He stood, staring after her with his mouth turned down. She couldn't help but replay his last words in her head. Were people in town talking about her? Is that how life would be if this relationship became something more? Would she be viewed in a negative light because of her association with Striker? Worries swirled around her brain and took up some of the space that had been occupied with positive thoughts only moments ago.

She forced herself to push the worry aside, determined not to be a downer for tonight's event. It was important for the club, they needed a reason to celebrate and take their minds off the trouble with the Grimms for one evening.

Not everyone would be at the party. At least three men would be on surveillance tonight, trying to find out exactly what was going on within the Grimm's walls. The club needed some intel they could use in their favor, to turn the tables on the rival MC.

Lila sighed and rested her cheek against Striker's back. When she inhaled, the leather smell made her smile. The negative consequences to staying with him seemed to far outweigh the positives, and she wanted to soak up every morsel she could before reality came crashing down around her like an old building hit by a wrecking ball.

Chapter Twenty-Two

By the time they arrived, the party was already in full swing. Striker hooked an arm across Lila's shoulders, and drew her to his side while they walked toward the entrance. He never neglected an opportunity to touch her in some manner, a fact that thrilled her, and one she was quickly becoming addicted to despite her misgivings about their relationship. He communicated with touch, and could sooth her as well as arouse her.

"You ready for this, babe?" He looked sexy tonight, dark and a little dangerous in deep blue jeans with a black button up shirt under his cut.

"Of course." She winced at the slight squeak in her voice. So much for hiding her anxiety about her first biker party.

"Right." He tugged her along toward the door. "You and your old man spend a lot of time at wild biker parties back in DC?"

"Har har, Mr. Hilarious. Just because I didn't hang out with bikers then doesn't mean I can't hack it now."

He chuckled, and gave her a quick kiss on her neck. "Have I told you how smokin' hot you look tonight?" The words were whispered against her ear.

Lila wore ass-hugging black leather leggings with a shimmery silver halter. The top ended about an inch above her pants, and showed off a peek of bare stomach, and the neckline had a deep V that revealed more than a hint of cleavage. Black leather ankle boots with a silver zipper and three inch heels completed the outfit. At Striker's request, her hair was down and flowed past her shoulders. Her style was very different from most of the women here, but she liked to think of it as biker chic. Striker seemed to approve, and that was all she cared about. "I think you may have mentioned it right before you felt me up as we were trying to leave."

The grin he gave her could only be described as wolfish. "Want a repeat?" he asked, wagging his eyebrows up and down suggestively.

Lila laughed and lightly smacked his arm. "We're already thirty minutes late, it will have to wait until later. Good thing you have a room here."

They arrived at the door, and Lila took a fortifying breath. Here goes nothing. Striker stepped in front of her, and turned, facing her. He slid his hands into her hair and held her still. "Seriously, babe, don't worry. I'm sure this will be different from any party you've been to, but I promise you no one will bother you. I'd kill them. Okay?"

"I know, Striker. I always feel safe when I'm with you. I'm really not worried."

He held the door and she stepped into the building. The clubhouse was packed. Bodies were crammed in everywhere she looked. Waiting for Striker to follow gave her eyes a chance to adjust to the dark smoky atmosphere of the open space. As she gazed around, Lila had to clench her teeth to keep her jaw from hitting the floor. Women wearing little more than their skin were everywhere. They danced out on the floor, danced on tables, and danced on laps. Actually dancing might have been too formal a word. Gyrating or writhing was probably more accurate.

Some of the women were doing way more than dancing. She saw couples making out, groping, and a few she couldn't help but wonder if they weren't doing even more. The whole place reeked of cigarettes, a bit of marijuana, and booze. A good majority of the partiers seemed more than halfway drunk already. Okay, Striker was right. This was not her scene at all, and she instantly felt out of place, like a shy kid on her first day at a new school.

Striker's arm slid around her waist, and she turned until she faced him. "You look terrified, Doc," he said chuckling.

"I'm not. It's just, well I'm—" She rolled her eyes at her own foolishness. Striker kissed her and she felt slightly better. "Who are all these girls?"

"Some ol' ladies, some local girls who just come to party, and strippers."

"Ah, strippers." Lila rolled her eyes again. "Of course. Sorry, lost my head there for a minute. Who doesn't have strippers at their parties?"

Striker winked at her. "Come on, wild thing." He guided her to the right side of the room where a row of square tables was lined against the wall. When she spotted Marcie and Hook, Lila felt herself relax. Their table was devoid of strippers, and Marcie had all her clothes on, which Lila took as a good sign.

As they drew closer, Marcie hopped up and rushed over to greet them. After accepting a hug and peck on the cheek from Striker she focused on Lila. "Hey girl! Are you freaking out yet?"

"She's good, Marce," Striker answered for her.

"I'm good," Lila parroted.

"Sure you are." Marcie laughed. "I'm sorry I didn't think

to give you the four-one-one on parties around here. With all Hook's drama, it didn't even occur to me to warn you about what you'd be stepping into." She linked her arm through Lila's and drew her away from Striker, toward their table where two empty chairs sat waiting for them.

When they reached the table, Marcie resumed her position next to Hook. He slung his arm across her shoulders, and pulled her close to kiss the side of her head. "Sit down, Lila," he said as he gestured to the two empty chairs. "This area is where those of us with a ball and chain hang during these parties."

With a roll of her emerald eyes, Marcie smiled at Lila. "It gets pretty crazy out there. A lot of the guys who come here with their ol' ladies hang off to the sides like this. Although I know for a fact that these two," she said, pointing her thumbs at Striker and Hook, "and a few others who aren't into the whole strippers gyrating in their face thing, hang out over here just because."

Lila moved to sit in the empty chair, but Striker snaked an arm around her waist, and hauled her onto his lap. He settled her against his broad chest, before he rested his hands on her thighs. After giving her waist a squeeze, he pressed his mouth to her ear. "See, not so bad over here. Like Marcie said, it's been a long time since I was over there in the madness. Gets old after a while."

"Not quite the badass you pretend to be, are you?" she teased, earning her a nip on the ear. "Hey." She giggled. "That hurt!"

"You want a drink, gorgeous?"

"A beer would be good."

"Hey, Kid!" Striker bellowed.

"Yeah, VP?" A tall, lanky young guy with buzzed blond hair and a prospect patch jogged over. Lila recognized him as

182

the prospect that was with her the day she was attacked at the hospital.

"Couple of beers, and four shots of tequila."

"Sure thing." He jogged toward the bar.

Lila raised an eyebrow at him. "Thirsty?"

"We're late, we have some catching up to do. Besides, we're planning to crash here tonight. Might as well make the most of it."

The prospect returned after a minute with shots and two beers as requested.

"Thank you." Lila gave him a smile when he placed their drinks on the table.

"No problem, miss," the prospect said as he beamed at her. "You sure are pretty."

Jester chose that moment to amble up to their table, his arm slung around the shoulders of Gumby, who leaned heavily on Jester for support. "Bring me one of those, prospect." He pointed to the tequila shots. "And it's doctor, not miss. And stop flirting, asshole. She's sitting on the VP's lap for Christ's sake." He slapped the prospect on the side of his shaved head. Pretty damn hard in Lila's opinion, but she kept her mouth shut.

"How're ya feeling, Gumb?" Marcie asked with a wink at Lila. Gumby's cut was hanging off one shoulder, his typically impeccable hair was mussed and pointed in multiple directions, and there was something pinkish all over his collar. Was that lipstick?

"I am feeling great, doll. You gonna save me a dance?"

"I don't think so, bro, you can barely stay on your feet. Don't need you breaking my woman's toes or knocking her down," Hook answered for her with a snort.

"Seriously, Gumby, maybe you should sit down or something before you pass out, and Stitch has to glue your head back together," Marcie suggested.

Jester unwound his arm from Gumby's shoulders, and shoved him down into the vacant chair. Gumby leaned his head against the wall and his eyelids dropped shut.

"Well, so much for the birthday boy." Striker laughed. He handed Lila a shot and pushed the other two toward Marcie and Hook. Kid had returned with Jester's shot by then, and they all lifted their glasses. "To Gumby. Let's hope he makes it to thirty-five and one day."

Lila tossed back her drink like a pro. After she placed the shot glass back on the table she saw four pairs of wide eyes trained on her. "What? Did I spill it or something?" She looked down at her shirt, but didn't see any liquid.

"Damn girl, you keep surprising us," said Jester. "I totally expected coughing and watering eyes."

"I like tequila," she said with a giggle. She may like it, but she wasn't used to it, and it went straight to her head if that giggle was any indication.

Jester just smirked at her as though he could see right through her.

"Let's dance, girl." Marcie stood and grabbed Lila off Striker's lap. "We can stay toward the edge, away from too much of the craziness, plus then our men can watch." With a wink for the table, she whispered that last part in Lila's ear.

"I love to dance!" she told Marcie, joy evident in her voice. "Before I moved out here I took all kinds of dance classes. Once I even took a pole dancing class." She'd never told anyone about that. Her passion for dancing was a well-kept secret. Unless it was ballet or ballroom, it was unacceptable in high society.

"No way, girl! I can't wait to see what you got. Make sure you dance in full view of Striker. He will love that, and you'll reap the benefits later on." Marie giggled, obviously feeling the effects of whatever she'd been drinking, and wagged her eyebrows up and down in Lila's direction.

Lila laughed out loud at Marcie's outrageous suggestion, and realized she was feeling the warm glow of a buzz as well. They reached the open area used as a dance floor as the music changed to a tune with a pulsing beat that flowed through Lila like the throbbing of her blood. She immediately started to move. Caught up in the tempo, she lifted her arms over her head and swayed her hips in a seductive rhythm. Her eyes fluttered closed, and she lost herself in the music.

"Damn, girl, you got some moves! You need a job?"

A throaty feminine voice broke Lila out of her trance, and, while she didn't stop dancing, she did look around to see who had spoken to her. Next to Marcie was a woman, probably in her mid-twenties, wearing a painted on black leather skirt that barely covered her ass and what was basically a black leather bra with a black, long-sleeved fishnet top over it. She was tall for a woman with generous breasts and a completely flat stomach. Platinum hair tumbled down her back in long waves making a striking contrast to her black outfit. She was a knockout.

Marcie giggled again as she hugged the woman. When she pulled away, Marcie turned the woman in Lila's direction. "Lila, this is Jaci, she bartends at Black's, which is where many of these girls dance. Jaci, this is Dr. Lila Emerson. Don't think she's looking for a new job, hon, though I do think she'd draw a crowd."

The song changed again, and a slower more sultry sound filled the air.

"Oh my bad." Jaci laughed, and winked a perfectly made up eye at Lila as she inclined her head toward where Striker was sitting. "Looks like you'll at least be putting on a private show tonight."

Lila turned, still moving in a slow, sensual manner, designed to entice. Striker rose from his seat and stalked straight toward her. There was no other word for it. He approached her like a panther tracking his prey, hard, powerful muscles shifting under his clothes. His normally ice blue eyes deepened with lust and promise. An obvious erection he didn't try to hide strained against his zipper. A distant part of Lila's brain registered shrill whistling and catcalls from Hook and Jester, and she felt her cheeks heat with the slow burn of desire.

Lila didn't know if it was the alcohol or the fire in his gaze that made her lose her inhibitions, but as Striker drew closer, she slid her hands down her body, and rocked her hips to the music in a way that left no question as to what she wanted from him. When he reached her, his arm shot out. Long fingers slid into the waistband of her leather pants and yanked her body to his. Flush against her, his hot, aroused form moved them to the music.

"Where the fuck did you learn to move your gorgeous body like this? Shit babe, you've got every man in the room rock hard and panting, and you don't even know it."

She gave him a sexy smile. "Can't tell you all my secrets."

The song changed, and Striker shifted, positioning one of his legs between hers so that her heated center, which was quickly growing damp, rested against his thigh. One of his callused hands molded around one round globe of her ass while the other slid under her shirt searing the smooth skin of her back with its heat. Their eyes met, and she wound her arms around his neck to play with the hair at the base of his head. The smoldering intensity in his eyes mesmerized her, and their bodies moved as one to the music, rocking and grinding.

The hard expanse of Striker's jean clad thigh rubbed against Lila's mound and sent delicious jolts of pleasure through her core. It wasn't enough. She tilted her pelvis, pressed closer, and ground herself down on his thigh in search of relief. Their mouths met, and his cock twitched where it lay trapped between them at the same time her pussy clenched with need.

They were barely dancing anymore, and about two seconds away from making love on the dance floor. Lila knew somewhere in the back of her mind that she should be mortified by her behavior. She felt self-conscious kissing him in public, and here she was ready to fuck him in front of his club and a bunch of strippers. But she didn't care enough to stop, she was too far gone, needed him too much.

Lost in her lust, Lila didn't notice he had maneuvered them to the back corner of the dance floor. He broke their mouths apart and stepped back a fraction, steering her around a corner and into a long dark hallway, which led to the back exit. A dim glow lit the hallway from one light bulb near the exit door. It was bright enough to see the hallway was empty and to see some of Striker's features, but low enough they could hide in the shadows.

"I need to make you come." He thumbed open her pants, separated the fabric enough to get his hand inside, and sank two fingers into her tight channel. "Damn baby, you are so wet for me."

"Yes," she hissed with a jerk of her hips as his fingers curled inside her. Pleasure invaded her brain until she could think of nothing but the amazing sensations shooting form her center. "I need you to make me come."

He chuckled and melded his mouth to hers, trapping her bottom lip between his teeth before his tongue soothed over the slight sting.

Lila wasn't able to keep still. She shamelessly rode his hand in the hallway where anyone could walk by at any time. She was beyond caring. Maybe she'd regret her actions when her head cleared, but for now she glided on a wave of lust and need so consuming all she could think of was release.

"More, Striker. I need more. Fuck me, please. I need to feel you fill me up, all the way, not just your hand."

"Jesus, baby, do you have any idea how fuckin' sexy you are? I'm never gonna get enough of you." With rushed movements, he unbuckled his belt and shoved his jeans down far enough to release his iron hard shaft. His arms slid under her thighs and he lifted her with minimal effort. "Wrap these beautiful legs around me, baby."

Lila didn't waste any time locking her ankles around his back, and reaching for his cock, to position him at her entrance. As he rammed into her, Lila's head fell back against the wall and she cried out. There wasn't anything in her life that made her feel as good as she did when Striker was inside her. Everything negative faded away, and her world was just...right.

He held still for a moment, which allowed her time to adjust. The burn and stretch of his penetration drew a whimper from her throat, and in a flash, the need for him to move overwhelmed her.

"Please, Striker," she begged as she tried to move her hips on his cock.

Striker must have sensed what she needed because he pistoned in and out with a frenzied pace.

In mere seconds, Lila flew into ecstasy. Her legs clamped around his body to clutch him as close as possible as she came apart. Her body bucked and shook. Electricity shot from her core, out through her entire being. Striker fused his mouth to hers stifling what would have been an epic scream of completion.

Lila was so caught up in her own intense orgasm she barely registered Striker when he followed her over the edge with a final powerful thrust.

"Holy shit," she whispered as she floated down from the high. "I have never experienced anything like that in my life. I don't know what came over me."

His forehead rested on her shoulder, and his torso kept her anchored to the wall, the only thing preventing her from collapsing on the floor in an exhausted heap. With a chuckle, he reached back and unwound her legs from his waist. "I don't know either, but I sure as hell liked it. You gonna be able to stand if I set you down?"

"Maybe."

Striker placed her feet on the floor, and stayed with her until she proved she was steady. "No regrets?"

She thought for a millisecond. Did she regret the most intense sexual experience of her life? No. But she did regret that she didn't regret it. "No, Striker, no regrets."

Just when they finished covering themselves, the door at the far end of the hallway opened and Jester strode in. He zeroed right in on them, and his face broke out in a wide grin. "Oh good, you're done."

Lila's eyes bugged out of her head, and her jaw dropped. "You saw us? Oh my God," she sputtered. She wanted to crawl in a whole and die.

"No worries, Doc. As soon as I realized someone was making use of this lovely hallway, I stepped outside." He approached them with a smirk on his face that made her suspicious.

Lila attempted to smooth her now tangled hair back in place, and tried to clarify. "So you didn't see anything?"

"Got an eyeful of Striker's white ass."

"Did you like what you saw, motherfucker?" He slugged Jester in the arm and the bigger man winced.

"Ow, brother, that fuckin' hurt. I was a gentleman and made sure not to look at anything of Lila's below the face." He rubbed at his arm.

She breathed out a shaky breath of relief. Sounded like he only saw enough to figure out who was making use of the hallway.

"I do have to say one thing though."

"What's that?" Striker asked, his voice laden with warning.

Jester turned to Lila and gave her a wicked grin. "Girl, the look on your face when you come is fuckin' beautiful."

With that parting shot he took off down the hallway, and narrowly avoided being grabbed as Striker lunged for him. "Asshole! Want me to gouge those eyes out?"

Oh. My. God. Lila sank against the wall and covered her face with her hands as the reality of what just happened set in. Sex against the wall in the MC clubhouse? She was a doctor, a pillar in her community, and the daughter of a powerful businessman, not a woman who had sex in a public place with a criminal. In the back of her mind she knew she was being unfair to Striker, emphasizing that one aspect of him, but she was starting to panic. She barely recognized herself anymore, and part of her worried she was too far down the rabbit hole to find her way back to who she was supposed to be.

Chapter Twenty-Three

Gumby's party turned out to be a huge success, and the club seemed to benefit from a night away from the stress of the conflict with the Grimm Brothers. Not that everyone had had a night off. Late in the night, after Lila had fallen into a deep, orgasm-induced sleep, Striker had slipped downstairs to meet with the prospects who'd been staking out the Grimm's clubhouse that night.

Jackal hadn't been spotted once since they started the daily watch. Snake, however, was ever present and appeared to be fully in the position of power. That meant any deals or pacts they may have agreed upon with Jackal were null and void. And now that the psychotic serpent was leading the Grimms, chances of a peaceful resolution to their problems were slim.

The club could handle a bloody war if that's what was required. It wasn't ideal, but they would survive it, and probably come out on top. Especially if there was any chance the Grimm Brothers were divided over Snake's rise to power. What Striker couldn't handle, was a continued threat to Lila.

They'd made love again last night. This time slowly, the frenzied need out of their system. They'd lingered, explored, and worshiped each other for hours, ending in an explosive climax that had shaken him beyond the physical. Striker was in deep with Lila, but her worth was so much greater than his. His biggest fear was that if this continued, his lifestyle would destroy her.

Heavy thoughts weighed on his mind while they rode back to his house. Flying down the highway thorough the open desert on his bike with Lila's arms tight around him, and her body snug against his back was quickly becoming his favorite activity. The vast desert scenery soaring by as the bustle of town grew distant had always been something he enjoyed, and he found it even better when Lila experienced it with him. Most experiences seemed to be that way.

Unfortunately, his deliberations, caused him to let his guard down, and a glance in the mirror revealed three bikes spanning the width of the road about a quarter mile behind them.

Shit.

They could only be Grimm Brothers, and that meant he and Lila were fucked. Images of Hook's bloodied face flashed in his mind along with the knowledge of what they could do to Lila. Fuck! He should have had a few of his brothers ride with them. They didn't stand a chance without backup.

Maybe he could outrun the Grimms. They were just a few miles from his house, and Striker knew this area like the back of his hand. The Grimms weren't as familiar with it, and there was a small possibility he could lose them. Just as he prepared to gun it, three more bikes pulled out, and formed a barrier across the road ahead of them. They were completely boxed in, six on two, well really one. There was no way Lila could take on any of them.

Striker slowed, leaving as much space as possible between

his bike and the motorcycles up ahead. Lila tensed around him as he braked, and he knew she'd spotted their company.

When the bike came to a complete stop, Lila released him, and sat stiff and straight as an arrow behind him. Before he dismounted, Striker discreetly reached around and checked that his nine mil was easily accessible. He didn't miss Lila's slight intake of air when she caught site of the weapon.

Up ahead, the three Grimm Brothers climbed off their bikes and removed their helmets. He recognized two of them. Snake was in the center and Casper, Sergeant at Arms —or at least he was under Jackal—for the Grimms stood to his right. Striker had had a few dealings with both of them in the past, but couldn't say he knew either of them on a personal level. The third guy he did not recognize.

Once he was off the bike he turned to Lila. "Stay next to me the whole time. Right with me. Close enough to touch me. I'm not leaving you on the bike because I don't trust those three behind us."

Lila's head whipped around and she inhaled at the sight of the additional Grimm Brothers lined up about two-hundred feet behind them.

"Look at me, baby."

She turned her head back to him, and he saw the stark fear in her wide chocolate eyes. "Do exactly what I tell you, got me? Keep your mouth shut at all times. I'm very serious. Do not say a word. These guys will not like a woman speaking up, so just don't say anything. I don't know what they want from me, but I'll do everything I possibly can to get us out of this."

"Striker." She whimpered, her eyes glassy with unshed tears. The look of terror on her face killed him.

He placed a finger across her lips. "Mouth shut, baby. If they do get you, and something happens to me, you do whatever the hell you have to do to stay alive. Do not fight them. Do not give them lip. It will only make it worse for you. I promise you my brothers will come for you if the worst happens."

Lila nodded, and swiped at a stray tear that escaped.

Damn, she would tough it out. Not many women he knew would swallow their fear and keep the panic hidden. He gave her a quick, hard kiss, grabbed her hand, and marched toward the waiting Grimm Brothers. Time to face the music.

"Snake," he said to the other VP when he was close enough to be heard without yelling.

"Striker," came the reply. "Pretty lady you got there."

Striker clenched his jaw so hard he thought his teeth would crack. Snake was a sadistic bastard, and he knew the quickest way to fuck with Striker would be through his woman.

"You stopped me on the road to tell me my ol' lady's pretty? Coulda sent me a card."

Snake laughed. "Nah, just trying to start the conversation on a friendly note. We got some business to discuss."

Lila was frozen beside him. Her hand gripped his as though she could make this all disappear if she squeezed hard enough. He kept her positioned on his left side, a little bit behind him, to shield her as best he could while his right arm was free to go for his gun if necessary. Not that it would do him much good. It was six on one. He'd be shot dead more than once before he could inflict much damage.

"We already discussed business with Jackal. Made a deal, and left on pretty good terms. Our business is done."

Snake shifted his eyes to Lila, and Striker swore she stopped breathing. Snake could intimidate the feathers off a bird.

"We've had some updates to our leadership since then. I'm

gonna be making a few other changes as well." His mouth curved up in a grin and he laughed. The sound made Striker's blood ice over in his veins.

Striker had been ninety-nine percent certain Snake staged a coup, but hearing the man confirm was unnerving. "You really are a slimy asshole, aren't you? You live up to your name well."

Snake's smile grew even more sinister. "Jackal got soft. I ain't. A lot of our members agreed." He shrugged.

A lot, but not all. That was the one thing the No Prisoners might be able to take advantage of.

~ ~ ~ ~

Lila's chest felt tight and she struggled to keep her breathing even, and not allow her body to quake with fear. She had to keep her shit together if there was any chance of helping Striker get them out of here in one piece, and she wasn't about to do anything to make this worse for him. That thought alone allowed her to keep her cool and do as he asked.

Was this it? Was this what she could expect of her life if she stayed with Striker? Constant violence and fear? Lila had responsibilities. She was a respected physician. People in town depended on her to provide their medical care, and now to help keep their kids safe and free from injury. She could not run around with outlaws who acted like the life of others had no value.

Snake was a chilling man. Tall, well over six feet, with straight, jet black hair hanging to his shoulders, he towered over everyone on the road. A wicked scar ran diagonally from the middle of his forehead, down to his cheek. Running up the right side of his neck was a large tattoo of a snake's head with its mouth open, fangs out, ready to strike. Lila couldn't help but wonder how far down his body the snake extended.

What unnerved her the most were his eyes. They were so dark she wondered if he was wearing black contacts to make himself look more intimidating. If so, it had the desired effect. He gave the appearance of a soulless demon, and was not someone she wanted to spend any time alone with.

"Maybe we should have discussed business before you attacked my guy, and before you terrorized my woman." Striker's hand flexed in hers and she realized how hard she clung to it.

Snake exchanged a look with the man to his right. Lila didn't know his name, but he was another daunting character. Short for a man, she guessed no more than five foot six, he looked like he'd blow over on a gusty day. Not a single hair grew from his head, and, combined with his pale skin, he reminded her of an egg. In looks he was the polar opposite of Snake, yet she had the impression he was just as deadly as the larger man.

No one said anything for a time, and Lila's anxiety ramped up. The day was growing hotter by the second. Heat from the sun beat down on the group, and she felt a bead of sweat roll down her spine. Lila itched to glance over her shoulder and check whether the three men behind them had advanced forward. Not knowing how close they were made her feel vulnerable, as though they could grab her at any time, and she wouldn't be prepared.

Snake ignored Striker's comment, and crossed his arms over his massive chest which gave him the appearance of an impenetrable wall. "You have something of mine, and I want it back."

"What the fuck are you talking about? I don't have shit of yours." Striker's voice raised a notch at the accusation. He sounded confused. Was he really ignorant of Snake's claim?

If possible, Snake's eyes grew even colder. "You sure as fuck do, or at least one of you No Prisoners does. Two-fifty large of something that doesn't belong to you."

What? Two-hundred and fifty large? Lila didn't have a clue what he was talking about. She remained at Striker's side, a step behind him so she couldn't see his face or get a read on what his thoughts were, but he seemed to follow the conversation better than she did.

"Come on, Snake, you're wasting everyone's time here. You know we ain't in that business. Why the fuck are you sniffing around us for this? Check with one your junkies, they probably got greedy. Most aren't known for making the best decisions."

It clicked for her then, drugs. They were talking about drugs. Apparently Snake thought the No Prisoners had taken two-hundred-fifty-thousand dollars worth of drugs from the Grimms. That was a serious accusation, she knew people killed for less, and had no doubt these men would kill to get their product back. They were in some serious trouble.

This was so far out of Lila's realm of experience. She felt beyond terrified just standing there, and wished she could do something. She never should have agreed to get involved with the MC. There were many qualities about Striker that Lila admired, but his lifestyle wasn't something she could handle.

"Our warehouse was broken into, the prospect on watch was laid out, but not before he recognized a No Prisoners' cut."

Shit, that sounded pretty damning. Striker tensed beside her, probably thinking along the same line. The only hope they had was the knowledge that the Grimms wanted their drugs back. That meant they'd let them go so they could take the message back to the club. Right?

In the next instant Snake waved both hands in their direction, and the two men who flanked his sides moved toward them. Snake stared straight at her. "I think I'll take something as collateral until I get my merchandise back."

Oh my God, did they mean to take her with them? In one fluid motion that left her head spinning, Striker shoved her fully behind him, yanked out his gun and aimed it straight at Snake's head.

The urge to cling to Striker, wrap her arms around him and bury her face between his shoulder blades was overwhelming, but she refused to have her presence cause any more trouble than it already did. She heard a few clicks behind her and it was a reflex to turn and look. The three men behind them hadn't moved any closer, but each of them had a serious-looking gun trained directly on Striker. Oh God.

"I suggest you lose the gun, Striker, unless you want the lovely Dr. Emerson to watch us end you, before we take her with us, that is."

Anger poured off Striker in waves. He tossed his gun to the ground, far enough out of reach to satisfy Snake, and turned to her. No words were spoken, but she knew what he wanted to tell her. Do what they say, don't make waves, stay alive. There was no way in hell she'd let him die trying to protect her. The next few moments were going to be critical to their mutual survival, so she gave him a slight nod to convey that she would follow his lead.

"Lila will take your message back to the club. You don't need her. I'll go with you while they investigate your claims."

Snake laughed. Lila was getting sick of the maniacal sound. "Aww. Isn't that sweet, boys?" He looked at his men. "Striker must really care for the good doctor. No, I think I'll stick with my plan. Having her as my guest will keep you motivated."

Still behind Striker, shielded by his body, Lila started to shake. Would they rush forward to grab her? Would they shoot Striker? She was afraid to move, didn't want to draw any further attention her way though she knew her efforts were futile.

"Dr. Emerson, step out from behind Striker. Five steps to your right."

Her breath came out in a whoosh of fear. "Fuck off," was on the tip of her tongue but she held it back. Striker could be shot at any time, and they'd both be totally screwed.

So softly she almost didn't hear it over the pounding of her heart Striker spoke. "Do it, baby. I promise I'll get you out of this."

The moment she stepped away, Snake's men converged on Striker. One stopped about a foot away from his left side with a gun trained on Striker's head while the other halted right in front of him. Without warning he slugged Striker once in the stomach followed immediately by a punch to the face. His eye swelled instantly and blood poured from his nose.

Doubled over, Striker swore viciously, but didn't fight back. Why wasn't he fighting them? He was a fighter, hell he was named for it, and he could probably flatten these two assholes in one second flat. Then it hit her, if the attention was on him, it was off her. He didn't fight back because he couldn't lose his focus on her and what was happening to her. He looked up, directly at her, and she felt sick to her stomach.

"Doctor, please join me over here."

Lila shifted her gaze to meet Snake's head on. She refused to cower in his presence no matter how much she quaked on the inside. It was as though she stared into a pool of nothing. No emotion registered in those black eyes, and he gave away no hint of what was to come.

She walked forward, until she stood about two feet from Snake. He wrapped a hand around her wrist and pulled her against his side. Tears filled her eyes, but she forced them away. When they made it out of this alive she could cry for days.

Striker's rage was palpable, as though it was another person standing in the road with them. He would tear Snake apart at the first chance he got. He rose to his full height and diverted the attention back to himself.

"If you want to keep that hand, you'll take it of her, motherfucker." His voice was practically a snarl.

Snake removed his hand from her wrist, but placed an arm around her shoulders as he faced Striker.

Lila was so tense she feared she might snap under the weight of Snake's arm.

Snake let out a short laugh. "I don't think you're exactly in the position to make demands, Striker. I am, however, and I want my shit back."

Striker took a step forward from his position between the two Grimm Brothers. "If you're right, and it was a No Prisoner, it was not club sanctioned. It was a lone wolf grab. I'll find who did it. If this isn't bullshit, I want the fucker as much as you do."

Snake released her, and moved toward Striker. Relief at no longer being touched by him nearly buckled Lila's knees. "I imagine you do. I want my product returned. You better pray it's all accounted for. And I want the man responsible delivered to my club."

Holy shit, would Striker agree to that? He would be signing a man's death warrant for sure, and probably a horrible and painful death at that. As Lila looked on in horror, Striker nodded. "You'll get him. He may be a bit dinged by the time he makes it to you, but you'll get him."

"You have until tonight. We'll meet out near the abandoned mine off Route Forty. Midnight. You bring my shit, you'll get your ol' lady unharmed. You're one minute late, or don't deliver, well, let's just say I'm without an ol' lady of my own right now."

Lila's stomach rolled at Snake's threat. She couldn't meet Striker's eyes. The fear and uncertainty was too great.

Snake mounted his bike then turned to Lila. "Hop on, Doc. Time's a wastin' and your man has shit to do." He winked an emotionless eye at her. "Make sure you hold on real tight."

Somehow Lila made her legs carry her to the bike, and she climbed on behind Snake. Her options were to hold onto him or to fall off, so she had to touch him at least a little. Her hands trembled and bile rose in her throat as she gripped Snake's sides. She kept her torso as far back from him as she dared while keeping herself on the bike.

With a raise of his hand, Snake signaled to his men. All five of them lowered their weapons and returned to their bikes. Lila still didn't look at Striker as Snake led the pack and rode out.

Chapter Twenty-Four

Goddamn it. This was Striker's nightmare. This was the exact reason he never should have dirtied Lila with his hands. The very second the Grimm Brothers pulled away, Striker snatched his gun and hopped on his bike. He tore back toward the clubhouse. Most of the guys should still be there.

What the hell was he thinking, getting involved with her? Lila didn't deserve any of this shit. She was the very essence of goodness, and in a few short weeks his life had stained her. Christ, there were countless people alive today because of Lila, because she used her skills and knowledge to save them. No wonder she looked at him with such revulsion when he agreed to hand over the thief. She was a healer, and he was a killer.

When he got her back, he wanted to wrap his arms around her, and hold her forever, so nothing could ever hurt her again. Then he wanted to strip her, and take his time loving every inch of her, erasing any memory of Snake's touch from her mind. He wanted to watch as she came apart in his arms while he poured himself into her welcoming body.

What he needed to do, though, was distance himself before he poisoned her. Because of him she would spend over twelve hours with a sadistic son of a bitch. He assumed she'd be done with him, never want to speak to him again, and she'd be smart to walk away.

Striker made the thirty-minute trip in nineteen minutes. Dust and gravel flew across the lot as he came to a harsh stop in front of the clubhouse.

"Who the fuck is that?" Jester's pissed off voice carried through the open doors of the garage bay.

As he killed the engine, Striker saw Jester stomp toward him.

"Striker? Why the hell are you tearing in here spraying shit all over? You're the one who usually bitches at people for pulling that."

Striker dismounted and jogged toward the clubhouse. "Need you inside. Now!"

"Jesus Christ, bro! What happened to your face?"

Striker hadn't given much thought to the beating he took from Snake's men. He glanced down at the blood splattered across his shirt. When he saw it, the pain in his face registered, but he ignored it. It didn't matter. Nothing mattered beyond finding out who betrayed the club so he could get Lila back before the trauma of being Snake's captive destroyed her.

"Do you need me to call Lila? Have her come check you out?" Jester increased his stride length to keep up with Striker.

"No I need you to get the fuck inside."

"Striker your face is all busted up, at least go clean it off."

"No time for that shit." He ripped the door open, and stormed into the clubhouse. Shiv was at the bar with Hook and Acer who both jumped up when they caught sight of

Striker's battered face.

"Christ! What happened to you?" Shiv was the first to speak.

"My face doesn't matter."

"Sit, Striker." Shiv tried to push him into a chair.

"I don't need to sit." Striker shook of his president's hold.

"I wasn't asking you." This time Shiv was successful in shoving Striker to a chair. "Jester, grab him a wet towel to clean his ugly face. Acer, get him a drink."

A moment later, a glass with an amber brown liquid appeared before him, the near full bottle next to it. "Drink it," Shiv ordered. "Calm your shit down, and tell us what the fuck happened."

He threw down the drink hoping it would help him get the words out. When Shiv held out the bottle to refill Strikers glass, he shook his head. If he was going to pull this off he needed all cylinders firing. "Lila and I were ambushed by six Grimms on the way to my house."

"Fuck!" Shiv bit out. "Doc okay?"

Striker shook his head as he stared into the empty glass. Fear for her clogged his throat, and he felt tears fill his eyes for the first time since as far back as he could remember. "No. They took her." His voice sounded rough.

"What?" Jester roared as he returned from the bathroom with a wet cloth. He shoved it in Striker's hands and began pacing.

Striker used the warm towel to clean the blood off his face. The skin around his eye felt puffy, and throbbed with a sharp ache, but he ignored it. He could breathe without difficulty so his nose probably wasn't broken. There were much bigger problems to tackle.

When he was done he tossed the towel under his chair. "Looks like Jackal is no longer in charge. Don't know how it happened, but Snake is running the show now."

Shiv paled a bit at that news. "What a fuckin' mess. This blows our deal right out of the water." He grabbed the bottle and took a long pull.

"It gets worse. Snake claims one of us stole a fuck ton of drugs from the Grimms. Gave me until midnight to find the drugs and hand over the guilty party. Lila is collateral."

Silence filled the room for a long, tense moment.

Jester stopped pacing and gaped at Striker. "You coulda told me Snake had a sex change and I wouldn't be as fuckin' shocked as I am now. Think he was shittin' you?"

Striker turned his glass over and slid it back and forth between his hands on the table. "I think he believes one of us did it. Whether or not it's true, I don't know."

"And if we don't deliver on time?" Shiv asked.

Striker looked him right in the eye. "Says he's in the market for a new ol' lady."

Expletives came from each man as Striker's meaning sank in.

"Damn, I'm sorry this touched your woman, Striker."

Striker looked at Shiv. The older man sat with his head rested on his hands, which were propped up by his elbows on the table. In that position he looked tired, defeated.

The men were quiet for another moment before Acer spoke. "Okay, so we get on this fast, find the fucker, strip his patch, and toss him to the Grimms. Saves us the trouble of getting rid of him."

Striker nodded. "I agree, though I told Snake to expect him in less than perfect condition. I want a few shots at him before we hand him over."

They all nodded.

"Who do we look at for this? I don't even know where to fuckin' begin." Shiv shook his head. "Never would have thought one of us would do something like this."

Striker dropped his head. What a disaster. They were sentencing a brother to death, a fact that Lila had clearly picked up on. The way Lila had stared at him when she realized the guilty man would be handed over to the Grimm Brothers was burned into his memory. Horror and disgust had been written plainly all over her beautiful face. But worse, was how she wouldn't even look at him right before Snake rode off with her. Striker knew that as long as he lived he'd never scrub the image of Lila on the back of Snake's bike from his brain.

"I have an idea who it is." Jester spoke, and his words crashed Striker back into the moment.

Each man gaped at him.

"Do you fucking know something about this, Jester?" Striker's voice was deadly, warning the other man what would happen if he'd been keeping something of this magnitude from him.

"No, VP. No fucking way I'd let something like that slide. And I could be completely wrong about my suspicions, but I think Rock might be using."

"Rock? You're shittin' me." Rock was a newer member, who had received his patch a little over a year ago. Striker was surprised, he'd been one of the best prospects they ever had. Took all the shit they gave him as though it was nothing. Not for one second would Striker have guessed he was using drugs. "Why do you think that?"

"Few times we've been out on runs, I thought he might be high. His behavior's been gettin' erratic. I also overheard him talking about money troubles."

Striker considered Jester's words. He looked at Shiv to gauge his reaction. Shiv reached into his pocket and drew out a thick cigar. His eyes were sad as he lit it. This would weigh heavily on him, that he let a man into the club who could hurt their family.

"He has been off lately. I knew he was having money troubles as well, and just figured he was stressed. But now that I think about it, he definitely could have been stoned." Acer shook his head in disgust as he added his thoughts.

"Big leap from doing some drugs to stealing two-hundred-fifty thou worth of product from the Grimms." Shiv puffed out a stream of smoke and watched it swirl toward the ceiling.

Jester let out a low whistle. "Two-fifty? Shit, no wonder Snake's on the warpath. We'd tear their club apart if the situation was reversed."

Striker nodded. Jester was right. Had someone stolen that much from the No Prisoners, they'd be on the receiving end of a full out attack. Difference was, they'd never go after someone's ol' lady as payback. There were just some lines you didn't cross. Sort of an outlaw code of honor. Snake didn't seem to buy into that. "Obviously we need to be one hundred fucking percent sure about this. The Grimms aren't going to just give him a spanking and let him walk."

"I think we should straight on confront him." Acer snagged the bottle from Shiv and took a swig. "He's fucked up right now. If it's him, I think he'll piss himself to get back in your good graces."

"Do it now. At his house. This way we can see if he has the shit there. Get Gumby and Hook in on the deal as well. We gotta move fast. Bastard only gave us twelve hours." Shiv looked at Striker as he issued the order.

All three men nodded. "There will need to be retaliation," Striker said. "We cannot let this slide. They have my woman. I don't even want to think about—" He stopped, unable to complete the sentence. He had to believe Snake would hold up his end of the bargain and leave Lila unharmed until the deadline. Otherwise, he wouldn't be able to function.

Shiv's hand landed on Striker's shoulder with a firm squeeze. "He'll pay for this, son. I promise you that. But you need to promise me you won't go cowboy on us and try to take him out yourself. When the time is right we'll cut that slithering bastard's head off, but we'll do it right. You hear me?"

Striker would be lying if he said the idea of going after Snake on his own hadn't crossed his mind, but Shiv was right. It would be smarter, and safer, to plan the retaliation as a club.

"Loud and clear, Pres." He leaned forward in his chair. "Okay boys, let's go catch us a traitor."

Acer and Jester walked out to the bikes leaving Shiv and Striker at the table. Shiv stood and pulled Striker up for a fierce hug. He slapped him on the back as he whispered, "Your woman's tough, and about as smart as Einstein. She'll be okay brother."

A hint of a smile ghosted Striker's lips at Shiv's words. "Thanks, man."

Chapter Twenty-Five

An hour later, Striker, Gumby, Hook, and Jester convened outside Rock's front door. Acer waited on his bike at the edge of the driveway. The neighborhood was shit. Someone needed to guard the bikes and keep an eye out for trouble. Acer drew the proverbial short straw.

Striker glanced at Rock's house. He used the term house lightly. Rock lived in the trashy part of town, in a rundown two-bedroom shack. It looked like crap on a good day, but today it looked even worse. The front had two windows, one on each side of the door. Boards covered one window while the other had a large crack straight down the center.

It made sense now, the dilapidated house, and the less than desirable neighborhood. Rock pissed all his money away on drugs. Damn, he'd seemed like such a great addition to the club, and Striker couldn't get over the idea of his betrayal.

Rock had a great personality, always joking and upbeat. He was a favorite with the ladies as well, although Striker couldn't imagine any of them coming back to this hole with him and deciding to spend the night.

Shaking his head in disgust at the entire situation, Striker used the side of his fist to pound on the door. The house remained quiet though they knew he was home. He'd partied last night with a few other guys who told Striker Rock left with a broad, taking her back here.

Striker limited the number of people who knew about the possibility of Rock's betrayal to the group that was here at the house and Shiv. Until they were certain, there wasn't any point in rattling the whole club.

After a minute he nodded to Jester who tried the doorknob. It was locked, but the door was so shoddy that one good shove from Jester's giant frame and it popped right off the hinges. Oh well. There was a good chance Rock wouldn't have a need for that door much longer anyway.

The foursome strode into the quiet house, and all stopped short when the appalling conditions became apparent. Striker had been inside once, about six months ago, but for what, he couldn't recall. He remembered the place was a dump, but what they saw in front of them was beyond disgusting. Fast food wrappers littered the floor along with empty beer and liquor bottles. One tall standing lamp was lit in the corner, and provided a fair amount of light since the lampshade appeared to be missing. The natural light was limited with the boarded window, and a smoky haze swam through the air.

"Jesus." Gumby held an arm across his nose and coughed. "This place smells like shit. What the fuck is going on with him?"

"If I had to guess, I'd say he was high more often than not these days." Jester ventured into the room and peered down at a coffee table littered with hypodermic needles, rubber tubing and burned spoons.

"Looks like you were right about him, Jest," Striker said, his voice filled with revulsion. "Fucking idiot. Let's find him, and see if Snake's shit is here. Christ, what a fuck up."

The men hazarded deeper into the house, toward Rock's bedroom. Striker arrived first, and nudged the thin door open with his foot. He wasn't going to touch a damn thing in this filthy building if he could avoid it.

When he stepped into the room, he turned his attention toward the bed. Sure enough, Rock was passed out face up on the mattress with one arm thrown over his head. A sheet covered the lower half his body, and the other arm lay at his side. Track marks dotted the crook of his elbow, and even more drug paraphernalia topped the nightstand next to the bed.

A woman slept next to Rock, sprawled out face down, with her naked ass on display.

Gumby was next to wander in, with Jester and Hook on his heels. "Well lookie here!" Gumby said as he gleefully rubbed his hands together. "Rock got himself a little action last night. Nice ass. Too bad she's probably a crack whore."

He moved around the bed, and lingered over the woman's prone form. Neither she nor Rock stirred despite the fact that the men made no effort to be quiet. Gumby bent down and ran his hand over the woman's ass. "Grade A," he said with a smirk before he lifted his hand only to bring it down with a sharp crack against the woman's rounded cheek.

A shrill cry sounded through the room, and she shot up in bed. With wide, frightened eyes the woman turned over and scooted back toward the headboard. Gumby kept the smirk on his face as he looked at the rest of the guys. "Ooh, front's not quite as nice boys."

The woman was probably attractive at one point. Now, however, the effects of prolonged drug use had taken an obvious toll on her. Her face was haggard, aged her before her time, and her limp blonde hair hung in her face, a stringy mess. She shrieked again, and attempted to rip the sheet

211

from Rock to cover her own body. Her face reflected stark terror, and she trembled as her gaze bounced between the four men staring at her.

Finally, Rock stirred. "What the fuck, bitch?" he mumbled, eyes still closed. "There a fuckin' fire or something?"

Gumby picked a cheap-looking dress up from the floor by his feet, and tossed it to the woman. "Get the fuck out, honey. We need to talk to your man."

She snatched the clothing from Gumby's hand, and ran from the room with the sheet wrapped around her. "He's not my man," she spat out. "Asshole was so stoned he could barely get it up." The men's snickers trailed behind her as she fled.

Jester hooted with laughter. "Hear that, Rocky boy? I think a limp dick means you're doing too much of that shit." Jester's mega phone voice seemed to clear any lingering sleep from Rock's head. His eyes popped open, the pupils dilated wide.

"VP. Shit, did I miss church? Something wrong?" Rock seemed unconcerned that he was nude, and no longer beneath the cover of the sheet.

He had to know why they were there, but if this was how he wanted to play it, then fine, Striker could play this game. "Get dressed and come out to the den. I don't want to have to stare at your dick while I talk to you. Stay with him, Gumb." He wasn't taking the chance that Rock would escape out the window.

"Sure, VP."

Striker moved toward the door with a signal for Jester and Hook to follow him. As they left, he heard Gumby talking to Rock. "Come on asshole, I don't want to see your tiny dick either. Get your ass up. You're about to have an interesting day."

When he was dressed, Rock joined them in the den. Gumby lingered near the mouth of the hallway, arms crossed, one shoulder against the wall. Hook guarded the front door in much the same position, and Jester stood off to the left of the couch in front of the boarded window. All exits were covered.

"Sit your ass down." Striker pointed to the couch.

Rock looked uneasy, and wasted no time trying to get on Striker's good side. "Sorry about the mess, VP. I haven't been here much to clean it up." His eyes darted between the four men as he spoke.

He was a sight. A thick and uneven beard sprouted from his face, and his clothes were ripped and stained. Black grease caked under his fingernails, and deep purple rings of fatigue resided under each of his eyes. He looked like he hadn't slept in a week, and probably hadn't showered in as long.

"I don't give a fuck about this shithole, Rock." Striker stood in front of the couch with one booted foot braced on the coffee table. He leaned forward and rested his elbow on his bent leg.

"Yeah. I know why you're here." Rock waved a hand back and forth in front of him indicating the drug supplies on the table. "Look, brother, I swear I only do it once in a while when I'm partying. It's really no big deal. I'll stop." He wiped his hands on the front of his thighs repeatedly, a nervous gesture that didn't go unnoticed by Striker.

"You broke a club rule. A big one. No one gives a fuck about a little weed, but this hard shit?" He waved toward the table. "It's unacceptable."

Rock swallowed, and started to bounce his leg in place. "I'm really sorry, brother, I swear it won't happen again. You're not gonna try and take my patch are you?"

Striker ignored the question in favor of his own. "Grimms approached me. Actually, they ambushed me when I was with my ol' lady." Striker let that sink in for a few seconds before he continued. Rock stopped moving, but that was the only indication he gave of any knowledge of where this conversation was going. "Turns out they are missing a fuck load of product. Snake claims a No Prisoner is responsible. Know anything about that, Rock?"

All color leached out of Rock's face at Striker's inquiry. To Striker, that was as good as a confession, but he wanted to see how this would play out. Would Rock man up and own it or would he pussy out and lie? It wouldn't change the outcome, but it would help Striker further understand the kind of man who would deceive his brothers.

Rock went with door number two. "VP, brother, that would be suicide. I wouldn't shit on my patch like that."

Beads of sweat popped out along his brow and rolled down his face. Striker looked to Jester and gave him a subtle nod. Jester took one step toward Rock, cocked his arm, and rammed his fist into the other man's ashen face. "Call him brother again, and I won't stop until you're dead. You are no brother of his."

"Care to revise your answer?"

Rock broke down. He bent forward and covered his face with his hands as sobs shook his body. Blood ran unchecked from his nose, but Rock paid it no attention. Words tumbled out of his mouth so fast, Striker barely made out what he was trying to say. Something about owing money to his dealer and how sorry he was. All bullshit in Striker's opinion. The excuses didn't matter. He was done.

"Jesus, stop crying like a little bitch." Gumby pushed away from his spot on the wall.

Striker held a hand out to halt Gumby's progression.

214

They'd get their retribution, but it would be done according to club policy.

"You sell it yet?" he asked Rock, his voice low and deadly.

Rock stopped crying, and leaned against the back of the couch looking utterly defeated. He shook his head. "I have a meet set up tomorrow, supposed to unload it then."

Striker just stared at him.

"It's all under the bed."

"Fucking idiot." Jester pushed off the wall and strode toward the bedroom. After a moment he yelled, "Should be able to fit it all in our saddle bags." He came back into the den with packages of heroin in his hands. "I'll load it up."

Rock turned a bit green and looked like he might get sick. Striker moved in front of him, and leaned in, inches away from Rock's face. He wanted to make sure Rock knew the extent of his fuck up.

"Snake has Lila." Striker said it with a calm he didn't know he still possessed. Hatred for this man burned through his gut like an iron poker straight from the fire. That he could put his own selfish needs above the needs of the club, of his family was unthinkable. He was a coward and a traitor, two things Striker loathed.

"Oh shit." The words were barely a whisper.

"For that alone I would have killed you. But, you're in luck. I made a promise, and I can't kill you."

A look a relief crossed Rocks face, and Striker took perverse pleasure in dropping the final bomb. "That will be Snake's job."

Striker saw the moment Rock realized the club planned to turn him over to the Grimms. He bolted up from the couch, and charged toward the front door. Striker reflexively punched him in the face, and he went down as hard as his name suggested.

"Damn that felt good." Striker rubbed his knuckles and turned toward Hook. "Tie him up, then get a prospect out here with a van to take him to the warehouse. Have everyone else meet there in an hour."

He strode toward the door and exited the house, walking straight toward his bike. After he filled Acer in, he threw a leg over his bike, and took off toward the warehouse. He needed a few minutes to collect himself. Right now he was in a tailspin.

What kind of leader was he if he couldn't sort out the good men from the bad? And what kind of man was he if he couldn't protect his woman? Now that he had a moment to think about something beyond discovering who betrayed the club, fear for Lila assaulted him. The only way to make this up to her would be to leave her to live her life. For the first time in his own life, Striker wondered how he'd get over walking away from a woman.

Chapter Twenty-Six

All patched members arrived at the warehouse about an hour after Striker left Rock's house. The guys had secured his hands behind him with zip ties and knocked him around a bit, at least that's how it looked. A prospect drove him in the back of a van to the warehouse, where he now sat in a chair in the center of the room begging someone to let him go.

Dried blood covered the skin from his nose to his chin, and Striker felt satisfied knowing he'd had a part in that. Rock's cut had been removed, and lay on the ground in front of him. The brothers gathered around the chair in a circle, and the room was abuzz with speculation about what happened.

Shiv stomped his booted foot on the ground loudly to get everyone's attention. "Looks like everybody is here, so let's get started. The longer we're all here, the more attention we risk. We received some unfortunate information from the Grimm Brothers. About a quarter mil of product was stolen from them. Snake claimed it was one of us."

A murmur of shock and disbelief ran through the room, and Shiv held up a hand to quiet the irate group. He went on to explain the ambush on Striker and Lila, the deal made with Snake, and Rock's part in causing the situation.

"We need a unanimous vote to take his patch back. He'll be going to Snake either way, but we decide if he does it as a brother or not."

There was no way in hell he'd keep his patch, the vote was just a formality at this point. He'd turned against his club, nearly started a war, and got an ol' lady abducted. No fucking way he deserved to call himself a brother.

"All in favor?"

Every hand in the room shot up immediately. Each man bore varying degrees of disgust and anger on their faces.

"Stand him up." Shiv stepped forward, and retrieved the cut from the floor. He turned to Striker and held it out. Typically, the president stripped the No Prisoners' patch from the cut. "You deserve to take this one, Striker."

Satisfaction flowed through him, this would go a long way toward easing his fury. Striker drew his knife from his boot. The sound of ripping leather echoed through the quiet warehouse as he sliced along the back of the cut. It was a fulfilling noise, and he stared right in Rock's guilty face as he did it. When it was done he, walked over to stand in front of Rock. "Ready, boys?"

According to the bylaws, when a member had his patch stripped he had to take one punch from each club member. If he fell, they were allowed one kick each. Striker started it off. He plowed his fist into Rock's face once again, and ignored the man's pathetic pleas for forgiveness. He wouldn't be finding that here.

Striker stepped back, and watched as each of his brothers delivered a nasty blow to Rock. He fell to the ground after the fifth hit, and the remaining men used their boots to inflict the punishment. Rock cried out as each man made contact, but no one showed any mercy.

When it was over, Rock was a bloody mess, lying

unconscious on the ground. "Go get the prospects from outside. Have them toss him back in the van." Shiv spoke to Gumby, who jogged outside. Three prospect came in and dragged Rock out by his feet.

Striker rubbed across the back of his neck. At some point during this miserable day the muscles had knotted and a dull ache settled between his shoulders. He should have been able to spot the weak link in the chain before it broke. Rock slipped past his defenses and made it through a year of prospecting. It never should have happened.

~ ~ ~ ~

Lila's nerves were stretched so tight she feared she'd shatter if she tried to sit down. She'd been at the Grimm Brother's clubhouse for about seven hours, and didn't have any idea what was going on outside the four walls she'd been locked in.

As soon as they'd arrived at the Grimm's clubhouse she'd been dragged off the bike and into a small room. The door wasn't locked, but there were two men standing guard outside. She knew this because after two hours of sitting in a room by herself she'd been brave enough to try and open the door.

She'd recognized Mohawk immediately from the night he came to the hospital, and when he winked at her she slammed the door closed and sat back down on the floor. She should be grateful they left her alone, but she was going crazy wondering what was happening.

The room they held her in was bare, no furniture, no windows. Just four blank walls that closed in on her a bit more with each passing minute.

When the doorknob turned Lila couldn't suppress a yelp of fear. The door swung open and Mohawk filled the doorway with a grin on his face. "Sorry, princess, didn't realize you were so jumpy. Snake would like the pleasure of your company in his office."

Oh God. Why was she complaining about being left alone?

Mohawk stayed in the doorway as Lila passed. She had to turn sideways and press herself against the doorframe to avoid rubbing against him. When she squeezed by she heard an audible inhalation and his arm came down to block her path. "Mmm, lady. You smell good. Striker buys you the good stuff, huh?"

"I buy it for myself, asshole." The words were out of her mouth before she thought better of it. His comment caused some of her fear to be replaced by anger.

"Oh well, excuse me, *doctor*. Sounds like Striker lets his woman have a little too much freedom. Me? I like my women obedient. You know how to obey, Doc?"

"Enough! I asked you to bring her to me, not make a move on her." Snake's voice came from somewhere down the hall.

"Yes, sir. After you, princess." He extended his arm down the hall, and Lila walked in the direction of Snake's voice.

When she stepped into his office he pointed toward a chair opposite him at the desk. "Sit. Close the door on your way out," he called to Mohawk.

Lila sat in the indicated chair, her posture stiff and rigid. Snake, on the other hand, looked right at home. He leaned back in his chair and hefted his boots onto the desk, crossing his legs at the ankles.

"Just wanted to check in, Doc. How are you enjoying our hospitality?"

"Well, considering I was supposed to be sipping a margarita on the deck, I can't say that I'm thrilled with this turn of events." Where was this defiant side coming from? Striker had warned her not to mouth off to Snake. His MC wasn't like the No Prisoners. Women were not treated with respect.

Snake frowned at her retort, and she wished she'd kept her mouth shut. "Well, Doc, I'll fill you in on how this is all going to go down. We'll leave here about eleven and head out to the abandoned mine. If Striker manages to find what was stolen, and gets it there by midnight, we'll make an even exchange, and I'll hold up my end. If he's so much as ten seconds late, you and I will leave, and the rest of my crew will open fire on the No Prisoners. Either way I feel it's a win for me."

All the hair on Lila's body rose as Snake spoke. His eyes shone, as though the idea of gunning down the entire MC pleased him. Lila wanted to reach across the table and claw his eyes out of his head, but she remained motionless, frozen with fear for Striker and fear for her own life. The life that she had just taken control of and started to love.

"You listening to me, Lila?"

She started and looked at Snake again. "Yes."

"Good. I wanted to present another option to you." His eyes grew hooded and his tone lowered. "As I said, I'm without an ol' lady at the moment, and, well, you intrigue me."

Lila's skin crawled and her mouth dropped open in shock and horror.

"I'd like you to consider staying here regardless of tonight's outcome. Though I'll warn you now you'll need to be a little more, shall we say, willing to accommodate."

Lila jumped up. She couldn't stay in his presence another second without becoming sick. "Please bring me back to that room now. I'll just wait there until it's time to leave."

"You'll consider my offer?"

Was he crazy? "Sure."

He nodded. "Good." He stood and called out. The door opened, and Mohawk escorted Lila back down to the room.

After he closed her in, she sank to the floor and covered her face with her hands. Hot tears burned behind her eyelids but she blinked them away before they could fall. How had her life spun so out of control as to get to this point?

She needed to make a plan. That's what she did before she moved to Arizona and it helped her keep her sanity and sort out her feelings. And right now she needed to plan a way to end her relationship with Striker.

His life wasn't what she wanted. Lila wanted to work at the hospital. She wanted to run her sports safety program and live a quiet life. She wanted to meet a sedate man with a nine to five job who would give her a few kids and grow old with her. A frown crossed her face. That all sounded so dull.

It wasn't dull. It was safe. Smart. True, Striker had a lot of qualities she admired in a man. He was intelligent, loyal and worked his ass off for the club. He also supported her work and her project at the high school one hundred percent. Not to mention she was wildly attracted to him, but being with Striker was neither safe nor smart.

That's exactly what she would tell him. She not only needed to feel safe, but she needed to make intelligent life choices. She couldn't choose a path where people would whisper behind her back about the company she kept. She couldn't choose a man who could end up in prison or dead. He'd understand. He had to realize all these things were true.

With a sigh, Lila closed her eyes and rested her head against the wall. She felt a fraction of a percent better at having come up with a plan to fix one part of this out of control situation.

She didn't realize she'd fallen asleep until she heard a chuckle from right above her. When she opened her eyes and looked up, Mohawk's grin filled her vision. "Wakey, wakey, princess. It's time to roll."

Chapter Twenty-Seven

Lila kept her eyes closed while Snake sped through the night toward their meeting location. When she was with Striker, riding at night was one of her favorite activities. Tonight the blackened sky felt anything but wondrous. It felt like a shroud, and she couldn't bear to look at it.

The bike slowed, and then came to a complete stop, and Lila finally allowed her eyes to open.

"You stay on the bike until I tell you," Snake ordered, swinging his leg off the motorcycle.

She pushed a button on her watch and glanced down at the glowing face. Eleven twenty. Snake had wanted to arrive before Striker and the No Prisoners. He'd said it would give him the upper hand.

Lila took a breath, and wiped her palms on her jeans. Her heart danced a nervous rhythm in her chest and she felt a bit dizzy. This exchange had the potential to turn into something deadly.

Still astride the bike, Lila checked out her surroundings. The night was so dark it was almost impossible to see more than five feet from her face. As she stared straight ahead she thought she saw something flash just a bit ahead of them.

Was that—

In the next instant Lila's hands flew up to cover her face as she was blinded by the high beams of a staggering number of motorcycles. Oh my God. The No Prisoners had arrived before Snake, and were lined up across the road. There had to be at least sixty bikes. Who were all these guys?

"Your shit is halfway between us, off to the right. It's all there. As is the other package we agreed on." In that moment, Striker's commanding voice was the most comforting sound she'd ever heard.

Lila looked off to the right where headlights of a bike illuminated packages of drugs stacked neatly behind a bruised and bloodied man. She gasped at the sight of him, and her first instinct, as a healer, was to run to him. But she tamped down the impulse, and tried to locate where Striker's voice was coming from. The lights were too bright and she couldn't see a thing.

"Lila, baby, walk straight across to me. Once she's here, Snake, you can take your shit and leave."

Snake stood about fifteen feet ahead of her, his face a mask of fury. He had to feel humiliated by Striker's show of force. Satisfaction flowed through her. His hands clenched and unclenched at his sides. Good. She hoped the bastard was embarrassed by how Striker beat him at his own game.

Lila scrambled off the bike and started toward the lights. She wanted to run, but was afraid to move too quickly. As she walked, she heard Snake yell after her. "Too bad, Lila. We coulda had fun."

She shivered with revulsion at the thought.

"What did you do, Striker? Call in the National Guard?" Snake called across the gap.

When Lila drew close enough to see over the glare of the lights, she was shocked to discover how many men accompanied Striker. There were more bikes than she'd originally thought, and looked to be about a hundred men. Who were they?

"You should try being nicer to people, Snake. You might make some friends that way."

Lila still couldn't see Striker, but she searched the crowd noticing that each man wore a No Prisoners cut. The patches on the front indicated different locations, Vegas, Joshua Tree, Santa Fe.

After another two steps she swung her gaze up and down the line again and locked eyes with Striker. He stood right in front of her. A wave of relief hit her with the force of a semi when she saw him standing there looking fierce and protective. The flood of emotion was so strong that she stumbled and would have fallen if Striker hadn't reached out and grabbed her.

He crushed her to him, and she wrapped her arms around his waist just as tight. "I've got you, Lila. You're safe. Did he hurt you?" Striker whispered against her ear.

"No. Scared me a bit, but mostly they left me alone in a room. Who are all these people?"

He chuckled in her ear. "Family, baby. We put in a few calls to charters in nearby states. They rushed here right away. My bike is right behind us. Go sit, and we'll be out of here soon."

His family. The moment the word came of Striker's mouth all the pieces fell into place for Lila. She released her hold on Striker, and moved toward his motorcycle. When she was seated, she looked at the men who'd come to support him. They stood together in a row, weapons trained on the ten Grimm Brothers who'd come with Snake, an impenetrable wall.

A family was exactly what they were. Not a conventional

one, but one that instilled loyalty and respect. She had a conventional family. Two parents, a sister, and all the high society perks she could ever want. But they didn't support each other, they weren't loyal to each other, they probably didn't even love each other.

This group of outlaws had her back more than her own blood ever had. They respected Striker, they loved him, and while Lila was with him that extended to her as well. No matter what happened, this family would take care of each other. They would be there for each other no questions asked. They'd ride hundreds of miles in one day to rush to the aid of a brother and his woman.

A warm feeling of support and acceptance replaced much of the fear she'd felt throughout the day. Where before she'd been prepared to walk away, convinced there was nothing here for her, she now saw the opposite might be true. This could be everything for her.

She looked up, surprised to see Snake and his gang riding off into the night. Lost in her own musings, she'd missed the final words between Striker and Snake. It didn't matter. For now, it was over, the score settled and she was free to resume her work and her life.

As she watched Striker approach the bike, and his brothers mount up and ride off she smiled at him. She wanted him in her life, him and this crazy family that came along with him. The good, and the bad.

It didn't matter if people in town didn't understand their relationship. Lila had spent over twenty years concerned about what others thought of her. It was time to give that up. What mattered was how she felt about Striker, and she was pretty sure she was in love with him. The rest was just details they could work out together.

"You ready to go home?"

She let out a weak chuckle and reached for his hand. "I was ready to go home yesterday morning."

Striker didn't laugh at her attempt at a joke. He didn't smile or take her hand. The man who had held her like he couldn't breathe without her just seconds ago was gone, replaced by a hardened version Lila didn't recognize. What had happened in the five minutes she'd zoned out?

Without another word, Striker climbed on the bike and they drove off. Lila had the distinct impression something had shifted in him, something that affected his feelings for her.

Chapter Twenty-Eight

As he drove them back to his house, Striker steeled himself for what he was about to do. When he first saw Lila tonight, walking across the distance from Snake's crew to his, her head held high, he realized he loved her. But keeping Lila alive, and in one piece, was infinitely more important than either of their feelings.

Once he was home, Striker climbed off the bike and waited for Lila to do the same. When her helmet was off, he followed her into the house. She stood ramrod straight and stiff, no doubt a result of his cold treatment.

"I need to go to the clubhouse to talk to Shiv. He stayed behind, and I need to fill him in, in person. Plus we have a lot of brothers staying in town and I need to help get them settled." His words were clipped, emotionless.

She nodded, but remained silent.

"Jester and Hook are on their way to stay with you. Don't know when I'll be back, but they won't leave you alone." He walked to the kitchen without another word.

Striker reached out to open a cabinet and noticed a slight tremor in his hands. His body was reacting to the unfamiliar emotions that filled his head and his heart. It wasn't acceptable. He needed to get himself under control.

With a grunt of frustration, he snagged an open bottle of Jack Daniels, sunk into a chair at the table, and took a long drink. Lila stood in the doorway and came into view as he lowered the bottle. Her arms were folded across her chest and a frown of disapproval was clear on her face.

"You gonna polish that off before riding back to the club?" she asked, worry deepening in her voice.

"Doesn't concern you." He was being a complete asshole, but he didn't know how else to put some distance between them. He should have guessed Lila would see through his bullshit though.

"Striker, what are you doing?" Lila moved to the table and sat beside him, resting her forearms on the flat surface.

He decided there was no point in dragging this out. "Lila this isn't going to work. You can't make it in my world. We might as well not kid ourselves." He took another hit of the Jack. This time when he placed the bottle back on the table she snatched it up. After a long drink of her own, she moved to the sink and upended the bottle. The contents flowed out and into the sink with a splash. "What the fuck are you doing?" he roared as he jumped to his feet.

"Don't you think we cheated death enough for one day? I watched you get assaulted and thought you were going to be shot in front of my face. Now I'm supposed to sit here, and worry that you'll be splattered all over the highway?" She sounded near tears.

He was such a piece of shit. If he thought he didn't deserve her before, he sure as hell didn't after the way he was treating her now. She'd been held by Snake for over twelve hours. She kept her cool the entire time, no matter what she must have been feeling inside.

Now, her concern was for him, not the fact that she'd been

touched and taken by a sadistic monster. And how did he thank her? Not by holding her and loving her as she deserved, but by shoving her away with both hands.

"Lila, I saw you. Saw how you looked at me when I said we'd hand over the thief. You were disgusted with the fact that I could turn someone, a brother, over to Snake. Well, baby, that's who I am. That's what I do." No longer having a bottle to busy his hands, he stood and paced the kitchen. "You can't handle that. You can't handle me. There's no point in pretending otherwise."

This wasn't what he wanted, and the heart he rarely allowed to feel cracked a bit more as each word left his mouth.

"That's what you do, huh? An everyday occurrence? Your brothers usually fuck you over, fuck your club over, and you're just there to take them all out? Because it looked to me like ninety-nine percent of them love you and would lay down their lives to support you."

"That's not what I meant." He ran a frustrated hand through his hair, and continued to prowl around the kitchen.

Lila stepped in his path, and placed her hands on his chest to halt his motion. Her touch grounded him. It was the only thing that kept him from flying apart with the rage and fear tearing at him. Another man had touched his woman, in front of him, had rode off with her on the back of his bike, and he'd been powerless to do anything but watch. Fuck no, he didn't deserve her.

"Seems to me you're disgusted by the whole thing as well. It's a horrifying situation, Striker. How was I supposed to react? Doesn't mean I don't get it, don't understand what you had to do. You have an obligation to protect your club, your brothers."

He looked at her incredulously. Was she for real?

"Whoever it was, he damn well knew the risk, right? No way he thought he'd get out alive if he got caught. I'm not even in the MC and I know your code. You don't betray the club. I know that, and while yes, it's upsetting, I can accept it. You seem to be the one having trouble with that."

Why couldn't she be like other women he knew? Why couldn't she scream at him for getting her kidnapped by his enemies? Why couldn't she throw something at him, and tell him what a scumbag she thought he was? Of course she had to be rational and accepting of him, making it that much harder to walk away. Suddenly the impact of the whole day crashed down on him. Betrayed by family, ambushed by his enemies, it tipped him over the edge.

"God damnit Lila," Striker yelled. "He had his fucking hands on you. Do *you* understand that? He took you right from me. I was helpless to stop him. Can you imagine what he would have done if we hadn't figured out it was Rock?"

Her eyes widened and filled, but she held back her tears. He felt a warring sense of shame and satisfaction knowing he got to her. "I understand exactly what would have happened, Striker. As you said, I'm the one he took."

"So why the hell don't you hate me? Why aren't you kicking me in the nuts and damning me to hell? This is me, Lila. I'm an outlaw, I'm a killer. My loyalty is to my MC family, and I will destroy anyone who gets in their way. You do not belong here, and you're crazy if you think you can deal with it, can deal with all the shit in me." He got right up in her face as he ranted. Now that the beast was unleashed, he couldn't seem to reign it back in.

~ ~ ~ ~

Lila lost the battle to remain stoic, her heart cracked with every word he said, and a lone tear slid down her cheek. She swiped it away as she tried to come up with something to say to get through to him. The rational side of her knew he felt responsible, knew he was worried for her, and knew it had killed a little part of him having to turn a brother over to the Grimms, even if he'd been betrayed in the worst way, but the emotional side of her that was in love with him was starting to win out.

She turned and walked into the living room, needing a second to collect herself, but Striker followed.

He advanced on her as he raged, and she backed up until she hit the wall, pinned on the receiving end of his tirade. "I can handle you Striker. I'm not afraid of you, of what's inside you."

With a snarl, he grabbed her hands and pinned them above her head on the wall. His face was so close she saw the different shades of blue in his eyes. They were filled with guilt and anguish.

"You really think you can handle me like this? You still feel the same way about me knowing I sentenced a brother to death? When I come home with this darkness, and need to fuck it out of my system, you gonna handle that? What about right now? You gonna let me fuck you like this right now?"

"Yes, Striker. I'm here. Take what you need from me. It doesn't scare me. You don't scare me. I'm strong enough to be what you need, what we both need."

He stared at her for a beat before he crashed his mouth down to hers. The kiss wasn't gentle, but she didn't need or want gentle right now. She wanted to feel alive and vital. Just as her need for air became too strong to deny, Striker pulled his mouth away. "I'm so sorry baby, you don't deserve this from me."

All the fight seemed to have gone out of him and what was left was raw emotion. He opened his mouth to speak again, but Lila pulled him into another kiss before he could say anything. He wasn't listening to her words, maybe she could show him with her body how she accepted him, loved him, and needed him. How she would be there to fight the demons with him, and in the times when he couldn't fight them himself, she'd fight them for him.

Striker's erection nestled against her core and she moaned into his mouth. Before long, it wasn't enough. Striker pulled her from the wall and propelled her forward, bending her over the back of the couch.

She gripped the top of the cushion and felt him yank her pants down. A thrill of excitement rippled through her as the sound of her panties tearing filled the room. Out of the corner of her eye she saw the tattered remains fly over the couch. Against the fabric, her nipples hardened, and her pussy clenched in anticipation of his invasion.

"Don't make me wait, Striker." As soon as the words were out of her mouth, he powered into her with one strong thrust. "God." He groaned. "You're wet." It was as though he finally believed everything she'd said when he felt the proof of her words in her body's response. He sagged, and rested his head on her back, his shaft embedded deep within her.

"Because I want you." Her voice was fierce. "Fuck me, Striker. You need this. I need this. We almost died or worse today. I need to feel you inside me, to feel alive. We'll deal with the rest of the bullshit later. Right now I just need to feel you move inside me."

Not waiting for him, she drew her hips forward, then pushed pack and impaled herself farther on his cock. After that neither of them spoke. He hammered into her furiously, as though he could imprint himself on her, and she reveled in it, meeting him thrust for thrust.

With adrenaline still coursing through them and emotions

running high, there was little room left for finesse and patience. It was raw and intense; he fucked her like a man possessed. It wasn't long before she came with a sharp cry as ecstasy flooded her system. The pleasure Striker gave her on top of the fear from earlier propelled her into an orgasm so powerful tears fell from her eyes.

Above her, a primal roar rang out, and knew the encounter had been just as earth shattering for Striker. Exhausted, Lila's arms were unable to bear her weight anymore and she collapsed over the back of the couch. Her breaths came in ragged pants, made more difficult when Striker's heavy body landed against her back as though he couldn't hold himself up either.

He must have heard her crying because he suddenly drew back. "Oh my God, Lila, did I hurt you? I knew—"

She stood, managed an awkward turn, and almost laughed at the picture they made. Striker's pants were down at his knees, his now soft cock dripping with their combined fluids, and his bruised face held an expression of concern. Her jeans were down as well, only barely past her ass, and who knew where the remains of her panties ended up. Lila was afraid to catch a glimpse of her hair. It had to be a tangled mess.

The look of self-loathing on Striker's face made her heart squeeze. "No, Striker," she said. She stepped into him and wrapped her arms around his powerful body. "You gave me exactly what I needed."

He stood still, and didn't return her embrace. "But you were crying."

"It was intense," she answered with a shrug.

Finally, he relented, and enfolded her in his arms. He brought his mouth to hers for a deep kiss that ended when they heard the rumble of pipes coming down the street.

"That will be Hook and Jester. I'm not sure how long I'll be, but they will stay the whole time."

She watched as he made himself presentable again. There wasn't enough time to shower, and she'd never admit it out loud, but she liked the idea of him wearing the scent of their love making for the rest of the night. She, however, planned to shower. It would at least give her something to do besides stare at Hook and Jester while Striker was gone. For now, she righted her clothes so she was decent when they came in the house.

Striker was so handsome. He moved with the easy confidence of a man secure in his power and position. It hadn't been long, but he'd become everything to her, and she already felt she needed him in her life just as much as she wanted him there. The thought was a bit unsettling for someone who had gotten used to being in charge and independent.

He looked up as he finished buckling his belt. "We have a lot to talk about when I get back. I need to think about some things before this goes any further." He let out a heavy sigh. "I've never cared enough about a woman to want to do right by her. And that's what I'm doing now, trying to do the right thing for you, Lila."

"Who the hell do you think you are?" she spat out, anger surging at his statement. "You don't get to decide what's right for me, Striker. I do that. So think all you want, but think about what it is that you want, not what you think I need. I'm perfectly capable of making those decisions for myself."

He chuckled and held up his hands in surrender. "My bad. I'm sorry."

Lila blew out a breath and her anger dissipated. "Let me just say one thing and then we can talk when you get back."

"Okay." He eyed her as though he thought she was trying

to trap him.

"I sat in a room by myself most of the time I was in the Grimm's clubhouse. It gave me a lot of time to think, and I had decided that this thing between us was over. I was going to tell you as soon as I got away from them. And then I saw you, and your brothers, who came from all over to help you, and I realized I was being a fool. You have a family that loves you, and will have your back no matter what. If you weren't deserving of that, you wouldn't have it. They respect you, and love you because you're a good man, Striker. I realized that instead of pushing you away because I'm afraid or because it might be difficult, I need to pull you closer. There's strength in numbers. Together, and with your family, we can have something important."

She couldn't believe it when she saw Striker's eyes fill. "Christ, Lila. There isn't a thing about you I don't think is amazing."

A pounding on the door interrupted anything further he might have said to her.

"It's open," he hollered.

Seconds later Jester and Hook entered the room. Lila was sure they could sense the tension. It was so thick it was practically visible. She didn't care who saw them. Being taken by Snake changed her outlook on the small things. Lila grabbed Striker and pulled him to her for a passionate kiss. She wanted him, and wasn't above playing dirty to get him. Might as well send him off on a positive note.

When the kiss ended she shifted her head so her mouth was pressed against his ear. "I love you, Striker." It may have been a mistake to make herself so vulnerable to him, but she wanted him to know what he'd be walking away from if he chose to do so. Her vision blurred, and she turned away before he could respond.

Rattled by her own weepiness, Lila walked into the bathroom. She locked the door behind her and turned on the water to give it time to warm up. After stripping down, she stepped in the steamy shower, and finally let the tears flow.

Chapter Twenty-Nine

Striker couldn't believe what had just transpired between him and Lila. The most emotionally charged sex of his life, culminating in one of the most intense orgasms he'd experienced, all initiated by him being a colossal asshole. There was a mountain of unsaid words between them, and he had so much to make amends for, he wasn't sure where to begin.

The entire time he'd been raging at her, Lila fought for them, instead of fighting him, and she looked gorgeous doing it. Face flushed with suppressed anger, eyes shining with what he now knew was her love for him. Her body had been taut with tension, a body he'd been unable to keep from touching, taking.

"Lila holding up okay?" Hook was the first to break the silence. The concerned look on his face spoke volumes. He'd always been very protective of women. It went back to a bunch of shit from his childhood. It was no surprise that the first question he asked was about Lila's wellbeing.

Striker shook his head, and rubbed a spot on the left side of his chest where a small ache had formed. "I don't know, brother. Some serious shit went down today. I don't think

239

she's had a chance to process it all."

"How about you? You holding up?" This time the inquiry came from Jester.

"Don't know that either, bro. I'll be back as soon as I can. Shouldn't take long."

"Don't worry, Striker, we'll watch over your woman." Hook spoke again.

"Thanks." He bolted into the kitchen, snagged his gun off the table, and strode back out the front door as Jester and Hook plopped down on his couch to wait for Lila.

~ ~ ~ ~

Wrung out after her crying jag, Lila dragged herself out of the shower. She was sure Jester and Hook didn't care what she wore, so she threw on a pair of yoga pants and one of Striker's many Harley Davidson T-shirts. As she pulled the soft fabric over her head, the smell of him surrounded her and made her feel embraced by him, something she needed in this uncertain time.

She toweled off her long hair, and secured it up in a high ponytail. Since she wasn't in the mood to dry it fully or put on makeup, it looked like she'd run out of ways to avoid going out to the living room.

With a fortifying breath, Lila opened the door to the hallway and started toward the den. Both men looked up as she came down the hall, staring at her as though they were expecting her to break down. "Hey, guys. Can I get you a drink or anything?"

Jester rose and walked to her. He slung a long arm around her shoulders, and steered her toward the couch where he encouraged her to sit. "No, doll. We can help ourselves if we want something. Sit and relax. By the way, you look about nineteen in that outfit. I like it." He bobbed his eyebrows up and down at he as he spoke.

His antics had the desired effect, and she laughed, easing the tension in the room and the tension in her body. "Thank you, Jester. I needed that."

"You doing all right, honey?" Hook asked.

Lila took a moment to answer. "I think so. Can I ask you guys a question?"

Hook raised an eyebrow at her.

"What happens now? With the Grimm Brothers I mean? I kinda zoned out at the end when I was sitting on Striker's bike." Her stomach clenched while she waited for his response. If he told her they were still in danger from Snake, she might just break down.

Hook rubbed a hand over the stubble on his chin. "Well, hon, I'm not going to lie to you and tell you we're all best buds now, but I think things will be calm for a while. Snake agreed to abide by the terms of the deal we set with Jackal." He shrugged as he continued. "His word probably means shit, but he's got enough on his plate with taking control of his club."

"What do you mean?"

"From what I've heard, the Grimms were pretty split as far as loyalty, half loyal to Jackal, and the other half helped Snake overthrow him. I'm guessing he cleans house, and gets rid of Jackal's supporters. Whether he'll replace them or not remains to be seen. He'll be too busy dealing with his own shit to mess with us for a while. Some of those guys are not gonna go quietly."

Lila blew out a breath. "Good. That's good."

Hook leaned back on the couch, and propped his feet up on the coffee table. "Are you gonna be able to make peace with what you saw go down today?"

"You mean the guy you turned over to the Grimms? Does it really matter how I feel?"

Jester joined in the conversation. "It matters to Striker. We are all aware when we patch in, that the MC becomes our life, our family. Everything we do is in support of the club. We are also aware of what happens if we betray that patch.

"We don't run drugs Lila. That's something our club decided long ago because of the violence and destruction it brings to the community. Not to mention we'd become an easy target for the cops. We are far from saints, but we don't seek out violence."

Hook took over where Jester left off. "To commit an act that goes against the charter is bad enough, to commit an act that harms our club, and puts our families in danger, is an unforgivable offence."

Lila nodded, she understood all this, and even accepted it. Didn't make the situation any less horrifying.

"Trust me, Lila," Jester said. "The guy that did this did so fully aware of what would happen if they got caught. If Snake didn't claim him we'd have taken care of it ourselves."

"Jester." Hook's voice held a note of warning.

Lila waved him off. "It's okay, I truly get it. I'm not going to freak out over this, nor will I tell a soul." She paused, not sure if she wanted to continue.

"What is it, hon?" Jester asked.

"I'm just worried about Striker." She was a little embarrassed to put her emotional cards on the table in front of them, but she'd started down this path, and might as well see it through. Lila cleared her throat. "I mean this was a serious betrayal by someone he trusted. Yesterday the guy was a brother, today he's a traitor, and now he's probably dead. I know he feels some kind of misplaced responsibility as your vice president."

Hook huffed out a laugh. "Hon, you're going to make one hell of an ol' lady."

Her eyebrows drew down. "How so?"

"Here we are, all worried you're going to think we are a bunch of barbaric murderers, and you're mostly concerned about how Striker will deal with all this. You're a good woman, Doc."

Her face heated as they both looked at her with respect and appreciation.

"It does wear on him, a lot," Hook said. "Having your goodness in his life is going to bring him peace, help him sleep at night. I've already seen it calming him."

Lila looked away as she recalled their earlier argument. Her presence in his life seemed to be doing the exact opposite. Striker appeared overly troubled by her, not comforted as they claimed.

Jester shifted to the couch, and sat next to her. One baseball glove sized hand reached out, and drew her head to his shoulder. "Whatever you're thinking, knock it off. I don't know what happened before we got here." He chuckled. "Though I can guess by the torn panties on the floor over there."

"Jester! What is it with you?" She buried her face in the bulk of his arm as the humiliation of him catching them for the second time washed over her.

Jester threw back his head and cracked out a laugh. "I get a kick outta making you blush, Stitch. But let me finish. I don't know what Striker said to you, but I want you to remember one thing. All this shit that's happening? Worst part for Striker is that it touched you, that he couldn't protect you from it."

"Jester's right, Doc. Give him time. Striker will pull his head out of his ass."

Exhaustion set in, and her eyelids became heavy. "What makes you think he has his head up his ass?"

"I've known him a long time, hon. I can guess how he's reacting to his feelings for you. Go ahead and doze off, Doc. We're not going anywhere until Striker gets back." Hook rose from the couch. "I'm gonna grab a beer. Want one, Jest?"

Jester nodded at Hook, snatched the remote control from the coffee table, and skimmed channels until he found a documentary on something motorcycle related. Lila didn't bother to pay attention.

She allowed her eyes to drift closed, and curled her feet up on the couch, with her head against Jester's substantial shoulder. The events of the day caught up with her, and she felt drained, both emotionally and physically. She should probably head on into bed, but wanted to be out in the den when Striker returned. Not to mention, she wasn't sure which bed she should sleep in tonight.

Chapter Thirty

The scene that greeted Striker when he walked through the door had him smiling his first genuine smile since leaving the clubhouse with Lila the morning before. No one noticed him, which allowed him a few seconds to observe the trio.

Jester sat in the center of the couch with Hook at the right end. The TV was on with the volume turned down low, just loud enough to make out what was being said. A UFC fight played on the screen, and the guys argued over who was a better fighter in voices barely above a whisper. Lila lay curled up on her side with her head pillowed on Jester's shoulder as she slept. Someone had covered her with a blanket.

He liked to give Jester shit for being affectionate with Lila, but it was in a brotherly manner, and there wasn't anyone he trusted to take care of her more than the two men on his couch. There was no way in hell Jester would ever try to move in on his woman.

Both men glanced up at him as the door clicked shut. Without a word, he entered the living room and scooped Lila up off the couch. He took a moment to enjoy her soft, warm weight cradled in his arms as he moved toward his bedroom.

"Striker?" Her voice was groggy with sleep, and slightly

confused. "You're back?"

"Yeah, baby, I'm home. I'm going to tuck you into bed, then I gotta talk to the boys for a few minutes, but I promise I won't be long."

When he reached his room, he nudged the door open with his foot, and turned to fit them both through. Gently, he laid Lila on the mattress, and brushed soft kisses over her face.

Lila looked at him with troubled eyes. "I wasn't sure you'd want me in here tonight."

"I always want you, Lila. It was never about me not wanting you," Striker whispered, and kissed her once on the mouth. He hated that he put doubts in her mind about how much he desired her. "Wait up for me."

When he reached the living room, both men stood, and Hook nodded his head toward the front door. "Want to talk outside? I could use a smoke."

"Sounds good."

They filed out the door and stood in the driveway. The air still held a hint of warmth from the heated day. Hook pulled out a pack of cigarettes and inclined it toward Jester who grabbed one.

"What the fuck, man?' Striker asked as Hook stuffed the pack into his pocket.

"You think your doctor lady is going to let you smoke?" Hook laughed as he asked the question.

Striker made a point to look around dramatically. "You think she's watching out the window? Give me a fucking cigarette."

"Your funeral man, just don't tell her I gave it to you. So what's Shiv's take on all this?"

Striker blew out a stream of smoke and watched it swirl into the dark night. "He's in agreement with us. Lila's safe and unharmed, but that doesn't address any of the shit that happened before Snake snatched her. We can't let his attack on Kenny and you slide," he said with a nod to Hook. "Makes us look like pussies. But he also agrees we have plenty of time to plan something smart while Snake's preoccupied with his club's shit."

An evil smile grew across Jester's face. "Damn, it will feel good to take that fucker down a few pegs."

"You ain't kidding. I could easily tear him apart, but I'd like to see his club crumble around him first." Striker watched Hook drop his cigarette down and crush it under the heel of his heavy boot. Orange sparks drifted up from the ground and glowed bright against the blackness of the night.

All of a sudden the need to be with his woman slammed into him with a force that almost stole his breath. "Thanks for staying with Lila. I'm gonna head back in."

Hook and Jester nodded. "No problem, VP," Hook said. "We'll take off, let you and the Doc have some time. She's a good one, brother."

His words were light, but there was a warning to his tone. He liked Lila, his wife liked Lila, and Hook would have something to say if Striker hurt her. Hook gave him a manly hug, and slapped him on the back before he climbed on his bike.

Jester did the same. "None of this is on you, Striker."

Striker took one last drag before he tossed his cigarette to the ground, and made his way inside to be with his woman. He found her curled on her side, staring out the window at the quiet and starry night.

He spared a moment to study her unseen. She still wore his shirt, which engulfed her upper body and ended just below the seductive curve of her hip. Her legs were bare, the smooth, skin nearly glowed in the dark of the room, like a beacon calling to him. Reflected in the window, her face was tight with worry, and guilt sliced at him for causing her to doubt his feelings.

It was only a few seconds before she realized she was no longer alone and rolled over. An entire army of men couldn't have kept him away from her in that moment, and she must have felt the same because she sat up and reached for him with welcoming arms.

Their mouths met in a fury of passion, and the simmering flame that always burned for her ignited into a wildfire. He fused his mouth to hers, so hard that for a second he worried he might bruise her tender lips. But she moaned and clung to him with a desperation that echoed his.

Striker shifted, and pushed her back down to the bed. He settled his body over her. Lila's soft form cradled his much firmer one in all the right places. Her breasts cushioned the hard planes of his chest, her thighs clasped his sides, holding him tight to her, and her heated core burned into the rippled muscles of his stomach. It was the perfect metaphor for their relationship, her soft, comforting, him hard and willing to kill to protect her.

He tore his mouth from hers, and sucked in air before grazing her jaw with his teeth. When he reached the spot just below her ear she shivered, and Striker smiled at the familiar response. He continued down her neck, trailing kisses until he met her collarbone. Gently, he laid his head on her chest and listened to the steady rhythm of her heart.

Lila had been panting and squirming beneath him, one hand fisted in his short hair, while the other stroked his back, but she froze when he rested against her. "Striker? What is it? Why are you stopping?" Her voice was breathless and a slight tremor alerted him to her unease.

"There are two main reasons we don't tell the ol' ladies any club business."

She remained tense beneath him, and he lifted his head to press a soft kiss to her lips. Some of the starch left her, and Striker shifted his weight slightly to the side, so he was still flush against her body, but wouldn't crush her with his weight.

"What are they?" Her calm tone encouraged him to continue.

"First, is so the cops leave them alone. They don't know anything, so there isn't any point in dragging them in for an interrogation, and trying to turn them against the club. They can't be arrested for withholding information, or forced to turn evidence against the club, because they just don't have it and never will."

Lila nodded. The light from the moon shone through the window, illuminating her face and making her look beautiful, despite the serious expression she wore.

"The second reason, is so that our enemies have one less reason to snatch them. Again, no point in taking someone and trying to torture info out of them if you know they don't know anything."

She winced at his last statement, and he experienced a moment of guilt for being so blunt, but he needed her to fully understand where he was coming from.

"With you, we ignored our usual practice in favor of letting you help us out. You know things about the club that I'd never normally tell you because you've been helping us with medical needs. You're vulnerable to the police, and rival clubs. This involvement with me could literally destroy your life, Lila. You could end up in prison, dead, or even worse."

Understanding flashed in her eyes, and he blew out a breath of relief, confident that she was catching on to what he was saying.

"Striker," she began.

He silenced her with a kiss. "Hold on, let me finish. I found out what it felt like to have someone get to you. When Snake took you, and there wasn't a goddamn thing I could do about it…" His eyes closed and he shook his head, fighting the onslaught of emotion the memory resurrected. "I felt a rage I can't even describe. It was like a beast inside me clawing to get out. I always stay in control of my emotional shit, and yesterday I wasn't. You do that to me."

Striker wasn't entirely sure what he was trying to convey to her, he was so out of his element. This was why he normally limited his involvement with women to sex only. That wasn't an option here. It was like Lila had cast some kind of spell over him.

"I get it, Striker." Lila stroked through his hair, the gesture comforted and soothed his battered soul. "I felt the same way when they hurt you and pointed a gun at your head. The same things you worry about happening to me could happen to you. Hell, they are more likely to happen to you."

She was right, and the realization surprised him. He hadn't given any thought to what it would be like from her perspective, or any of the ol' ladies for that matter. They frequently dealt with the threat of their men being arrested, incarcerated, and issues with rival clubs. They handled it much better than he had.

"It's something we'll both have to find a way to deal with if we want this to work, and I don't know about you, but I feel this is worth the risk."

He closed his eyes, enjoying the play of her fingers over his scalp.

"I love you, Lila. But part of me thinks if I love you, I shouldn't drag you into this shit." Jesus, he couldn't believe he was having his conversation. He was turning into a pussy. If his brothers' found out, they would torment him mercilessly for the next fifty years.

"I recognize the risks out there for you, the very realistic and scary risks, and while I may hate that there are so many threats to you, if I want to be with you, I have to accept it. You have to do the same. If something were to happen to you, it would kill me," she said, her voice thick with emotion. "But it would pretty much kill me if you walk away now. So I'd rather reach out and grab what we could have, for as long as possible."

Tears started to track down her face. The sight of those tears twisted his gut. He did not want her to cry for him. "Baby, please don't cry," he whispered as he reigned soft kisses on her forehead, her eyes, her cheeks, and finally her lips. "I can't stand it."

"We can take extra precautions, Striker. I'll always listen to you, do whatever it takes to stay safe, and make you feel confident about my safety."

Lila was the perfect ol' lady for him, always so calm, and logical. She reasoned through problems to find workable solutions instead of freaking out and causing drama. He dealt with some deep shit as the VP of an outlaw motorcycle club, and knowing he could share his burdens with her was powerful. He could count on her to keep her cool no matter what he had to unload. She was the only woman who could ease the demons in his soul, and he'd be the worst kind of fool to let that slip away.

Done talking, he took her mouth again. This time there was nothing easy about the kiss. This time he poured all the need and desire he had for her into the act. As he continued the assault on her mouth, his hands worked the shirt up her body until her breasts were bare. Under him, Lila moaned and widened her legs, rocking her pelvis against him. God, he loved when she did that, as though her body was seeking him out of its own volition.

"Put your hands above your head. I want you to keep them there. Move them and I won't be happy."

Lila raised an eyebrow at him, letting him know he pushed her boundaries. But after a split second of hesitation, she slid her arms above her head and gripped the edge of the pillow. Her compliance touched something deep in him.

"Good girl. I want to spend some time on this gorgeous body, and your hands just make me lose my focus. Close your eyes and don't move your hands. I promise you'll be rewarded for your obedience."

Lila watched him for another second before letting her eyes flutter closed. Fuck yeah. Her trust humbled him. She lay defenseless before him, eyes closed and breasts thrust toward him like a submissive sacrifice and his dick, which was as hard as a steel pipe, twitched painfully in his pants.

"This is gonna be fun."

Chapter Thirty-One

With her vision blocked and arms above her head, Lila felt exposed and vulnerable. It was a foreign sensation. She wasn't sure she had ever trusted a lover enough to be at their mercy. A quiver of nerves warred with the excitement in her belly.

"Last rule," he whispered in her ear. She hadn't realized he moved and jumped slightly as his breath swirled over her ear. "No talking. You can moan and you can scream, but no talking until you are ready to beg me to fuck you."

Until she was ready? Hell she felt ready to beg him right now.

"You can't ask me to go faster, can't ask me to go harder, and can't ask me to move left or right. You take what I give you until there is no possible way you can stand not having me inside you. Understand?"

With a nod, she moaned. His words made her sex flood with moisture. He'd barely touched her, yet she was so turned on she felt ready to combust.

"Good girl," he said again.

One large hand splayed over her abdomen, sending warmth through her body. He took his time and slid one palm up her torso, pausing to rest between her breasts. Her nipples ached for his touch. Having his hand so close to them without knowing if or when he'd touch them, was pure torture.

"You're so beautiful, Lila," he whispered.

Lila gasped. His lips hovered above one breast. When he spoke, his heated breath puffed on her nipple. She arched up, her body taking over, making her breasts seek his mouth. Her nipples were hard points of unfulfilled desire. Afraid he'd stop completely, she had to bite her lip to keep from pleading with him to suck her.

"I have this drive, this need to possess you in every way." As Striker spoke, he ran his tongue around one areola, so close to what she needed, but not quite there, just more torture designed to drive her out of her mind. "You're mine, and the fact that another man threatened that, touched you, sets off something dangerous inside of me." The other breast was treated to the same maddening attention.

She let out a low sound, part desire, part frustration, and part need. This was so much more than making love. The things he was saying? He was claiming her, mating with her, letting her know she belonged to him now.

Without warning his mouth clamped down on a nipple and he sucked, hard. After being so turned on, the sensation was almost beyond what she could tolerate. Pleasure so intense it bordered on pain exploded from her breast, and she was helpless to stop the scream that erupted from deep within. His mouth moved to the other side, lips, teeth and tongue worshiping her as she writhed beneath him.

Lila grew wetter by the second. Were she still in control over her thoughts, she may have been embarrassed by the amount of fluid easing between her legs. But, as it was, she focused completely on the delicious sensations that rocketed through her body. Her entire being centered on the twin peaks, and Striker's attention to them.

After what could have been five minutes or an hour, Striker abandoned her breasts, and trailed his mouth back down her body, nipping and sucking along the way. Never had a man spent so much time on her pleasure without thought for himself. When he reached his destination, he lifted each of her thighs, placing them over his shoulders with his head positioned between.

For a few seconds Lila felt nothing, heard nothing, and grew a little nervous. She was wetter than she had ever been in her life, saturated. Maybe it was too much. Maybe he found it unappealing. Then she heard him inhale slowly as though she was a fine wine he wanted to savor.

"Fuck, baby, you smell amazing. You are drenched. Do you have any fucking idea how it makes me feel when I see your body telling me how much you want me? I'm trying to get myself together so I can take my time with you, but you're making it very hard."

She knew how hard it was, she'd felt the evidence against her leg when he'd tormented her breasts. Her mouth opened to make the sassy retort, but at the last second she caught herself and shut it, remaining silent.

"You're being very obedient. I like it."

In the next instant Striker took a long sweeping lick through the folds of her pussy, up to her clit, where he sucked it lightly into his mouth.

That was all it took. Her orgasm slammed into her without warning, like a runaway freight train. Somehow she managed not to scream his name, but she did make a sound that was a cross between a wail and a moan. Unable to keep her arms up any longer, her hands fisted into his hair to pull him closer, or push him away, she wasn't sure.

Striker acted as though he didn't realize she just had an explosive release. Shoving his tongue into her channel he fucked her with his mouth. This time, Lila did scream, she was so sensitive from the previous orgasm that the jabs of his tongue inside her were barely tolerable.

Striker was relentless, giving her no time to recover before he drove her right back up again.

Lila's head thrashed back and forth on the pillow, and she bucked and jerked beneath him, completely out of control. She was seconds from coming again, and wanted him inside her this time. With a cry of need, she yanked Striker's head up by his hair, and met his eyes. He looked wild, and a little out of control as he raised one eyebrow and speared her with a questioning look.

"Fuck me, Striker," she begged. "Please. I need you to fuck me. Now."

He rose. With her legs still over his shoulders, his muscles bunched and flexed, making him look every bit the alpha male he was. He held himself over her, a hand on each side of her head as his shoulders pushed her knees toward her chest. "Position me." His voice was rough and dark.

Immediately, her hand sought him out. Her entire body trembled in anticipation as she wrapped her fingers around his impressive girth. Lila decided Striker needed a bit of his own torture. She squeezed and stroked him, enjoying the feel of the soft skin over his hard length.

"Lila," he rumbled out the warning.

With a sassy smile, Lila guided him to her opening. He wasted no time. Almost before she could register him moving, he impaled her.

"Striker." She whimpered.

"I know, babe, I know." He stilled for a moment, his forehead rested on hers. "You ready, baby?"

"God, yes."

He needed no further prompting. Striker pulled back until he was almost completely out, and then roughly pushed back in. A harsh cry ripped from her mouth. The sound seemed to spurn him on and he plunged in and out of her like a madman.

"There's no going back, Lila. This is it. You'll never have another man."

"I don't want to go back, Striker. There's no man I could ever want as much as I want you."

"I gave you a chance to walk away, to save yourself, and you didn't take it. You're mine now, Lila. This makes you fucking mine," he ground out, never letting up his furious pace. "Say it."

"I'm yours."

"Whose? Who do you belong to Lila?"

"You, Striker! I'm yours, Striker. Oh God," she cried when his hand slid between their bodies and found her clit.

"Damn fucking straight," he said before he captured her mouth in his for a rough kiss that matched the pace of their lovemaking.

"Harder," she managed to say between heaving breaths. She needed to feel his full strength pumping in and out of her.

"Yes ma'am," he quipped, as he forced her knees even farther toward her body, and powered into her, deeper than she thought possible. "Christ, I love you, Lila."

The moment she heard the words ripped from his throat, pleasure crashed in a wave that overwhelmed all her senses. Lila yelled his name over and over again as she came. She curled her fingers into his ass, holding him to her as though she could meld their bodies. Her pussy clamped down on him, and she spasmed and shook for endless minutes. Above her, Striker swore, stiffened, and jerked as orgasm claimed him as well.

Lila sagged into the mattress, spent and sated. Striker collapsed next to her and rolled to his side, tucking her tight against his sweat-dampened skin. They lay silent, each breathing hard for many minutes while their bodies cooled and calmed.

Lila had nearly drifted off to sleep when she felt Striker's hands stroking over her. They skimmed up her ass and snuck around to the front. Wetness, evidence of their lovemaking, coated her thighs and he let out a low groan when his hands encountered it. With slow strokes, he rubbed a finger over the tender flesh between her legs, and her eyes popped open. "Striker, you're still hard."

He chuckled. "Yes, baby, I'm aware."

"How is that even possible after…that."

"I'm pretty much hard around you twenty-four-seven."

Lila smiled and enjoyed his touch until a familiar smell tickled her nose. "Striker, have you been smoking?"

"Smoking? What?"

Lila didn't believe his phony innocent tone for a second, but when he lifted her leg and slid into her from behind, she lost all conscious thought, and climbed toward ecstasy once again.

Chapter Thirty-Two

A buzzer sounded, and the heavily padded players jogged off the turf field for a fifteen-minute halftime. Tonight was the third home game of the high school's football season, and Lila's sports safety and concussion program was in full swing.

She made a habit of attending the home games to answer any questions the coach may have should someone be injured. By mid-season, she hoped he'd feel comfortable performing a basic concussion assessment and be able to make the appropriate recommendations.

"Dr. Emerson, thank you again for the hours of work you've put into our team. The new equipment is wonderful and I feel much more confident handling injuries after studying your pamphlets." Lila looked at the salt and pepper haired coach who approached her, his hand outstretched to shake hers. The evening was warm and sweat coated his brow.

"It's been my pleasure, Coach Reynolds. This is an issue I'm passionate about, so I've been overjoyed at the enthusiastic response to the program." She gave the middle aged coach a warm smile as she grasped his hand. He'd been so receptive to any advice she had to share. At one of their planning meetings he'd mentioned a student athlete who'd graduated last year had developed a seizure disorder after suffering two untreated concussions in one season.

"Looks like you've generated interest from other schools as well. Wouldn't it be great if you could grow this throughout the county?"

Great was exactly what that would be. None of the Crystal Rock Falcons had been injured in tonight's game, which she was grateful for, but a player from the opposing team had slammed head on into another player, and went down hard.

Coach Reynolds had jogged over to assist their coach. He walked them through the concussion assessment that Lila had educated all the coaches at CRHS on, and the guidelines for determining whether a student could return to play.

When the opposing coach requested a copy of the printed information, Reynolds had pointed him in Lila's direction. "I'm meeting with their athletics department next week to start educating them on concussion prevention and management as well as the importance of equipment maintenance and replacement of worn gear."

Excitement zinged through her blood each time she thought about it. Months of hard work were finally paying off, and it seemed like the program was growing, exactly what she'd hoped for when she created it.

"You staying for the second half of the game?" he asked her.

"I'd love to, Coach, but I have another commitment this evening."

"Well it was nice to see you. Enjoy your evening, and your weekend."

"Thank you, Coach Reynolds. Please say hello to your wife for me."

He smiled at her as he sauntered back toward his team. Two sharp toots on his whistle indicated to the players that halftime was almost over.

Lila glanced down at her watch to see how much time she had. Tonight was the third Friday of the month, which meant she'd be attending the mixed martial arts fights the MC hosted. This would be the second time Lila went, and she had to admit she'd loved the first one. Watching Striker in the ring had been an exhilarating experience. By the time he won his match, she had been embarrassed to confess she was fully turned on.

Striker was the epitome of male animal grace when he fought, completely in command of his powerful body. Lila was aware Striker was in amazing physical shape from the many times she'd seen, touched, and tasted his body, but seeing him pushed to his limits was something else entirely. She couldn't keep her hands off him after the last match, and was excited for a repeat performance.

One of the No Prisoners owned a gym on the edge of town, and most fighters in the area used his place to train. The club shut the place down on the third Friday of each month for Friday Night Fights, as the event was called. It was a pretty significant production, with fighters convening from all over the state to participate. Afterward, the MC hosted a party in a big vacant lot behind the gym. The men barbequed and drank while women flocked to them.

Lila stood on her tiptoes and stretched her neck in search of Jester. He was supposed to meet her here, and follow her to the gym. When she didn't see his giant frame towering over the rest of the spectators, she decided to make her way to the parking lot and wait for him.

She'd only taken three steps, when a clammy hand on her arm stopped her progression. "Dr. Emerson, I'm so glad to see you here. I haven't seen you in weeks. I'm so sorry I couldn't be at the last committee meeting. Mother's hands were acting up. You know how her arthritis gets. Would you care to sit with me for the second half of the game?"

Lila rolled her eyes heavenward, and counted to five before she turned around. Earl White was a sweet man, but his clinginess was wearing on her. Each time she saw him, he glued himself to her side, and smothered her with his questions and offers of assistance. She'd politely declined numerous invitations to dinner, and if they persisted, she'd have to use a stronger approach.

"Earl, it's nice to see you. Thank you for the offer, but I'm actually on my way out. I have another engagement." She gave him a polite smile that felt forced, and started to turn back around.

His face hardened, and Lila felt a split second of unease. Each time she turned him down in the past, his face had filled with a deep sadness, and she felt guilty for denting his sensitive ego. Tonight there was no hint of melancholy, but his eyes sparked with anger and his mouth pressed into a firm line. "You're going to see *him* aren't you?" He spat the words through clenched teeth.

Lila sighed. She really hated to do this to him, but perhaps it was time. Maybe if she spelled out her relationship with Striker for Earl, he could finally move on. "If you mean Striker, Earl, then yes. You know I've been dating him for months now."

Earl's expression didn't soften as he stepped closer to her. "It's a mistake, Lila. He's a mistake. You need to stay away from him before something happens to you."

A small shiver coursed through Lila. His words seemed more threat than concern. "Listen, Earl, I'm flattered that you care for me, but maybe I need to make my position perfectly clear. Striker and I are pretty seriously involved. Last week I officially moved in with him. You may not approve, and I apologize if this is blunt, but it's really not your concern."

He leaned forward. He wasn't tall for a man, but at such a close proximity, Lila had to tilt her head back to view his face. "Striker is a criminal, Lila. A lowlife, dirt bag criminal, just like that group of bikers he leads. They are nothing but a bunch of losers who belong in jail, and—"

"Earl! That's enough." Lila put sufficient snap in her voice to stop his rambling. The last thing she wanted was to cause a scene in public, but she wouldn't abide by him speaking to her in such a manner. "You know nothing of our relationship, and I'd appreciate it if you kept your opinions to yourself in the future. All you know about the MC is hearsay and rumors. They have become family to me, so please do not speak ill of them in my presence. I won't tolerate it."

Earl had lost a fair amount of weight, and his skin reflected a grayish pallor that she'd not noticed before. It had only been two weeks since she'd seen him at a committee meeting, but since his campaign to get her to go out with him had ramped up, she tried to avoid him, and hadn't taken a close look at him. He had a sickly appearance. Anemia maybe. Possibly a cardiac issue.

"This is the last time I'll warn you, Lila," Earl ground out.

Where had this outraged man materialized from? Earl was always so meek and nervous, but today he seemed angry beyond reason.

"Is there a problem, Stitch?" The loud voice rumbled from above her head and just behind her. Lila turned and craned her neck farther, to peer up at Jester. He stood directly behind her, hands on his hips and a scowl on his mouth. Lila again had to resist the urge to roll her eyes, this time because she knew Jester was trying to intimidate poor Earl.

She shook her head and narrowed her eyes at Jester. "No, no problem. I was just coming to look for you." She turned back to Earl who stared down at his worn sneakers. He once again had the look of a man beaten down by life. "Enjoy the rest of the game, Mr. White. Please think about what I said."

Without waiting for a response, Lila spun on her heel and looped her arm through Jester's, giving a firm tug toward the parking lot. He didn't budge. When she shifted her gaze back to his face she noticed he still frowned down at Earl. The man may have been a nuisance, but few deserved to be on the receiving end of Jester's ferocious glower. Lila pulled a bit harder this time. "Come on, Jester. I don't want to be late."

The only reason she was able to move his oversized body was because he allowed it. He turned and walked to the parking lot with her, a beefy arm thrown across her shoulders.

"You know, Jester, it's been over two months since the incident with Snake, and he's kept to his part of the deal. Don't you think you guys can lay off the hovering a bit? I can't go anywhere without one of you tailing me. It's cramping my style."

He laughed at her and gave her shoulders a squeeze. "Cramping your style, huh? Hon, you might as well get used to it. I don't think Striker is ever going to forget what happened. You just may have a tail for the rest of your life."

"Lovely." She grumbled. It got old, always having someone follow her around, but she knew Striker had been frantic with worry when Snake took her. If this gave him peace of mind about her safety and security, she'd tolerate it.

"The Grimms aren't our only enemies, Stitch," Jester reminded her.

When they reached her car, she noticed Jester had parked his bike behind her, boxing her in.

"I'll move out of your way then follow you to the gym."

"Okay, just give me a few seconds." Lila took a quick peek around, and, not seeing anyone, she started to shimmy her stretchy maxi skirt down her legs.

Jester's jaw dropped in shock, and he threw an arm up across his eyes. "Jesus, Doc! What the hell are you doing? You can't take your clothes off in front of me. Striker will remove the eyeballs from my head, slowly, with a rusty knife. I thought we were friends!"

Lila cracked up as she drew the Falcon's Football T-shirt over her head, and tossed it in her back seat. "Jester, relax. I have other clothes on underneath. I wasn't going to wear a high school football shirt to the fights. You can open your eyes. I promise I'm not naked."

Jester spread his fingers and peeked through the opening between his pointer and middle finger with one eye. Then he dropped his hands altogether and reached into her car. "Oh, hell no!" he spat out as he stuffed the T-shirt and skirt back in her arms. "Put this back on. You cannot go like that. Your ass is practically showing in that skirt thing, and your boobs are definitely showing."

Lila choked back a laugh as she looked down at her outfit. Sure her black leather skirt would need a map to find her knees, and her red halter showed some cleavage and molded to her body like a second skin. But as far as MC parties went, her outfit was tame. "Jester, you're exaggerating. Besides, every woman I see you with is pretty much wearing little more than underwear. Why are you acting all papa bear?"

"I have a lot of money riding on Striker's match tonight. Once he sees you in that, he won't be able to concentrate for shit. The only thing he'll care about is knocking the teeth out of the men who are staring at you. And, doll? That will be all of them."

"Then I guess you better make sure Striker sees his opponent take a good look at me." Inside, she was almost giddy. This outfit had been chosen with the express purpose of driving Striker crazy. Good to know it would have the desired effect.

Jester opened his mouth to speak, then closed it again. "Hmm, that may not be a bad idea, Stitch."

Lila couldn't help it, she doubled over laughing at the serious look on Jester's face. He just rolled his eyes at her. "Get in the car, wench. You're the one who didn't want to be late."

"Okay, okay. I'm going." Lila held her hands up in surrender after she swiped at the tears brought on by her laughter.

"Know this though, babe. I lose money tonight because of you, there's gonna be hell to pay."

Chapter Thirty-Three

Jester entered the gym with a cardboard box perched on his shoulder. Striker assumed Lila was behind him, but couldn't see her small frame around Jester's massive one. With two fingers in his mouth, Striker blew out a shrill whistle, and raised a hand to wave Jester over.

"You want this on the table, Stitch?" Jester called over his shoulder as they navigated their way around the octagonal ring in the center of the room. Last month, she'd worked with the injured fighters, serving as a medic of sorts. She patched up their bloodied noses and split lips, and determined if anyone required more intensive medical care or a trip to the ER. Lila enjoyed it, so the owner of the gym agreed to make it a regular thing. The box Jester carried was full of bandages, gauze, and whatever additional supplies Lila needed to keep them from falling to pieces.

He spotted Lila before she noticed him, and, holy shit, his woman looked hot. A black leather mini skirt stretched across a firm ass that just begged to be squeezed. On top, a red shirt that might as well have been painted on cupped her breasts, and showed off just a hint of cleavage, enough to remind him what awaited his attention under the fabric, but

267

not enough to be indecent. On her legs were sheer black stockings.

While she was still unaware of his presence, Striker crept over, and pressed her against the nearest padded wall. She let out a startled yelp then smiled when she realized who had her pinned.

"Hey, baby," Striker said as his mouth descended on hers in a searing kiss usually reserved for times when they could get naked as fast as possible.

Lila melted against him, and his brain tuned out everything but the feel of her tongue stroking in his mouth, the way her breasts pressed against his hard chest, and her hands as they glided up his back. He kissed her deeply, and groaned when she tilted her pelvis against him as though seeking to be connected. Another few seconds, and he'd forget they were in public, and rip her clothes off.

"Thank you," Striker whispered against her lips when he ended the kiss.

Her eyes were clouded with desire. "What for?"

Striker nipped at a spot on her neck, right below her ear then smiled against her skin when she shivered in response. She was always so responsive to him.

"Jester called me while he was waiting for you to pull out of the parking lot at the school. He told me what you said to your not so secret admirer. How we were your family, and you wouldn't tolerate him speaking poorly of us."

Red bloomed across her cheeks, and she fisted the soft material at the front of his T-shirt in her small hands. "I wasn't aware he overheard me."

"I know, baby." He continued to whisper words that were only for her ears. Friday night fights were something he loved, but tonight he wished he could be alone with Lila instead. "What you said? I'm not sure how to tell you what it means to know you feel that way."

Cheeks still pink, she smiled at him, and pressed a soft hand over his lips, stilling his words. "I meant it. And I love you. Kiss me again," she whispered before she pulled her hand back.

"Love you too, babe." He leaned in, and recaptured her mouth in a kiss rife with emotion and passion. This woman had come to mean everything to him, and he wasn't always the best at expressing it with words, but he could show her in a thousand ways.

Striker couldn't stop himself from inching his hands up the silken length of her thighs, until they were under her short skirt. When his hands encountered the edge of stockings, what little blood that remained circulating his body shot to his groin.

"Holy fuck, Lila," he rasped out as he tore his mouth from hers. "Are you wearing garters?"

One corner of her mouth lifted into a very seductive grin. "I am. With a matching bra and panties set. I bought them online. Can't very well go lingerie shopping with a guard dog following me everywhere."

"Christ." He ran a hand through his hair as he willed his dick to stand down. "Describe them to me."

"Black. Lace. Tiny. Sinful." She winked at him.

Striker groaned, and banged his forehead against the wall, next to her head. "If I let this guy take me out in the first round we can be going at it in your car in twenty minutes."

Lila giggled next to his ear. The sound made him smile. He loved to hear her laugh. "As romantic as that sounds, Jester would literally kill me if you threw your match."

"Oh, hell no! Are you shittin' me girl?" At Jester's loud exclamation Striker dropped his hands from under her skirt, and whipped his head around.

"Look at him, panting after you already. And garters? Jesus. I warned you, Doc. You lose me money, and we're gonna have a problem." He lowered his voice and continued to mumble to himself. "I knew he'd be panting after her like a damn bitch in heat once he got a glimpse of that outfit. And now, garters? Jesus."

"By the way," Striker said, his voice dropping even lower. "That outfit is smoking hot. One glance around the room, and I counted five assholes begging for a bloody nose. They need to keep their eyes looking elsewhere."

Lila giggled again, and playfully swatted him away. She was pleased he appreciated her efforts. Happiness shone from the wide grin on her face. She lifted her gaze, and their eyes met. A wealth of unspoken emotion passed between them in that moment.

"Oh, baby, I'm sorry. Not much blood running to my brain at the moment. I didn't even ask how the game went."

"It was great! The coach of the opposing team asked if I'd come and educate their athletic staff about my concussion program. Can you believe it? I'm so excited!" Her voice rose with proof of her elation.

Pride swelled deep within Striker. There were so many things he admired about his woman. Her passion for and dedication to the work she did was high on the list. "Of course I can believe it, Lila. You've worked your ass off for this. I won't be surprised if it spreads throughout the entire state."

He loved the bright smile that lit her face. She was proud of herself too, as she should be.

"Don't you have a match to prepare for? Jester's already on my ass about my outfit, if you lose this fight because you were out here instead of warming up, he may ban me from all future fights."

Striker nipped at her bottom lip, swollen from their earlier lip lock. "Jester needs to find his own woman to stare at, though it is hard to look away from you in this getup."

"You better get moving." She placed her hands on his chest and gave a little shove, but he wasn't ready to release her just yet.

"I need a kiss for good luck, babe. I gotta make this a quick match. The faster I pound this guy, the faster I can see what's under this skirt," he said as he bobbed his eyebrows up and down.

With a grin, Lila leaned forward and pressed her mouth to his. He loved the feel of her lips on him, anywhere on him. He swept his tongue into her mouth to deepen the kiss, but pulled back before he was ready to end it.

"Okay, maybe that was a bad idea. You're too fucking sexy babe." He gave her a quick smack on the ass, which drew a sharp laugh. "Walk me to the locker room."

Jester waited just outside the locker room door, a deep frown on his face. He didn't say anything as Striker pushed through the door, but he growled at Lila when she paused in front of him. Striker heard her laugh, followed by, "Jester, stuff it. I'm not scared of you. Relax! Maybe you need to get laid or something."

Striker sunk his teeth into his bottom lip to keep from cracking up at Jester's scoff. Life was pretty good right now. The threat from the Grimms had been eliminated, which meant he could breathe easier about the club's future, and Lila's future. True they'd lost a full-patched member, but he was glad to take care of that problem before it escalated and damaged his family. Now, he had a gorgeous, sexy, smart woman who was as hooked on him as he was her. Shit, all he had to do was beat some ass tonight and life would be damn near perfect.

~ ~ ~ ~

The night couldn't have gone better. Striker won his match in the second round when he sent his opponent crashing to the mat with a killer jab that knocked him out cold. Thankfully, the number of injuries had been minimal through the evening, so Lila was able to view the fights.

It surprised her how much she enjoyed watching the men fight, Striker especially. She'd never voice this to any of the guys, but it seemed like a well-choreographed dance. The way each boxer moved was fascinating, almost beautiful, as they harnessed the power of their bodies. Most fighters wore only shorts when in the ring, giving her an unobstructed view of their toned physiques at work as they fought. These men were amazing physical specimens, and watching their muscles ripple under their skin as they battled their opponent was no hardship.

Striker had a few new bruises, but that was the extent of the damage he sustained. After he won, he'd hopped down from the raised ring, and kissed her silly. Lila loved that he had no reservations about showing affection and claiming her in public, and had gone from being embarrassed to reveling in it. Coming from a background where you had to think about how every action would be perceived by society, she wanted to soak up each spontaneous touch and caress he gave her regardless of who was around to witness it.

The final match had ended about ten minutes ago, and Lila was just finishing up with the winner of that fight. He'd taken a nasty punch to the face that split the skin of his left cheek. Luckily for him it didn't require more than a few butterfly bandages to keep it together. Unfortunately for him, his cheek had swelled to twice its normal size, and turned a dark shade of purple that would stick around for a while.

"Okay, Rex, I'm done. It should heal up nicely, but you'll

be a little scary looking for a week or two," she said with a sympathetic smile for the fighter from a No Prisoners chapter a few hours away in Nevada.

"Thanks, darlin'. Didn't hurt a bit. You got some gentle hands. I can think of a few other uses for them if you're game." He gave her a molten look that probably worked on most women.

Lila laughed, and rolled her eyes at him, noticing Striker approach from the corner of her eye. He was freshly showered, and dressed in jeans and a T-shirt with his No Prisoners cut. He smelled like the masculine scented soap he preferred, and she took a second to enjoy it before she chuckled at the unamused look on his face. He must have overheard Rex's flirting.

Rex raised his hands in surrender as he encountered Striker's murderous glare. "Hey man, I ain't trying to poach your woman. Just paying the Doc a compliment is all."

"All right, you two. Fights are officially over. Behave." Lila said with a smile, confident it was all in good fun.

Striker slung an arm around her shoulders and pulled her close in a possessive manner. "You ready to head out back? I'm starved, and dying for a beer."

"I want to bring all this stuff out to my car first. It's parked out front," she replied indicating the box of excess medical supplies.

"I'll carry it for you if you walk out with me."

"No problem guys," Rex interjected with a wink. "I'll tell everyone to avoid your car for the next...what? Should three minutes be enough?"

Lila snorted out a laugh while Striker flipped Rex off. "Get the fuck out of here before I bust up the rest of your ugly mug."

Lila started for the door with Striker as Rex's laughter

followed them. She loved the banter between all the men. Most people would probably find it crass and vulgar, but it created a dynamic between the MC brothers that she found entertaining.

When she stepped outside, the chill in the air startled Lila. Even after almost a year of living in the desert, the drastic temperature changes from day to night still took her by surprise.

She hadn't tired of the wonder of the night sky. Constant activity in Washington DC was a distraction from noticing the splendor of the starry sky, and when you did notice it, the city lights muted its beauty. Out in the desert, one could stare at the vast spread of twinkling orbs for hours, and Lila had a few times while relaxing on Striker's deck.

In no time, night riding with Striker had become one of her favorite activities. There wasn't any experience that matched the feeling of flying down the highway in the dead of night. The combination of the seemingly endless desert surrounding them, with the infinite starry sky above, and the strong man beneath her arms was a recipe for bliss.

"You coming, babe?" Striker's voice brought her back to earth. He was about twenty feet ahead of her, just a few steps away from the car.

She chuckled to herself, and quickened her steps. "Sorry, hon, I got lost in the sky."

Striker used the key fob to pop her trunk open, and bent to place the box inside. He rose back up and turned toward her. In the next instant shock and fear slammed into Lila in equal measure as Striker gave a cry of pain, and crashed to the ground, his body convulsing as he fell.

What the hell? Lila had just enough time for her medically trained brain to wonder if a blow to the head during his fight caused a seizure when she felt a biting pain on the side of her neck, and a terrible surge of electricity traveled through her body.

Unable to control them, her legs gave out and she rushed toward the ground. She tried with everything she had to reach out her arms and brace the fall, but they wouldn't respond to her commands. Fiery pain coursed through Lila's system, and she thrashed uncontrollably on the way to the asphalt.

Panic set in, fueled by the realization that both she and Striker where completely helpless against whatever threat had reached them. Was it the Grimm Brothers? They'd given their word that the two clubs were square, but could Snake really be trusted to keep his word? Probably not. The last thing Lila remembered before her head hit the ground, and blackness set in, was two old sneakers in her line of sight.

Chapter Thirty-Four

Lila floated through a sea of seemingly endless darkness. Her head ached and her eyes felt like sandbags weighted them down. Trying to clear the cobwebs from her mind, she thought back to the last thing she could recall. Friday Night Fights. It had been a great night, at least the part she remembered. What happened after the fights? Why couldn't she remember going to the party? She wasn't usually enough of a drinker to black out and forget half the night. Was that what she did?

Shivers racked her body, and her brain registered the fact that she was cold. It took a few minutes to sort out the reason, but eventually she figured it out. She was supine on a bed without any blankets, and apparently she was only wearing her underwear. The second that thought ran through her mind the rest of the evening came back to her in an avalanche of fear and horror.

Holy shit! She and Striker had been tased in the gym parking lot, and now she was on a bed somewhere, practically naked. No longer foggy headed, her eyes flew open and she shot up with a gasp as pain sliced through her head. "Oh my God," she cried, panic lacing her voice.

"Baby, hey babe. It's okay. You're okay. Look at me." Striker's voice was a balm to her out of control nerves.

Lila turned and focused in the direction she heard Striker's voice coming from. "Oh my God," she exclaimed again. She attempted to rush to his side, only to be painfully jerked back to the bed when a metal cuff around her wrist halted her motion. "What the fuck?" Her voice was shrill and thready, and she sounded like she was about to lose her shit. It pretty much mirrored how she felt.

"Striker, are you okay? You look awful. What's happening? Where are we?" Lila frantically scanned the room trying to get her bearings.

They appeared to be in a small bedroom, in a house or apartment she wasn't sure. A twin size bed with an iron headboard was pushed into one corner, with a nightstand next to it. Lila's right arm was handcuffed to an iron rung, and allowed her to stand, but not tread more than two steps from the bed. A table lamp on the nightstand provided the only dim lighting in the room. Across from the bed was a tall chest of drawers, and in front of that was a chair that held Striker.

Her heart squeezed with fear as she took in the sight of him. He was slumped in the chair, bound to it with what had to be yards of duct tape woven around his midsection multiple times. His arms and legs were each secured to the armrests and legs of the chair. His head bobbed to the side as he fought to remain conscious. Jesus, someone had beaten the shit out of him. Blood tracked from his mouth, and his face had extensive bruising, but what worried her were injuries she couldn't see.

Lila was trained to work in high stress and crisis situations. She shoved her panic down and drew on that training, with a promise to herself that she could freak out like crazy later on.

In a voice that impressed her for its calm sound she said, "Tell me about your injuries, Striker. Did you lose consciousness at all?"

A small smile graced his bleeding mouth. "That's my girl. He went at me with that bat over there." He tilted his head toward the door where a bat rested in the corner. "Mostly bruises I think, maybe a few cracked ribs, but I'm feeling pretty dizzy, like I'm not going to be conscious for very much longer."

This was not good. He needed to get to a hospital. "You may be losing blood internally. Are you in pain?"

He snorted in response to that question. "Yes. It's hard to isolate because he wailed on me in multiple spots, but most of the pain is on the left side of my torso."

"Okay try not to move much. You need to conserve your strength, plus, if you do have broken ribs, you risk puncturing a lung with excess movement. If we can get out of these restraints do you think you could walk?"

"Not sure, gorgeous. He busted me up pretty good. But I'll sure as hell try."

His calling her gorgeous brought back the shocking fact that she wasn't wearing her clothes. "What happened to my clothes?" She glanced down at her nakedness, unable to keep her voice from wavering with fear. Did this sick asshole do more to her than just remove her clothes?

"No, Lila, he didn't." She looked up sharply, and met Striker's serious gaze as he tapped into her thoughts. "I was awake. He made me watch as he undressed you, but I promise he didn't do more. Though I'm not under the impression that will last, so we have to figure a way out."

"God, I'm so sorry you had to watch that."

"Don't worry about me, baby. Listen, when he comes back do not antagonize him. You do whatever the hell you have to

278

do to stay alive and escape. You hear me?"

Lila nodded at him as she looked around the room for… anything. Trembling from the cold she rattled the chain around her wrist testing its strength. There wasn't any way she was going to break it. "Who is it? A Grimm Brother?"

Just as she asked, the door flew open, and Lila's stomach bottomed out as she recognized their attacker. Earl White stood in the doorway and stared at her. She wished she'd paid more attention to the unease she'd felt during their conversation earlier in the evening.

Lila's heart pounded with such fast fury, she almost didn't hear him speak over the drumming sound.

"Dr. Emerson, you're awake."

His oily brown hair stuck out in all directions, his clothes hung off his thinner frame, and she thought again that he had the appearance of a chronically ill person.

What had the hairs on the back of her neck rising was the look in his eye. Lila had experience with mentally ill patients in the hospital. Patients who had gone off medication and were out of control, having psychotic breaks, but she had never seen a look in someone's eyes quite like the one she encountered now. It was a completely insane look, a look that told her she was in real trouble, because there was no way she could reason with him.

"Where are my clothes?" she croaked, using all her remaining strength to keep the hysteria out of her voice.

"You were dressed like a slut." White's voice was hard as he scolded her, not at all the mild anxious tone she'd come to expect from him. "I got rid of them only to discover you were wearing something even trashier underneath." He shook his head as though disappointed in her. "I left these on though because I didn't want *him* to see you naked." He choked out the reference to Striker as though disgusted by the thought of him. "I had planned to cover you back up, but there really isn't much point since we will be together soon."

Oh God. He was totally crazy. Was he planning to rape her in front of Striker? It would kill him. She could not let that happen. She needed to keep him talking while she developed a plan. "Why are we here? Why take both of us if it's me you want?"

Striker didn't look good. His head lolled to one side, and his eyelids repeatedly fluttered closed only to jerk back open as he fought to remain awake. Her question to Earl seemed to put a little fire back in Striker, and he glared at her. He'd asked her not to antagonize Earl, but she had to keep him talking.

Earl moved farther into the room, close to Lila. Her skin crawled as he reached out a hand and stroked it down her arm. She clenched her jaw until it ached to keep the scream inside her throat. She kept her focus on Striker. He was her touchstone to remain calm. Fury shone in his eyes and he seemed more alert now.

"I wanted to make sure he couldn't come after you of course. I don't know why you're with him. I tried to warn you, sent you texts, tried to scare you with my car." He shook his head and his shoulders slumped. "Didn't work. It just drove you to him. I'm sorry for that. When it became obvious you would just run to him with any threat, I knew I needed a new approach. I joined your committee to be close to you. My hope was that I could convince you to leave him, but you do nothing but sing his praises."

"Wait. What?" she asked in shock. "That was you? All of it? What about the man who attacked me at the hospital?" No wonder there had only been a few texts. They had mistakenly thought the threat left with the Grimms, when in reality Earl had simply changed his tactics.

Mr. White frowned. "I didn't attack you! I was trying to save you! To show you how dangerous it was to be a whore for a motorcycle club!"

"But the man had a Grimm Brothers tattoo." Lila's head spun as she looked down at Earl's hands. They were bare, no tattoos marred the skin.

"Tattoo parlor in Vegas airbrushed it on for me. They'd never heard of the Grimm Brothers. It scrubbed right off with alcohol. Smart huh?"

Lila's head spun as she listened to his explanations. The entire time the threat had been from this man? Because of the timing, they'd never even considered it could be anyone but the Grimms.

Lila glanced back to Striker. Her head pounded, and she was starting to feel a little woozy, but one look at him kept her going. She needed to figure out a way to get them both out of here. Striker needed medical attention, and fast. He had remained quiet, most likely thinking Earl would get angry if he spoke.

"Don't look at him!" Earl's voice rose, taking on a shrill quality. "What are you even doing with trash like him? I would have given you everything, done anything for you."

Suddenly Lila knew what she had to do. Bile rose at the thought of it, but she forced it down. It was the only way they stood a chance of escaping. With a shaky breath she sent Striker a look that she hoped conveyed how sorry she was for what he was about to witness. God, she needed to pull this off.

Lila forced her body to relax though Earl still had a hand on her shoulder. "Why do you think I'm with him? I had no idea who was sending those messages, and I was terrified. I needed protection."

A look of confusion crossed his face. "But I sent the notes because you went off with them in the middle of the night."

How long had this man been spying on her? "Of course I did," she said trying to sound incredulous. "Bikers showed up at my house in the middle of the night. I was terrified of what would happen if I didn't go along with them. I got sucked in from there. Do you know what it's like for an ol' lady? We're property. I had no choice. I've been living in fear for months now."

Striker wasn't buying this, was he? He looked furious. His hands gripped the armrests of the chair so hard, his white knuckles glowed in the dim light of the room. Sitting helplessly by while she was forced to deal with the situation had to be killing him.

Earl's gaze softened a fraction, and his hand stroked up and down her arm in what he must have thought was a soothing caress. In reality her skin crawled with revulsion under his fingertips.

"Oh, Lila, I screwed up. I'm so sorry." He sounded truly upset by the thought of her being with the No Prisoners against her will. "Here I was trying to get you away from them, and my actions drove you right to them. Can you ever forgive me?"

Was he for real? Forgive him? She wanted to drive a knife through his skull. "Of course I forgive you, Earl." She remembered something about using a person's name when in a crisis situation to make them feel validated and to humanize them. Maybe it came from a movie, but it didn't matter now. "I'm glad you're calling me Lila. You're usually so formal with me and this is nice."

He smiled, revealing yellowed teeth, and continued to touch her, moving his hand to rub her back. "I'm so glad you aren't mad at me, Lila. I've been so worried about you."

He was just crazy enough that her plan seemed to be working. As his touch grew bolder Lila's legs started to quake. She slammed her knees back to keep them from collapsing under her, and gave him a smile she hoped was sexy. "Thank you, Earl, for caring about me."

He stepped even closer, and wrapped both arms around her in a tight embrace. Lila gagged as evidence of his arousal rubbed against her naked belly. She lifted her shaking arms, and attempted to return the hug. "I'd like to be with you, Earl, but how can I touch you properly when I'm restrained?"

He pulled back a bit to study her face. His pupils were dilated wide and beads of sweat dotted his forehead. "I really want to trust you, Lila. I want to release you so we can be together. Do you promise you won't try to leave?"

She forced her lips to turn up in what she hoped was a sweet smile, and placed her free hand on his pale cheek. "Yes, Earl. I owe you now, for getting me away from the motorcycle club. I'm in your debt."

He considered her for a second, and she stood still, afraid to do anything that might indicate her deception. Earl reached in his pocket and fished out a key.

Lila's opposite hand flew to her sore wrist after he unlocked the cuff. She rubbed the bruised skin and fought to be smart and stick to her plan. The sense of relief at being unshackled was overwhelming. They had a shot now. She just needed to get Earl out of the picture.

Earl placed his arms around her again, and smoothed his hands up her back. Lila clenched her fists at her sides and closed her eyes. There was only so far she could take this, and despite what her brain commanded, her arms just wouldn't raise to return the embrace. When she opened her eyes, she locked gazes with Striker over Earl's shoulder. He gave her a small nod, and the minute gesture of approval fueled her, giving her the fortitude to continue.

Earl's hands stilled on her back, and he pressed a kiss to her neck. A shudder of loathing wracked her small frame, and she prayed he would interpret it as arousal. With her eyes on Striker, the only thing keeping her from breaking down, Lila forced a small moan from her lips in attempt to keep Earl distracted. She wanted him engrossed in his task so he wouldn't be aware when she made a move.

The muscles in Lila's arms and legs ached from the force required to remain still. She endured Earl's lips on her neck as he landed kisses along the column of her throat. He was sweating and she felt the clammy moisture against her skin. With a groan, he ground his hardness against her hip, and slowly trailed his hands around her body. When they closed over her breasts, Lila reached her limit.

In a lightning quick move, Lila lifted her knee, and rammed it into Earl's groin. He let out a tortured wail, and his hands fell from her body to clutch between his legs. The handcuff key, tumbled from his hand to the ground. Lila took advantage of his distraction, and shoved him toward the bed with all her strength. She grabbed for the dangling handcuff, and slapped it around his wrist with a satisfying click.

"The key." Striker's voice sounded weak and riddled with pain.

Lila spotted it on the floor, and bent to retrieve it. She had no idea where to stash it on her body so she threw it through the open door and out into the hallway. For exactly three seconds, Lila felt triumphant. Then she realized Earl could still reach her.

A cry of pain was ripped from her throat and fire lanced through her scalp. Earl fisted her hair in his free hand, and yanked her back. She cried out again as he ruthlessly backhanded her across the face, splitting her lip. It felt as though her entire face had burst wide open. Tears pricked her eyes, and she rose on the balls of her feet in an attempt to relieve some of the pain in her scalp.

~ ~ ~ ~

Striker feared he didn't have long before he passed out. The room swam before his eyes, and his body felt wrecked. A clock on the nightstand read two twenty-seven, or at least he thought that's what the blurry numbers displayed. Just four and a half hours since this fucker snatched them at the gym. Lila fell to the ground seconds after he did, and before he'd regained control over his useless muscles, Earl had stuck a needle filled with God knows what into his neck.

He'd woken up forty minutes ago when the sounds of Earl struggling to remove Lila's clothing crashed through his sedation. Earl had been muttering to himself about how Lila looked like a whore, and what a bad influence the club was on her. Striker screamed every obscenity he could think of at the fucker to draw his attention away from Lila's nearly nude body.

Earl had turned his anger on Striker, punching his face numerous times before he'd grabbed the bat from the corner of the room and did the real damage. Every breath was like a knife to the chest, and he guessed more than one rib was broken. The bat had connected with his stomach a number of times as well, and he worried Lila's prediction of internal bleeding was accurate. His entire body hurt like hell, but he'd done his best to downplay it for Lila's sake. She needed to keep her wits about her. He was helpless to free them, but he wanted to aid her in any way possible.

Now, watching Earl run his hands and mouth over the body he loved, he vowed the man would not survive to see another birthday. Striker would find a way to kill him, slowly if he had the chance.

Striker tried to channel the feelings of impotence into wrath. Lila was amazing, and his heart literally ached at what she had to endure to save them both. He vowed that she would never know another second of fear if they got out of this alive.

She was so strong. Where many women would have panicked and been hysterical, his Lila pulled her shit together, and tried her damnedest to take this fucker down.

Striker fought with everything he had to remain conscious. They would have to move fast if she incapacitated Earl. His respirations increased and his hands gripped the armrests so tightly he thought he might rip them right off as he watched Earl's hands move to Lila's breasts.

He continued to observe, powerless as Earl and Lila struggled for a few minutes. Earl shoved her hard, slamming her fragile body into the wall where he hit her again, this time a full on punch to the midsection. Lila cried out then doubled over, her body heaving as she coughed. He screamed at Earl, but this time Striker wasn't able to distract him.

In order to keep himself sane, Striker committed each thing Earl did to Lila to memory. He planned to do each of those things to Earl once he got his hands on him, only with greater severity.

"You fucking bitch!" Earl screamed in Lila's face. He wrapped his hand around her throat and lifted her off her feet. "I knew you were his fucking whore. I loved you!"

Tears streamed down her face, and she made a horrible choking sound. Earl still held her by the throat and her face turned an alarming shade of purple, but she continued to fight back. Reaching forward she clawed at his face, leaving a rake of fingernail scratches down his cheek. With a loud roar Earl threw her across the room. Her small body crashed into the dresser before it crumpled to the ground at Striker's feet.

"Lila!" Striker shouted. He struggled against the tape that bound him to the chair, ignoring the searing pain in his gut. Black spots swam in front of his vision, but he ignored that as well.

Lila coughed, and gulped air from her position on the floor. The one thing they had going for them was that she was now out of Earl's reach.

Earl started toward them, dragging the bed with him, his shackled hand wrapped around the iron rung. Where was his strength coming from? It could only be born of rage and insanity.

"Get up, Lila," Striker ordered. He blinked his eyes in rapid succession, trying make the room stand still.

Lila scrambled to her feet still hacking out a cough each time she tried to suck in a breath. She swayed a bit, and braced herself against the chair Striker was tied to. Earl drew closer, and screamed vulgarities at her as he advanced.

"The bat, babe. Get the bat," he whispered. Earl wouldn't hear over his own screams.

Their eyes met, and she nodded then hurried to the corner on the other side of the chair, where the bat rested against the wall. Striker thought she moved with a slight limp, but didn't have time to consider it further.

Lila grabbed the bat with both hands, her face a mask of agony, streaked with tears and black eye makeup. A loud battle cry erupted and she swung the bat, slamming it into Earl's head with a crack that would have made Mickey Mantle proud. The man collapsed to the ground in a heap and the bat clattered to the floor next to him.

Lila rushed to Striker's side. She knelt in front of him, and swiped her tears away even as new ones fell. With trembling hands, she reached forward and tugged at the tape around his forearms in a fruitless attempt to free him. "God, Striker, he used so much tape. It's going to take me forever to get it off. What if he wakes up?" Her voice was harsh, ravaged by the pressure Earl had exerted on her throat.

"Look at me, Lila," he commanded as he gazed down at her fear-filled face.

Lila looked up from the floor at his feet.

Her chocolate eyes gutted him. Terror, remorse, shame, and guilt stared up at him. All things he would have to help her battle once this was over. There was simply no time to address it now. "You did it, baby. He's down, and we can get out of here. There's a knife in my left boot."

She gave him a tiny smile. "I forgot about that." Lila pulled out the military style knife he always kept in his boot. More than once she'd teased him about it. Not wasting any more time, Lila sawed through the tape around his arms first, and in seconds he was free.

Before Lila moved down to his feet, Striker grabbed her face with both hands and drew it to his own. He pressed their lips together in a firm kiss. Both their mouths were bleeding and he didn't want to cause her any further pain, but he needed to feel her for just a moment. "Let's get out of here, baby. I'm not going to last much longer."

Lila pulled herself together, and liberated his legs and trunk from the chair. He rotated his wrists and ankles to get the blood flowing as renewed pain flooded his system. Shit, that hurt like a son of a bitch.

"Can you walk?" she asked.

"I think so. I may need to lean on you a bit, but first you need to find something to cover up with."

She peered down at herself, clad only in her lingerie.

"Shit, I completely forgot." She looked around as though searching for her clothes.

"They aren't here. I think he destroyed them. Grab something from that dresser."

A look of panic crossed her face, and she shook her head vigorously. "No! I can't put something of his on my body. I can't do it."

She sounded close to the edge, so Striker worked to keep his voice calm. "It's all right, baby. Help me get my cut off then you can take my sweatshirt. Just unzip it and slide it off me."

She shook her head again.

"I'll be fine Lila, I promise you. We need to roll before he comes around."

She moved toward him, and helped ease him out of his cut. Then, slowly, she worked the sweatshirt down his arms. They didn't really have the time to waste, but she was trying not to hurt him, and not to freak out, so he didn't rush her.

Once it was off, she slipped it over her own body. Striker leaned forward and fumbled with the zipper but was able to close the sweatshirt for her. It was long enough to cover her ass, but the garters and stockings were still visible. It would have to do. He didn't have a clue where her shoes were, but she could get by without them.

He slipped his cut back on, then struggled to stand and take a step forward. The world spun and he almost fell on his face, but Lila was there to take his weight. With Lila's arm around his waist, they hobbled into the hallway.

"I think he drove us here in your car." Striker gasped as his ribs screamed in pain. "Look, there on the counter." He pointed to a kitchen counter about fifteen feet away. "I think those are your keys."

"Oh thank God." Lila swiped the keys from the counter

and they staggered their way toward the exit. "Where the hell are we? I don't see a phone, and you need a hospital. Who knows where our cells are." Her voice sounded rough and raw, and he knew her throat had to be sore.

"Earl told me exactly where we are. Bastard bragged all about how he planned this, and how we're actually really close to the gym. Go there. Jester and Hook will take care of everything and get us to the hospital. You hit your head on the concrete and passed out. You shouldn't be driving at all. This road ends at a cross in about a mile. Take a right and the gym is about a mile and a half down on the left."

They struggled through the front door, and out into the night. It was cold, and next to him Lila trembled from the chill. The house they were in was small, a typical one story desert dwelling. There weren't any others on this road, at least not that they could see in the black of night.

Striker stumbled, and a groan of pain escaped Lila as his weight on her increased. "Sorry, babe. I think I'm going to pass out."

They were at the car, and instead of answering, Lila leaned him against it as she opened the rear door. She helped ease him inside, and encouraged him to lie down. "I need you to try and stay awake Striker. Talk to me as I drive."

He mumbled something in reply, and heard the car door slam as the world went black.

Chapter Thirty-Five

Fuck, fuck, fuck. This was not good. Striker needed to get to the hospital, and fast. Lila's entire body throbbed in pain. She hadn't said anything, but she was dizzy and her head pounded. There was a good chance she'd lose consciousness as well.

She'd never be able to drive all the way to the hospital. The best option was to do what Striker suggested, and drive back to the gym. The party should still be going strong, and his brothers would take care of them.

Petrified that Earl might wake up at any moment, Lila moved as fast as her aching body allowed. Her throat was on fire, her ribs throbbed from where they'd crashed against the dresser, and she thought her ankle was sprained. She worked not to fall into hysterics. That could come later.

Gingerly, she climbed into the driver's seat, locked the doors, started the car, and pulled out onto the dark road. For the first time since she woke up in hell, Lila had confidence they would make it. Earl was back in the house, hopefully still cuffed to the bed, and they'd made it out alive.

The MC would never call the cops on him, preferring to handle him on their own. She tried to feel guilty about that, but it didn't come.

Striker was right. The gym was very close, and within minutes it came into view. Lila sobbed in relief as the car drew closer to it. With a hard jerk of the steering wheel, she flew into the parking lot, and around the back of the building where the party was still going full blast. Lila laid on the horn to attract as much attention as possible. Tears blocked her vision, and she slammed the car in park.

With the last of her strength, she shoved the door open, and stumbled out only to look up and glimpse about fifty stunned bikers staring at her, and no less than ten weapons trained on her. "Help," she said weakly, swaying on her feet.

"Holy fucking shit! Lila? Put your weapons away! What the fuck happened to you?"

She glanced up again. Jester sprinted toward her, and she collapsed to her knees, loud sobs echoing through the quiet lot. She couldn't imagine what they all thought of her right now as she bawled on the ground bleeding, covered in bruises and wearing nothing but a sweatshirt and some lingerie.

Jester reached her in seconds, and scooped her into his arms where he cradled her against his enormous chest.

"Striker's in the back seat," she choked out between sobs. "He needs help immediately. I need some too. That crazy man who was my patient at the hospital, Earl White, took us from the parking lot. He was behind everything, the Grimms didn't do a thing." She turned her face, and buried it in Jester's shirt as the tears flowed.

"Fuck," Jester bit out. "Okay, honey, I've got you. You're safe now. Hook, I'm gonna drive Lila's car to the hospital. Follow us with a few other guys, and let Shiv know what's going on."

Hook nodded and sprang into action, motioning for others

to join him as he pulled out his phone.

Jester carried Lila around to the passenger side of her idling car. He tried to be gentle, but she was unable to stifle a whimper of pain when he placed her on the soft leather seat.

"Sorry, honey," Jester said with a grimace.

"I'm all right. Just go. We need to get Striker there fast," she rasped.

Lila rested her head back against the seat, and closed her eyes as she tried to stem the onslaught of tears. Now that she'd given into them, she couldn't turn them off. Jester folded his large body in to her little car, but she didn't react.

The continuous rumble of the car as he sped toward the hospital had a calming effect. When some of the fear finally ebbed from her system, other unpleasant sensations rushed in. Her head throbbed and her throat was on fire. A sharp, stabbing pain hit her midsection every time she took a breath and her ankle was swelling.

Striker remained quiet, in the same position she placed him in, sprawled across the back seat. Fear for him was eating at her. What would she do if something happened to him?

Lila forced those thoughts from her mind, and attempted to reposition her body in the seat, but pain caused her to gasp and remain as she was. Violent shivers racked her body. Shock was setting in. Jester noticed and cranked up the heat in the car before he reached out and folded her trembling hand in his much larger one.

She opened her eyes, and sent him a grateful smile. Jester gave her hand a squeeze as his voice permeated the quiet car. "I'm not going to make you tell me everything now, but I have a few important questions. You think you can answer them? Your voice sounds awful."

Lila nodded. "What do you want to know?"

Jester shot her a quick glance, before returning his eyes to the road. They flew down the highway at least thirty miles an hour above the speed limit. Police attention would be very unwelcome.

"Do we have a body to deal with?"

The question startled her. Since leaving the house, she hadn't given a thought to Earl White, but now she understood he needed to be dealt with. Lila assumed they wouldn't let him live, unless he'd managed to escape. The idea had dread racing up her spine so she pushed it aside. Perhaps later, when the dust settled, guilt and shame for her part in the retaliation would come, but now, with the taste of terror still lingering, in her mouth she wanted him to pay.

"A live body. He held us in a house, very close to the gym actually, only one about a mile down on Turtle Rock Way."

Jester nodded. "I know where that is."

"When we left he was handcuffed to a bed, unconscious, but I think alive."

Jester dug out his phone and relayed the information to someone, instructing him to head to the house, pick up the *motherfucker,* and stash him at the warehouse. The warehouse? Was that the building she'd gone to with Striker some months ago when Kenny had been stabbed? It felt like a lifetime had passed since then.

Jester hung up and took his eyes off the road for a beat to glance at her. "Hang in there, baby doll, we'll be there in five. I hate to ask this, but were you raped, Lila?"

The blunt question startled her. "Geez Jester, dive right in why don't you. No, I wasn't raped. Why did you assume that?"

Glancing at her quickly he said, "You're only wearing Striker's sweatshirt, Doc."

She looked down, yet again having completely forgotten

about her state of undress. No wonder she was freezing. "Shit, I keep forgetting." She turned away, unable to meet Jester's eye. "I, um, woke up handcuffed to a bed in my under things. He took off my clothes to torture Striker, but Striker said he didn't...you know." Her face flamed. It must have been beet red. Luckily it was dark in the car, and there was no way she would tell him how she came on to Earl to save them. She hadn't processed that herself yet.

"Good. Last thing for now, there's no way to avoid cops getting wind of this after you two show up at the hospital. Tell them you don't know who took you, act a little confused. Stall answering any other questions for now. We'll come up a plausible story for you. Got me?"

There was no point in playing dumb. This was how it was done in their world, a world she'd willingly joined. She'd play by their rules. "I got it."

They pulled up to the emergency room, and Jester jumped out of the car with orders for her to stay put until he got help. They made it. The world outside the car became fuzzy as Lila saw the ER doors whir open, and people rush toward the car. Certain that help had arrived for both Striker and her, Lila finally gave into the oblivion that had been threatening to pull her under.

~ ~ ~ ~

Striker did not come to slowly. He awoke with a jolt as his body was assaulted by pain, and his mind was flooded with terrifying memories. His eyes shot open and darted around the room immediately assessing for danger and seeking out Lila. Where the hell was she? Where was he? Had they made it to the gym?

He struggled to sit up only to let out a groan when his ribs screamed in protest.

"Easy there, brother. The docs did a lot of work to make

sure your ass stayed alive, so don't go fucking it all up." Striker turned his head to the right with a start as Hook's voice filled the room.

Hook was seated in a vinyl recliner next to the head of Striker's bed. He looked tired. How long had Hook been sitting there?

Striker's mouth felt like it had been blasted with hot, dry air for hours. "Lila?" he managed to grate out.

"She's safe brother. They kept her overnight to monitor her since she blacked out, but she's in better shape than you are."

Striker closed his eyes and leaned back against the bed. The relief was staggering. He didn't have a clue what was going on with his own body, but he was alive, and Hook didn't look worried, so he figured he'd stay alive.

"Listen, Striker. Now that you're awake the cops will be in soon. We're pinning all this shit on Rock. Blamed drugs, said he snatched Lila because we were kickin' him out of the club. We busted up his house to make it look like it happened there, and we scoured the other house. Story is he snatched her after the fights. Lila was able to free herself and call you when he stepped out for a while. You came for her, fought with Rock, and rescued Lila. Rock took off."

It was a good story. No one would ever find Rock's body, the Grimms would make sure of that. They could easily say he split to avoid the No Prisoners' wrath after snatching Lila.

"Your girl did good, man," Hook continued. "She had the cops eating out of her hand. Stuck to the story beautifully. Jester stayed with her, acting all mamma bear." He chuckled and shook his head. "Who knew he had such maternal instincts."

"She seem okay?" He didn't mean physically.

"Something ain't right. That's why Jest won't leave her

alone. Physically she's busted up, but nothing serious. Something seems off emotionally. She's real skittish." Hook had questions in his eyes. The guys must be dying to know exactly what happened in that house.

Striker closed his eyes as unpleasant memories assailed him. Lila had saved both their asses, but she'd paid for it. Watching her endure that pervert's hands on her body sickened him. The shattered look on her beautiful face when she awoke and realized she wasn't wearing any clothes was the same look she got when that piece of shit pawed at her. Striker knew it was a scene that would haunt his dreams for years. She was his woman. It was his job to protect her, and he'd been unable to do a damn thing beyond watch the horror unfold.

Everything she'd said to Earl was bullshit, and he knew it. Not for one second did he think she was with him because she was trapped. But he knew her well, and she'd worry he now doubted her.

Hook must have been growing impatient waiting for answers because he prodded Striker along. "She showed up at the gym wearing your hoodie, and not much else."

Striker swallowed down his disgust, and explained to Hook how Earl White ambushed them in the parking lot with his Taser, and filled him in on the rest of the story. When he got to the part where Lila saved them, he almost couldn't get the words out.

"You good, brother?" Hook asked.

It was hard for Striker to look at Hook while he reiterated the tale. The feelings of anger and inadequacy were too great. He nodded, and continued the story, staring straight ahead.

"Lila was fuckin' incredible. She played him like a fuckin' violin. Told him she was only with me out of fear, made him

feel like her savior. He fell for it hard, and uncuffed her."
Striker paused. He needed a minute to get himself in check
before he continued. For some reason saying it out loud was
worse than reliving it in his head. "She gave him what he
wanted. Came on to him, let him put his filthy hands all over
her. When he was distracted, she sent his balls up to his
tonsils."

He finished telling Hook the story, at least up until he
passed out. By the time he finished Hook looked almost as
irate as Striker felt.

Eyes narrowed, lips pressed together in an expression of
anger, and fists clenched, Hook leaned forward and spoke in
a low voice. "He was still at the house. Gumby took some of
the guys to check it out. They moved him to the warehouse.
Prospects are babysitting him until you're out of here."

Striker finally looked at him. Immense satisfaction welled
inside him. He was surprised. He'd assumed Earl would have
escaped somehow by the time anyone went back to check out
the house. This time around he would enjoy the moments
spent with Earl. The same couldn't be said for the other man
however. In fact, Striker could guarantee Earl would not fare
well in their next meeting.

Hook leaned back in his chair. "Did some digging. You
know how Acer is with computers. Not sure what he hacked,
but turns out our buddy Earl has a naughty past. Multiple
restraining orders against him. He was charged with
kidnapping, rape, and the murder of a twenty-year-old girl
three years ago in Mississippi. Case was open and shut. Some
sort of error occurred during the trial, and a mistrial was
declared. Bastard got off with nothing and moved here to
start over."

"Jesus." Striker ran a hand through his hair, possibly the
only part of his body that wasn't screaming in pain. He

should probably take something for it, but wanted to be fully alert when he saw Lila.

The conversation with Hook came to an abrupt halt when a sharp knock on the door grabbed their attention. Without waiting for an invitation the door opened, and Jester came through, pushing Lila in a wheelchair. She looked exhausted, dark rings rimmed each bloodshot eye. His heart squeezed painfully with the knowledge that he'd been unconscious while she dealt with the aftermath of their nightmare.

She still wore his sweatshirt, but someone had given her a pair of scrub pants to cover up her exposed lower half. A bulky boot encased her right ankle, and he assumed that was the reason for the wheelchair. Her poor face was a colorful mess, and her neck looked raw and bruised as well. But she was alive, and she'd never looked more beautiful.

Jester looked tired as well, and Striker was immensely grateful for his care of Lila. His loyal brother had stayed with her in his place the entire time.

Hook rose and pushed his chair into the corner of the room so Jester could steer Lila right next to the bed. He lowered the bedrail so she could reach Striker. With a nod to Striker, he and Jester quietly left the room, allowing them a few moments of privacy. It wouldn't last. The police would arrive any moment for his statement, and a nurse or doctor was bound to check in soon, but he was relieved to have a few minutes alone with her.

"Hey, baby," was all he said.

She reached out and slipped her small hand into his. Even after everything she'd been through, her skin felt baby soft and just that simple touch grounded him. Lila gifted him with a small smile probably meant to pacify him, however, it didn't reach her eyes. "I'm fine, Striker. Nothing that won't heal."

He wasn't fooled by her attempt at levity. "Lila, I'm so sorry you had to—"

"Striker, it's done. We're alive, and will both heal up just fine. No point in rehashing it," she said with another one of those fake smiles.

Striker wanted to pursue this further, but as predicted there was a knock at the door. His nurse bustled in with a syringe, and a stern lecture about the importance of taking pain medication in these early days. Deeper conversation with Lila was put on the back burner, and unfortunately that's were it stayed for the next few days, as they weren't able to get another moment alone.

Chapter Thirty-Six

Striker stayed in the hospital for three nights before he was discharged with a long list of instructions, including no motorcycle riding for six weeks. Lila almost laughed out loud when the nurse broke the news to him. There wasn't a chance in hell of keeping him off his bike for six weeks, but she supposed they'd cross that bridge when he felt better.

Overall, he was very lucky, they both were. She got off with a mild concussion, a severely sprained ankle that was now in a clunky boot, and myriad colorful bruises. Striker's injuries included several rib fractures, major bruising over much of his body, and a lacerated spleen. The internal bleeding from the injured spleen was what caused him to lose consciousness, and required surgery to be repaired.

While he was monitored for a few days in the hospital, Lila remained glued to his side. She was tired and sore, but refused to go home until he was released. From a medical perspective Striker was healing well, and completely out of danger, a fact she understood, but still she couldn't bear to be away from him.

Outwardly, Lila was confident her smiling facade looked believable. Inside, however, she was a mess. Each time her eyes closed, images of Earl's psychotic face flashed, and the sensation of his clammy hands on her body made her feel sick once again.

Lila replayed the instant she woke up, and realized her clothes were missing again and again. The most upsetting factor was the inability to forget the moment she noticed Striker duct taped to the chair, slumped over and beaten. She had barely slept in the three days since it all happened, and the strain of fatigue was starting to show.

Striker seemed unaware that she was so close to a breakdown, and for that she was thankful. His primary focus needed to be on rest and recuperation, not worrying about when she would fall apart.

Since he awoke in the hospital, they'd had about a total of five minutes alone. Police detectives came by multiple times, nurses and doctors zipped in and out of the room all day, and his club brothers or her coworkers were a constant presence. It was for the best, and kept her from having enough solitary time to really delve into what happened and risk losing her shit.

One question plagued Lila's mind, a question Striker could answer, but she hadn't voiced it yet. Partly because they didn't have a second alone, and partly because she knew bringing her concerns to light would cause her to give into the fear and push her over the edge into a meltdown. Where was Earl? Was he out there, possibly still a threat to them? Or had someone gone to the house and killed him? She needed to know before she could relax with the knowledge that the ordeal was truly over.

They were finally home, having arrived about two hours ago. Marcie had stocked the refrigerator and prepared a few meals for them, which Lila greatly appreciated. The thought of grocery shopping in public or standing in the kitchen to cook was not one she wanted to entertain.

Hook and Jester had driven them home from the hospital, and stayed until they were satisfied the two walking wounded could manage on their own. Thankfully, Lila was allowed to stand and walk around in her bulky ankle boot because there was no way she would have wanted to be hobbling around on crutches.

Now that their friends were gone, Lila hid in the bedroom, in hopes of avoiding the conversation they needed to have. Unaccustomed to being a coward, Lila gave herself a mental scolding and emerged from the room. She limped down the hallway in search of Striker.

Lila found him on the couch, his feet propped on the coffee table, head tilted back, and eyes closed. On his bottom half were a pair of gray fleece sweat pants, one of Lila's favorites. He looked so sexy in them when he roamed around the house barefoot and shirtless. Now, however, a plain black T-shirt covered his bruised and battered torso.

A coffee mug sat on the table, and Lila had a sneaking suspicion it wasn't full of coffee, or at least not coffee by itself. The men seemed to think the instruction of not drinking while taking pain medication was more of a suggestion than an order.

For now, Striker appeared to be asleep. Lila made her way to the couch as quietly as possible for someone with a large plastic boot, hoping to get the mug and return it to the kitchen.

As she bent to retrieve the mug, a hand closed over her wrist, gentle, but with intent, and she nearly jumped out of her skin. Since that terrible night, she'd been far too jittery.

"Baby, sit down. You know you shouldn't be on that foot so much."

Lila peered over her shoulder at Striker, and gave him

what she hoped was a convincing and cheerful smile. "I was just going to share your *coffee*," she said, stressing the word to make sure he knew she was on to him.

He ignored her admonishment, and tugged on her wrist. The boot impaired her balance, so she tumbled to the couch and landed with a soft bounce. When she was settled with her own feet resting on the coffee table, next to his, he placed a finger under her chin, and turned her face toward him, assessing her with his gaze.

He didn't say anything, and after a few seconds Lila squirmed under his penetrating glare. "What is it, Striker?"

"I want you to stop, Lila," he said stroking a finger down her black-and-blue cheek.

She knew exactly what he meant, but wasn't sure she could go there yet so she played dumb. "Stop what? Am I hurting you?"

"Lila." His tone held a warning that he saw right through her phony act. "You don't need to act like things are wonderful for my sake. I was there, and I know exactly what you went through. Let go, baby. I'm here, and you're safe now. You know, I really never thought this existed, but I love you, Lila. It's deep baby, all the way in here." He slid her hand under his shirt and pressed her open palm to his chest, over his heart. The warmth of his skin and steady thrum of his heartbeat reassured her. "Let me do my job of loving you."

He leaned close and gave her a gentle kiss, sliding his hand into her hair to hold her in place. Her hand remained on his chest and the rhythm of his heart picked up the instant their lips met.

Striker's tenderness was exactly what she needed for the cup to overflow. Tears flooded her eyes and spilled down her face. When he broke away, a loud sob erupted from where she'd buried her fears, deep within. Before she knew it, she was gasping for breath as she wept and clung his chest. His arms wrapped firmly around her, and he stroked her back, letting her cry it out. Lila was grateful he remained quiet. She couldn't have spoken if she wanted to.

~ ~ ~ ~

Striker's chest tightened as ragged sounds of anguish poured from Lila, but this was exactly what she needed. She'd smiled, and worked so hard to show everyone she was fine from the moment she rolled into his hospital room. But he knew better. He sensed she was clinging by a thread, and he'd just cut it with one swipe.

Striker wasn't sure how much time passed, but after a while, Lila's sobs calmed and her breathing became steady. Unsure if she was asleep, he sat and held her while he rubbed her back in a soothing circular motion. Eventually, she lifted her head and gave him a watery smile. Her bruised face, ravaged from the exhausting cry, still looked beautiful to him.

He drew her head to his shoulder, in no rush to let her go. After witnessing her being groped by a psychopath, he wasn't sure he'd ever let her go again.

When Lila finally spoke, her words were not at all what he expected her to say. "I'm so sorry, Striker. The things I said to him. And I let him touch me. You're the only man who is supposed to touch me, but I let him. And you had to watch." Tears streamed down her face anew, and she lifted her head until he could see her somber eyes. "Please know I didn't mean a single word I said to him."

Christ. Was this what had been plaguing her mind? "Baby, stop." Striker silenced her with a quick hard kiss. "You were incredible. The only reason we got out of there alive is because of your quick thinking. You did exactly what I'd told you, exactly what you had to do to keep us both alive. We can deal with the fall out. I'm more sorry than I can express that you had to endure that, but I don't for one second hold anything that happened in that room against you, nor do I believe a word you told him." He held her face tenderly between his hands, and stared straight into her eyes as he spoke. He needed to make sure she believed him.

"I wanted to die when he touched me. It was so much worse knowing you watched, yet having you there gave me the strength to do what I had to. Does that make any sense?" she sniffed and rested her head back down on his shoulder.

Striker tried to tamp down his reaction. She needed him calm, not murderous. "Watching him and knowing I couldn't help you was the single worst experience of my life. That feeling will be burned into me forever. I promise you, baby, that no one will ever hurt you again."

She burrowed closer, and pressed a gentle kiss to his chest. "What happened to him?"

Striker stiffened. He knew this question would come up eventually. It went against all his instincts to let her in on his plans for Earl, but she had been traumatized by the man and needed closure.

It wasn't a lack of trust. He believed in his soul that Lila would willingly go to jail before she betrayed the club, but he didn't want her to feel in any way responsible for Earl's fate. That was one hundred percent on the motherfucker himself.

"Striker? Is he out there? Do you think he'll come for me again?"

He sat up straighter, and gazed at her abused face, trying to decide how much to tell her.

"I can handle it. Just tell me. I won't freak out, and I won't repeat anything. Ever," she added with conviction.

"I know, baby. I trust you completely. I just don't want you burdened with any more bullshit." He gave her a sad smile. It would take her some time to get over all of this. Hell, it would take him some time as well, and violence had been a part of his life for as long as he could remember.

Lila remained quiet, and Striker couldn't deny her the resolution she needed. She deserved to know that Earl wasn't a threat any longer; she wouldn't need to look over her shoulder every time she stepped out of the house.

"We have him," he stated simply.

A look of confusion crossed her pretty face. "What do you mean?"

"Some of the guys went to the house and he was still there. They've been holding him until I'm well enough to deal with him." He was curious to see what she was going to do with the information, and was more than prepared to convince her Earl's fate was not her responsibility.

"I didn't know it was possible to feel fear like I felt when I woke up in that room. When I saw you tied to that chair... God, Striker. He would have killed you, wouldn't he? If we hadn't escaped he would have raped me while you watched and then killed you, probably me too."

It was said more as a statement rather than a question, but he answered anyway. "Yes, baby, that's exactly what would have happened. Acer did some digging, looks like he was responsible for the death of at least one other woman. Same situation, a woman he developed a sick obsession with."

Lila's face morphed into a look of disgust. "Well, then I'm glad it ends here. I won't lose a wink of sleep feeling sorry for him. What will you do to him?"

He shook his head. No way in hell would he give her those details. The idea of revenge and the knowledge that Striker was taking him out of the equation may sit well with her on the periphery, but she'd struggle with the details. He planned to make Earl suffer and beg for his life before he learned there was no way he would leave alive.

Once the dust settled, and Lila got over the immediate trauma, details about what happened to Earl would eat away at her. It was a guarantee. She was good. Her life was based around the notion of helping people, doing no harm. She would have to be satisfied with the knowledge that Earl was no longer a threat.

Striker cupped her face between his hands, and stroked her cheek with his thumb, enjoying the feel of her under his fingers. He needed more, wished he could strip down and feel her skin all over his, but neither one of them was in any shape for activities more strenuous than blinking.

"All you need to know is that he won't be a problem for you or any other woman again. I'm not going to give you details. Can you just trust that I will take care of you?"

She looked like she wanted to argue, but relented in the end. "Of course. I trust you with my life. I love you Striker." Tears filled her eyes again, but she held them back this time.

He kissed her, sliding his tongue into her mouth as she opened to him. As was typical, the kiss turned hot and needy within seconds. Striker speared his hands into Lila's hair, and devoured her mouth, shifting his sore body as best he could. He wanted to feel as much of her as possible. He pressed against her and continued to kiss her with abandon until he felt her flinch. Shit, he'd nearly forgotten they were both all busted up.

He pulled back to avoid hurting her further, and rested his head against hers. "Sorry, baby. I lost my head."

"That makes two of us."

"Shit, Lila, I want inside you. I want to fuck you hard, until neither of us has any room in our head for anything but intense pleasure."

Lila groaned. "Striker…"

He kissed her again, just a quick taste this time. "Come on, baby, let's get some sleep. The sooner we heal, the sooner I can sink into that hot pussy. It's the only way I'm going to be one hundred percent convinced that you're safe and here with me."

***

The next morning Jester and Hook came by in a van to take Striker to the warehouse. Lila put up a moderate fight, saying he wasn't in any shape to leave the house, but eventually she backed down, aware of how important this was. He'd originally planned to wait until he was fully healed to deal with Earl, or at least healed enough that he could beat the shit out of the man before killing him, but he didn't want this hanging over their heads any longer than necessary. He would have to amend his plans a bit, but in the end, Earl would still be dead, which was the important part.

He tried to walk as normally as possible from the van to the warehouse. Giving Earl the satisfaction of seeing him hurting and impaired was not part of the plan. Hook unlocked the doors to the warehouse, and instructed the prospects guarding Earl to wait outside. Gumby was there as well, and he remained inside.

Earl was duct taped to a chair much as Striker had been just a few nights ago. One of the guys had obviously beaten him, and he didn't look nearly as smug as the last time they were in a room together. His head hung down, but Striker could see he had some bruises on his face.

"Hey, Earl." Gumby smacked him on the side of his head and he jolted awake. "You got a visitor."

Earl's eyes grew wide with fear as he saw Striker approach.

"Cut him loose," Striker ordered Gumby.

"Sure thing, VP." Gumby sliced through the duct tape

with a knife.

Earl didn't try to stand. He just stared up at Striker. "How's Lila? I didn't want to hurt her, but you have her so brainwashed she doesn't realize how much I love her."

Striker reached out and grabbed Earl by the throat, much as the man had done to Lila. He wanted him to feel what she felt, to experience the same fear and pain. Earl made a choking sound and tried to pull Striker's hand away, but he was no match for the strength of Striker's hatred, even in his injured state.

Striker's body protested the action, and intense pain shot through his side. He ignored it, and squeezed, taking pleasure in the way Earl's eyes bugged and his face turned purple as he gasped and tried to draw in a sufficient breath. "How's Lila? Let's see, she has nightmares where she wakes up screaming, remembering your filthy hands on her. That what you want to know?"

Earl gasped and tried to shake his head. "No...you're... lying."

"You don't love her, you sick fuck. You have a perverted obsession with her just like you did with the girl you killed in Mississippi."

Striker released Earl's throat seconds before the man would have lost consciousness. Earl crumpled to the floor, choking and wheezing as he tried to fill his lungs with air. Striker wanted him to feel relief for just a moment, to think that maybe he wasn't going to die, maybe Striker would be merciful.

Earl struggled to his feet and looked at the men around the room. "I'll stay away from her. I promise." His voice sounded rough, similar to Lila's.

"Damn right you will." Striker pulled out his gun and pointed it at Earl's head. He waited for the moment Earl realized his death was certain. Once that inevitability was reflected in the bastard's eyes, Striker pulled the trigger once, turned, and walked back to the van. It was over. Lila was safe.

It was time to put this shit behind them and get on with their life together.

Epilogue

"Come here, babe. I want to show you something."

"I'm coming! Just grabbing another beer. You want one?" Lila called from the kitchen.

"Sure. You know I'll never turn down a chance to be served by my little woman."

Lila walked into the living room and gave a roll of her eyes. "Here." She held the beer out to him. Before he could grab it, she pulled it out of his reach. "Oh wait, I forgot to shake it up for you, let me do that now."

She laughed as Striker leapt over the back of the couch and lunged for her. "Don't even think about it, wench," he said as he caught her. With a playful growl, he hauled her over his shoulder and dumped her onto the couch.

When she stopped laughing, he joined her on the couch and pointed to a wall in the foyer, near the front door.

"Oh, Striker…" She looked at him, and the rest of her sentence lodged in her throat when she saw the look of pride on his face. "You didn't have to hang that up."

"Are you kidding me? Of course I did. You did a great thing for those kids, and they honored you for it. Fuck yeah, we're hanging it up."

Lila chuckled. His sweet and crass combination never failed to amuse her. "Well, thank you. I was surprised enough when the football team invited me to their end of season banquet. I never dreamed they'd give me an award." She glanced at the shiny plaque that now hung on her wall. It read, *We honor you, Dr. Lila Emerson, for your dedication and service to the safety and wellbeing of our youth.*

Three months had passed since the incident with Earl White. Three amazing months where she and Striker had grown closer, and connected in a way she'd never imagined. She had friends and a family she loved and who loved her, a job she excelled at, and a man she adored. Life was good and the damage inflicted by Earl was fading into a distant memory.

"Okay, I won't pretend I don't love it." She laughed. "But I'm even more excited by the fact that four schools in the county are using the program now."

"You're an amazing woman."

"Striker." Her voice was soft and her heart melted at the look of intense affection on his face.

"I mean it, baby. You are so much more than I deserve, more than I ever even thought was possible for a guy like me."

"You don't give yourself enough credit. So many people count on you, trust you, and respect you. You are a good man."

He didn't respond, but leaned in and captured her mouth with his. The kiss was sweet and ended before she would have liked. "Marry me, Lila."

Her eyes popped open, and she gasped. "What?!" She looked down at a black velvet box in his hand. Tears flooded her eyes, and she brought her gaze back up to his. "You want to marry me?"

"More than I want to ride my Harley. More than anything I've ever wanted." His voice was thick and caught on the last word.

The smile that erupted on her face was so large it hurt her cheeks. "Yes! Of course I will marry you. There is nothing I want more." She threw her arms around his neck and squeezed for all she was worth. She didn't even care what the ring looked like. Being bound to Striker was all that mattered.

A sheepish look crossed his face. "I probably shouldn't tell you this, but I have reservations for us tomorrow at that new restaurant I town. I was going to do this in a more proper way, but I just couldn't wait any longer."

Finally, she looked down at the ring and smiled. "I don't want a fancy dinner. I much prefer to be in our home. Everything about this is perfect."

With a sly smile, she stood up, moved in front of Striker, and dropped to her knees, settling between his powerful thighs.

He raised an eyebrow. "Don't you want to call and share the news with anyone?"

She shook her head. "No. I have something more important to do first."

Striker lifted his ass and allowed Lila to draw his sweats past his hips. She smiled when she found him hard and ready. She rose fully on her knees and reached for the hem of her shirt, drawing it over her head, revealing new lingerie she'd purchased. She knew just what her man liked.

"Damn, baby, you are the sexiest woman."

Lila just smiled and leaned forward, gripping his straining erection with one hand as she lowered her mouth to him.

~ ~ ~ ~

Striker hardened painfully the instant Lila dropped to her

knees in front of him. Then, when she whipped off her top and revealed the little scraps of nothingness she called lingerie, he nearly blew.

The heat and suction of her mouth closed over him, and he dropped his head back on the couch with a low groan. There was only one thing in this world better than the feel of Lila's talented mouth engulfing his cock, and that was sliding into her hot, wet pussy, something he planned to do in just a few minutes. He wasn't above letting her thank him for the ring first.

Lost in the pleasurable sensations, Striker nearly missed the sound of his front door as it started to open.

Lila jumped, and released his cock. She fell back on her heels and crossed her arms over her sexy breasts with a look of horror on her face.

"Whoever the fuck that is, if you take one more step in here I'll kill you."

"Oh shit!" Jester's voice sounded out, and he threw an arm across his eyes. Striker didn't give two shits if Jester saw him in the buff, but he didn't want any man's eyes on Lila. "Jesus, you guys are like fuckin' rabbits. Don't you ever take a break?"

Lila chuckled, her face bright red.

"Hey, dickhead, Lila just agreed to marry me, and we're celebrating. That okay with you?"

"No shit?" A grin broke out across Jester's face. "Well congrats, man. Lila, you could do better, but—"

"Get the fuck out," Striker yelled. He grabbed the remote control and hurled it in Jester's general direction.

"All right I'm going!" Jester backed out, and pulled the door closed behind him.

Striker looked at Lila and shook his head. She was on the floor, her mouth wet from sucking his cock, laughing hysterically. "This is becoming a nasty habit. Come here woman." He grabbed Lila under her arms, and twisted so she lay under him on the couch.

He reached down, and, finding her wet and ready, pulled the string of her thong aside. He entered her with one powerful thrust. The sounds of her needy moans filled the room, urging him into action. The last thought Striker had before giving himself over to the consuming pleasure, was that he couldn't wait to tie her to him for the rest of his life.

Thank you so much for spending some time in the No Prisoners' world. If you enjoyed the book please feel free to leave a review on Goodreads or your favorite retailer.

Want more from Lila and Striker? Sign up for Lilly's newsletter and receive FREE No Prisoners bonus content!
www.lillyatlas.com

Keep reading for a sneak peek at the next book in the No Prisoners Series.

Jester
Available November 1, 2016

Jester

No Prisoners MC Book 2

Chapter 1

Bile burned its way up Emily's esophagus, then straight back down when she refused to give in to her body's need to revolt. She was in trouble. Serious trouble. The kind of trouble that could result in her being wheeled from her house in a body bag.

"Johnny," she whispered. Her heart broke a little as the reality set in of how low he'd sunk.

Across the living room, her brother was bound to one of their kitchen chairs. Purple bruising mottled his face, which was swollen like a balloon, displaying the evidence of what must have been an awful beating. Each time Johnny inhaled, a pain-filled wheeze hit her ears. Rivers of sweat ran down his face and despite his limp posture, he quivered, no doubt craving the heroin that ran his life.

Her lower lip stung and she forced her jaw to relax and end the punishment her teeth inflicted. Whenever she was nervous, she bit her bottom lip, and right now she could have bitten straight through.

Four gun-toting, tattooed bikers took up residence in her living room. The house she'd spent her hard earned time and money turning into a home had been violated. She racked her brain, trying to think of a solution, a way out of this terrifying situation, but fear clogged her mind and nothing came to her.

"Well, Emily, what's it gonna be? We ain't got all fuckin' day." Snake's voice was dark and threatening. He towered over her, all six-foot-three of him. A single muscle in his jaw twitched and his eyes narrowed. But it was the way he stared at her that sent chills down her spine, like he took pleasure in her fear, got off on it even.

"I—" The words stuck in her arid throat, and she coughed. "I'll do whatever you need me to do. Just don't hurt Johnny anymore."

"There you go, boys. At least one of the Carver siblings ain't a complete fuckin' moron. She's pretty too." Snake winked at her. His tongue darted out and flicked back and forth before disappearing into his mouth.

Her breath stilled. The end of his tongue was forked and each half wiggled independently.

"Emily, shut up. Don't—" Johnny's slurred protest was cut short by a quick blow to his already battered face.

She winced as the short, wiry man, whose pale bald head resembled an egg, connected his fist with Johnny's face. Johnny's head snapped back, and blood sprayed from his mouth across the beige carpet like a geyser, seeping into the fibers. The crimson splatter would stay there, deep inside the wool, no matter how much she scrubbed. She'd never forget this moment—one more thing ruined by the trauma of the day.

"Stop," she cried out. "Please, don't hurt him anymore. I said I'd help you." Her voice cracked with the effort to hold back a sob.

Twenty minutes ago, Emily had bounced into the house

she shared with Johnny, elated that school was out for the summer. Teaching first grade was her true passion, but by the end of May she was beyond ready for the decompression time the summer months afforded.

Instead of beginning her much anticipated vacation, she'd been cast as a character in Johnny's nightmare.

Two steps into her home and a man grabbed her arm. She'd fought against his hold, but was no match for his strength. Snake then *invited* her to sit on her own couch while he presented her options. Comply with his demands, or watch Johnny die. Not much of a choice for someone who was more a mother to Johnny than a sister.

A firm hand took hold of her chin with a vice grip. Snake's eyes bore into hers, like two windows to nothingness. Black, soulless orbs that didn't reveal a hint of what was brewing behind them. He made a sound she swore was a hiss, and she prayed she wouldn't see fangs when he smiled.

"This is all very touching." Snake laughed and drew away, waving his hand back and forth between Emily and her brother.

He turned his head, the motion making the snake tattoo on his neck look like it was slithering. The inked reptile rose from his shirt and climbed up his neck. Johnny had talked about a man nicknamed Snake—before Emily knew Johnny was part of an outlaw biker gang—saying the man had a tattoo of a three-foot-long rattlesnake from his neck to his groin. The serpent's head moved as its master did, its mouth open wide, revealing two fangs that dripped with venom, ready to strike at any time. Even the way Snake moved resembled a reptile studying its prey, looking for weaknesses and an opportunity to attack.

"Perhaps, Johnny, you should've given more of a shit about your sister when you were stealing from me." He shook his head and tsked, much as Emily would when one of her first graders broke a classroom rule, except the consequences here were far worse. "If you'd done your job, and sold the merchandise instead of snorting it, we wouldn't have ever known you had a sister. But, lucky for you, she seems willing to step in and clean up your mess."

Story of her life. She'd been cleaning up after Johnny since he was a kid, years before their parents died.

Johnny was thirteen when their parents were killed in a devastating motor vehicle accident, just three miles from their L.A. home. Even as a young teen, he'd set a precedent for trouble. Small time offenses mostly; petty theft, smoking, hanging with a rough crowd. Life took a turn for the worse when, at seventeen, he was initiated into a gang. The Killing Machines, or KMs to Los Angeles natives.

Hours after she found out, Emily had them packed and heading east, finally stopping in the tiny, off-the-grid town of Sandy Springs, Arizona. They resided here for the past four years. Emily thought she'd been successful in removing Johnny from the temptation of drugs and gangs. For a while, he even held down a steady job busing tables at a local restaurant. But, at twenty-six, she was apparently still very naïve.

A few months prior, she discovered a wad of cash in his dresser drawer. After snooping around, she learned he'd quit his job, and was now a prospect for the Grimm Brothers MC. Dealing drugs, no less.

The mistakes he made didn't matter. She'd do anything in her power to help him. He was her only family, and she loved him.

"Okay, kids. Here's how this is gonna go." Snake rubbed his hands together and slid his split tongue across his bottom lip as he paced the distance between Emily and Johnny.

The small, quiet man who'd beaten Johnny—Snake called him Casper—smiled so big each tooth was on display.

Emily swallowed a groan. Whatever they were about to make her do was not going to be pleasant.

"I know a broad who lives over in Crystal Rock. She's gonna get you into a No Prisoners party tomorrow night. You, pretty Emily, are going to make friends, rub elbows, hell, rub cocks. I don't give a fuck."

Emily's head spun. What the hell was he talking about? A No Prisoners party? Was he insane? "Wh-what?"

"Emily!" Snake clapped his hands in front of her face and laughed when her muscles jolted. "Focus. I need you to cozy up to the No Prisoners. I know they're planning to fuck with me and I want to know how. You're gonna find out. In two weeks we've got a very expensive deal going down. The No Prisoners would love to see it crash and burn, and I need to know if they are planning something to interfere."

Emily shook her head, her mind racing with all the reasons this was a horrible idea. "I can't do that." This plan would never work. "Why can't your friend just do it?"

"Two reasons, Emily."

She hated the sound of her own name coming from his lips. Probably why he said it so frequently.

"She ain't the type of girl they share secrets with. She's the kind of girl they fuck. But you're so sugary sweet they'll be tripping over their dicks to get close to you. Besides, Trixie doesn't have the strong motivation you do." He grabbed Johnny by the hair and yanked his head back so Emily had a full view of his beaten face. "This is not a discussion. You need to concentrate on getting me what I need, so Johnny doesn't end up as buzzard food in the desert."

Why on earth would Johnny get involved with these men? One look at his dilated pupils, sweaty brow, and subtle tremors and the answer was obvious.

Addiction.

If only she'd been paying closer attention, maybe she would have noticed he was using again. Then she could have...what? He'd refused countless offers of rehab or counseling. His joining a gang had been the last straw after years on a never-ending merry-go-round of begging and pleading with him to get help. She'd thought moving was the answer, but his demons just followed them. She was clueless as to what else to do to help him.

"Two weeks, Emily." Snake wiggled three fingers in her direction.

Emily shook her head and her stomach somersaulted.

"Maybe I haven't made myself clear. You need a little more convincing?" Snake pulled a gun from the small of his back and pointed it at Johnny's head.

Her heart nearly pounded out of her chest, but her brother didn't react in any way. Had his self-worth decreased to the point where he no longer cared if he lived or died?

All background sounds blended together. Emily heard nothing but the rushing of blood in her ears. "No, no, no!" She leaped from the couch, hands out in front of her as though she could somehow prevent Snake from killing her only family. "I'll do it. Just let him go and I'll do it."

Snake laughed again. "I like you, Emily." He came to a stop in front of her and leaned down so his mouth was against her ear. His stale breath wafted across her skin and she shuddered in revulsion. The hand holding his gun wrapped around her waist, securing her in place. She froze as though she were standing on a landmine. "I'll let him go *when* you get me what I want," he whispered.

Tears flooded her eyes. She soaked in Johnny's image, memorizing how he looked: vulnerable, damaged, and lifeless. That image would need to be burned in her brain to drive her over the upcoming days.

Snake straightened and paced the room, waving the gun as if he were a conductor in a symphony instead of a murderous sociopath. Emily swallowed, her attention glued to the movement of the weapon.

"Johnny will remain our guest for the next two weeks. If you get me what I need, he will be returned to you. Take your time. Don't rush. Don't think you're gonna feed me some bullshit tomorrow, get your junkie brother back, and live happily ever after. He stays with me the entire time."

Damnit. Her first instinct had been to fabricate a believable story and disappear with Johnny.

Snake halted in front of her and stroked the muzzle of his pistol down her cheek. A bead of sweat rolled down her spine, leaving an itchy path in its wake. Frozen in fear, she ignored the minor irritation.

He tapped the gun against her cheek twice, before turning to his henchmen. "We're done here, boys. Load him in the van and let's roll. Emily, Trixie will meet you at the No Prisoners' clubhouse tomorrow night at ten. She'll know who you are."

Casper sliced at the zip ties that bound Johnny's limbs to the chair, while two men she'd forgotten were in the room came from behind her and gathered him up. They ignored his grunts of pain as they dragged him by the arms toward the door.

Emily prayed he wouldn't be stupid enough to try and fight them, but it wasn't necessary. His knees buckled and his head lolled, not an ounce of rebellion left in him.

Snake nodded at her and started for the door. "You'll be hearing from me," he called out before following his goons out of her house.

The instant her door clicked closed, Emily bolted to the bathroom and emptied the contents of her stomach into the toilet. After many minutes, the violent heaving subsided, leaving her weakened and exhausted. Sweat ran down her face, mixing with her tears and stinging her eyes.

How would she ever survive the next few weeks? How would Johnny?

About the Author

Lilly Atlas is a contemporary romance author, proud Navy wife, and mother of two spunky girls. By day, she works as a Physical Therapist at a hospital in Virginia. For years, Lilly has been daydreaming and plotting characters in her head while driving, showering, and sometimes when she was supposed to be paying attention to something else. She finally decided to get the ideas out of her head and into books.

Every time Lilly downloads a new ebook she expects her Kindle App to tell her it's exhausted and overworked. She's been waiting for the pop up asking to please give it some rest. Thankfully that hasn't happened yet, so she can often be found absorbed in a new book.

47865516R00185

Made in the USA
Columbia, SC
04 January 2019